This is Growing Up

Wild Child Reckless Book One
Juliet McKinley

Suddenly Juliet

To my Dad. You left us entirely too soon, and you are missed every day. This book wouldn't have happened without you.

To my husband, my very own book boyfriend. Thank you for always having my back and encouraging me to fly even when I felt like giving up. You are my everything.

To Morgan, Mia, EJ, Brandy, Holly, and the whole Fury gang. Thank you for being the best group of people I have ever known.

To my PA Gwen- Am I ungrounded now?

About the Author

An avid reader turned author of second-chance, steamy contemporary romance set in small towns, Juliet believes happiness comes from family, hot coffee and even steamier romances.

Juliet is living out her dream to write about what she knows - since she's living her own happily ever after in her very own small town in Texas with her husband (who's always glad to provide some inspiration for the sexy hero), children that keep her on her toes and a coffee habit that cannot be contained.

Prologue
Delilah

Present

"Thank you, Denver, and good night!" My voice rings out over the noise of the crowd as I toss out a guitar pick, plaster on a big smile, and step back from the microphone.

The stadium goes wild, fans waving signs and pictures, and I glance up, watching another barrage of flower petals rain down on us as we walk off the stage.

Passing my guitar off to a roadie, I roll my neck and shoulders, trying to work out the kinks left from performing for several hours. Another show, another city no different from the hundreds of others we've played over the last seven years. Security funnels us into a line while onlookers clamor to get our autographs, and we head out of the stadium signing hats, pictures, CDs, and more along the way.

My bandmates slap me on the back as we approach the tour bus. It takes minutes that feel like hours before we're safely secured inside. We split into our respective rooms and quickly change out of our "stage finery," or so we like to call it.

Standing in the shower, I lean my head against the wall. When I started this, I was so excited. Now, it's all I can do to get through each show.

Maybe I should take a break from touring?

After drying off, I stretch out my back again before putting on my favorite pair of faded black yoga pants. It's the little things in life that make you sigh in pleasure. I should not hurt this bad at twenty-three.

Everyone is laughing and joking around when we reconvene in the common area. My friends try to draw me into the conversation; my half-hearted answers and lackluster tone quickly exclude me. I grab a plate with a bottle of water from the table and walk to the seats farthest away from the noise.

The bus starts up, pulls out, and I sink back against the plush seat as my head leans against the window. I smell the boys making popcorn and gearing up for another *John Wick* marathon. I sit the plate on the seat beside me, no longer hungry.

Everyone else's chatter ebbs and flows around me, and I still can't find the energy to engage. Instead, I watch as we eat up the road, the miles growing between Denver and our next destination, Portland.

For three years, we've been touring—almost consistently since we left at eighteen. While the others have stopped home for the occasional visit, I refuse, choosing to remain at our compound in LA. The reality is I am terrified. I miss my mother, but I can't risk seeing *him*. He still runs his father's business in our small, sleepy town.

Our band is a close-knit family. Many of us have been together since high school. We do a lot of things, but we don't keep secrets. And what we definitely do not do is mention him.

I let out another resigned sigh. We're headed to Portland, but after that? *Like it or not, Texas, I'm coming home.*

Chapter 1
Delilah

Age Six

The moving truck is long and colorful as it pulls in front of the house next door in the midday sun. Hoping whoever's moving in will have a six-year-old girl like me, I run over to the magnolia tree by the fence and stick my face against the slats. Watching and waiting until, finally, the truck's doors start to open. A boy joins the mom and dad, and my heart falls. He looks to be around James's age. No other children pop out after him. Feeling decidedly cheated, I sit back against the tree and fiddle with a fallen magnolia blossom.

"Hello!"

I jump up so fast I trip over my feet and would have hit the ground if not for the voice's owner diving over the low fence to catch me.

"Oops, I didn't mean to scare you. Let's get you back on your feet!" He sets me right, and I stare at him. Unable to find my voice, I toe my shoe into the ground and glance at my scuffed trainers. "My name is Alex. What's yours?"

I cock my head to the side, looking up at him again. "Your name is X?"

The sound that follows makes me smile. There's sunshine in his laughter, and I'm happy just hearing it.

"No, Lil Bit, my name is Alex. It's short for Alexander, but you know what? You can call me X if you like. I don't mind."

I notice his eyes, so different from mine. His are blue like the spring sky over the lake in the morning, and mine are green like our yard before the sun scorched it. His hair is dark, black like the crows that Mom chased from our garden. Mine is red, like a penny you pick up for good luck.

"My name isn't Lil Bit. It's Delilah Rose—Delilah Rose Callahan. I'm six and my favorite color is purple."

"Hello, Delilah Rose Callahan. My name is Alexander Brian Stephenson. I think purple is awesome, but my favorite color is green." His smile turns cheeky as he tugs my long red hair, and I giggle.

I pivot to see James running up toward us before he walks around the fence and over to the moving truck. It isn't long before he's chatting happily with X. I follow behind them, listening as they go.

When we reach the back of the moving van, Alexander grabs a box and hands it to James, who turns and walks toward the front door of their house. I step up next and hold out my arms expectantly.

X chuckles and then hands me a case. "That's my guitar! I take lessons from my dad. Have you ever played guitar before?"

He unsnaps the lid and pulls the instrument out to show me. It sparkles in the sun, pale wood with a dark pattern in the middle.

I reach out a tentative finger and slide it along the front and over the strings.

"Do you know 'You Are My Sunshine'? Mama sings it to me." I've always loved to sing but singing while X plays the guitar is new and adventurous, and I'm entranced by the idea.

I gasp in amazement as he continues to play softly. I join in, my voice rising high above his until I realize I'm the only one singing now. I'm concentrating on the way his hands move over the strings. So much so I don't hear our parents walk up to the back of the truck.

"That was wonderful, baby girl!" my mother says, hugging me from behind.

I grin at her and turn to my dad. My smile falls when I notice he's in his uniform and has his go bag next to him. I can feel the tears welling in my eyes. I know what that means, and I don't want him to go.

"Don't be sad, my Rosie. I'll be home before you know it." He says this every time, but I never believe him. I miss him as soon as he leaves and he's always gone for months.

My dad catches me in his warm embrace, and I inhale the smell of grease and tobacco, which will forever remind me of him. Holding me close to his chest, he whispers reassurances into my ear, reminders of how much he loves me, how he won't be gone long, and other promises. I don't want to hear it, though. So I shove away from him, dropping to the ground, and race around the house.

I ignore my dad calling after me and climb up as high as I dare. You can't see me from the ground anymore. Then I lean back against the tree trunk and tuck my knees tight.

"Delilah."

I hear X's voice below me, and I gasp.

"C'mon down. Say goodbye. He's going to miss you so much!"

"Is your dad a soldier too?"

"No, but I know what it's like not to get to say goodbye to someone. It isn't a good feeling."

I climb down the tree, and when I reach the bottom, I see my dad waiting for me. I leap into his arms and my dad catches me and swings my body around, pulling me tight to his chest.

"I love you, my Rosie. My wild child. I'll be back as soon as I can. I promise." His voice is soft.

I lay my head on his shoulder, place my arms around his neck, and squeeze as tight as possible. As always, my dad pretends I'm choking him, dropping to his knees and falling backward.

Mom laughs as we both get off the ground, and Dad heads toward my brother, hugging him close and saying something in his ear. James grins before returning to the moving truck with X close behind him.

I smile, kiss my dad one more time, and yell, "Wait for me!" as I chase after the boys.

Meeting X when I was six may have changed my life's course. Still, the year I turned eight would forever destroy the world I thought I knew. It's the same year my dad died, and what I remember most is the sound of crying.

Dad was recalled overseas, and while he was granted leave several times during the first year, something happened, and he couldn't come home anymore. Mom says the bad guys were attacking more villages, and that my dad is needed to help keep other little girls and boys safe.

Knowing what I know now, I know it was more than that.

It's the summer just before school is supposed to start, and the days are long and hot, which means we all try to stay out of the heat as much as possible. That's when some men I've never seen before show up out front of the house. I watch them exit their shiny black car and walk up the drive. They're dressed like my dad, so I open the door for them even though Mom has repeatedly warned me not to do so if I don't know who's on the other side.

The taller one crouches down to look at me. "Is your mom home, sweetheart?" His voice is soft, and his eyes are kind.

Those eyes would haunt my dreams for years to come.

I run to get my mom from the kitchen. Mom follows behind me until she sees the men standing at the door. When I notice she's stopped moving, I turn around to see her staring at the men with what can only be described as fear on her face.

Who are these men? My mom is never scared.

The second man steps in from the doorway, and his movement catalyzes my mom's reaction. The glass in her hand hits the floor and shatters. It isn't long before she does the same. I freeze up as I watch my mother drop to her knees. I don't know what's happening but I do know it isn't good. Then I hear the pounding of feet on the porch as my mom begins to wail.

James and X come barreling into the house. X looks around and bolts back out, and James stands in the doorway, his hands clenched next to his sides. The first man turns to speak to my brother while the second calmly talks to Mom on the floor.

I still don't understand what's happening but know something is very wrong. Overwhelmed by the uncertainty, I rush up the stairs to my favorite hiding place in the back of my closet. But I can still hear my mom crying, so I pull a blanket over my head and cover my ears to block out the sound, rocking back and forth as I hum the tune to "You Are My Sunshine."

I'm not sure how much time passes. It could be minutes or hours, but at some point, I fall asleep. I wake up to X kneeling over me, shaking my shoulder. I sit up slowly, shoving my long red hair out of my face, and X maneuvers himself to sit beside me. I look over at him and my heart clenches. He seems so sad.

"We need to go downstairs. Something's happened. Come on, we have to go."

I grab his hand and follow him into the living room, where I see his mom holding my mom on the couch. His dad is talking to James near the kitchen. All conversation stops when we enter the room, which makes me nervous. X and I take a seat on the couch, and I tuck myself slightly behind his body, using him to shield me against the silence. My brother stares at us, but I don't recognize the look on his face.

At first, I thought he was mad, but for the life of me, I couldn't figure out why. I would see that same look on his face for years to come before I finally realized it wasn't directed at me but at our dad. For dying. For leaving us.

After a few minutes, Mom slides toward me and explains that my dad isn't coming home. I jerk my hands free, shake my head silently in denial, and leap to my feet. I back away from everyone before bolting out the door.

I will never forget the pain or the sound my heart makes as it breaks in my chest, the tears streaming down my face as I run as fast as possible. I can hear everyone shouting, but I don't slow down. I have to get away. I have to run this pain out. I have to find a way to get everything to disappear.

Little did I realize that nothing would make it disappear, no matter how hard I tried over the next ten years.

I stop when I find myself standing at my tree and start to climb up without a second thought. I want to get away. I want to hide. I want this to all have been a dream.

Perching my body on a limb, I let the tears fall from my eyes and hide my face in my knees. I sob so hard and long that my throat aches, and my eyes swell. When my tears have run their course, I climb back down, only to realize I was never alone. Sitting on the branch below me, his back pressed to the trunk, is X. I don't know how long he's been here, but his calm presence is the only thing that seems to ease the pain. The only place in my world that feels safe.

"It doesn't seem like it now, but it will be okay. I can't tell you how I know, but I know. One day, you will wake up, and it will all hurt less. You will always miss him, but the pain of losing him will get better. You have to trust me on this. Tell me you believe me," his voice whispers into the night.

"Dad was going to build me a tree house right here. It was supposed to be my birthday present." I know it's not the answer he wants, but everything seems impossible and large, and I don't believe his words.

How can I ever get past this hurt? The center of my universe just imploded like a black hole, and now everything will be sucked in until nothing is left.

"You will get your treehouse," X promises. "If I have to build it by hand, chopping down trees for wood, you will get your treehouse."

The day of the funeral gives us a muted-gray sky filled with sorrow and rain. It's as if the world is crying as I stand in the black dress mom picked out for me, next to James at the graveside, my umbrella trembling beneath the rapidly falling drops. I watch as the soldiers fold the flag before presenting it to Mom, who accepts it with tears streaming down her face. Mom looks older now, tired and pale instead of vibrant and lively. She doesn't look like my mom anymore.

I wonder if I still look like me...

James is positioned on the other side of me. He still seems so angry, and I envy his anger. I'm just sad, and I can't stop crying. Most days, I don't even want to get out of bed. My dad is gone, and he isn't coming back. I'm not prepared to face a reality that doesn't include him.

I'm so wrapped up in my thoughts that I don't notice the line of men stepping up to the grave until the first volley of shots rings out into the air. I jump and X steps up behind me, offering support as the second set sounds. My heart has crawled into my throat by the third and final set.

It's official. My dad is gone forever.

The reception following the ceremony is full of people, many I don't know, so I do what I do best. I hide. I'm at my limit and don't know where else to turn. I walk toward my room and see X standing on the stairs. Watching me. I go to move past him, and he follows, his guitar in his hand. He must have gone next door for it.

When we reach my room, we settle on the carpet, cross our legs, and he begins to play.

At first, he strums out a few silly tunes like: "Old MacDonald," "Bingo," and "The Wheels on the Bus." But when even those fail to hint at a chuckle, he tries something different.

The next song has no words. The melody is soft and low with an aching sadness. It expresses every feeling living inside me in an arrangement of notes that resonates with emotion. I curl up on my side, my head on a pillow, and cry to the haunting sound.

Chapter 2
Delilah

X and his dad take the rest of that summer to build my tree-house. They work on it tirelessly for weeks. I often see X outside measuring and cutting boards well past sundown. Even as our hearts protest, our lives seem to settle into our new reality by the time the project is complete.

Mom returns to working full time as a nurse at our local hospital. During her overnight shifts, we stay next door with the Stephensons. Mrs. Stephenson ensures we are fed and in bed promptly to get us to school the next day.

I honestly don't think we would have made it without them.

It's become routine to get off the bus and let myself into their house. We don't even knock anymore. This place is now our second home. We have keys and I have my own room, while the boys bunk together.

On my way to the kitchen, I spot X's guitar on the couch and stop. He doesn't usually let the instrument out of his sight when it's not in its case. I approach the couch and slowly run my fingers over the strings. The discordant notes make me cringe, and when I hear his voice, I jump back.

X laughs softly. "Nice try. We both know you're not sweet and innocent. It's been long enough. I won't fall for that anymore."

I stick my tongue out at him, which only has him laughing harder.

He points to the guitar. "Do you want to learn how to play? I could teach you, you know."

"I would love to learn, if you don't mind. Are you sure you want to teach me?"

X smiles, swipes up his guitar, and gestures for me to follow him.

We end up in my treehouse, where he places the instrument in my lap before ensuring my fingers are in the correct position. X then explains the strings, frets, and notes. He quizzes me on finger placement and general knowledge before teaching me how to actually play. We start with simple songs that are easy for me to follow.

I slowly build up to more challenging pieces with X guiding me. We practice every day. This routine goes on for months.

One evening, X sits me down and hands me a package. I look at him curiously as I turn it around in my hands.

"It isn't my birthday. What is this?"

"I know. It's your *un*birthday! Happy unbirthday!"

Chuckling under my breath at his silliness, I open the package to reveal a purple strap, sparkling purple picks, and several spools of replacement strings.

"X, this is amazing and so beautiful, but I don't have a guitar..." I glance up just as he removes a case from behind his back. It has a giant purple bow on it. I jump up and throw my arms around his neck. "Thank you. Thank you so very much," I whisper.

From that point on, the only constant thing in my life is my daily guitar practice with X in my treehouse. We spend hours playing and singing together. X has a decent voice. He claims mine is better and that *it will take me places*.

But I think he's the one who is really destined to leave our sleepy little town, not me.

Before I realize it, four years have passed. I'm twelve. James and X are sixteen. For James's sixteenth birthday, Mom gives him Dad's old pickup. I don't know what it is about that truck, but James finally stops looking angry and starts laughing and joking with me; it's like he's my brother again.

He spends hours cleaning that truck until the cherry-red paint glows. It's his pride and joy. He takes me to get ice cream and to the movies. He brings us all to the lake, and once during our Spring Break, he even gives me a ride to the mall.

X and James start to hang out more, go out late at night, and sneak home early in the morning. X and I don't practice that much anymore.

The summer I turn thirteen, I meet Jensen. He transferred from California to our little Texas town with his dad after his mom died. We immediately become best friends and are inseparable. We play, sing, and stick together. And we feel invincible.

It's the same summer the popular app VidReel drops. Users can record and post short videos using prerecorded music and filters.

Jensen and I decide to start a band and be *big town famous,* as he likes to say. That's how Wild Child Reckless is born, and we take over the back bedroom that used to be my mother's craft room.

My fourteenth birthday is a bright-blue sky and no clouds for miles. We gather outside for cake and presents. My brother has been asking me what to get me for months, and I finally break down and tell him about the recording kit I want for the band so that we can create better-quality videos to post on VidReel.

We've built a small following. Jensen and I play together, though I do most of the singing. Sometimes Jensen joins in on the chorus, but he's far shyer than I am. However, he's slowly coming out of his shell and has acquired some local groupies.

My Mom is off from work, a rare occurrence, and as we sit in the sunshine, I can't remember a time in the last few years when everything seemed perfect like this. I tilt my head back and close my eyes, soaking in the sun.

Jensen picks up a box and brings it to me before plopping down on the bench next to us. So I crack an eye open and turn to take the present from him.

"This is just a prototype. If you like it, we can see about making more—but I wanted you to have it for your birthday."

Ripping away the wrapping paper, I open the small box before jumping up with a gasp. Jensen made me a t-shirt for our band. I squeal as I hug him, then jump up and down.

Behind me, I hear both James and X clear their throats. I sit next to Jensen and lean against his shoulder, shooting them a dirty look.

Why are they both glaring at me?

"I LOVE IT! You know what this means? We have to post a new video! I have just the song! Want to go set up?"

"I've got my bass in the living room. I'll meet you in the studio."

As Jensen heads into the house, I run up to my brother and give him a huge hug. "Thanks for the gifts, James. They're the best! Where you got the money for the equipment, I'll never know! Thank you for setting it all up!" I hug X next. "Thank you for the new picks and strings! How did you know I wanted that new strap and case? I swear, sometimes I think you have my phone bugged!" I tease as I turn to run into the house, pecking my mom on her cheek as I go by.

Back in our studio, I find Jensen messing with the new equipment. He looks up and tosses me my phone when I walk into the room. "You have a new DM on VidReel. I checked it first—it's legit."

I've been getting some not-so-nice pictures from men on the app. So we decided that Jensen would check all the DMs before I see them. I pick up my phone and open the message. My eyebrows hit my hairline,

It's a guy from South Elgin West. His name is Grayson, and he says he's a drummer. He wants to know if we're looking for one and if he can audition. He could pack his travel kit and come by whenever we have time.

I look up at Jensen and shrug my shoulders. "We were talking about adding more to our sound. A drummer could be a good place to start. What do you think?"

Jensen tunes his bass, softly strumming the instrument while mulling it over. "I think it can't hurt anything. See if he can come by. We have that cover we've wanted to do. Adding drums would set it off."

I send a quick message to Grayson before grabbing my guitar. When my phone vibrates, I look before I think and get a face full of something I never wanted to see.

"Ahhh!" I yell and toss my phone, rubbing my hands against my shorts as if that will clean them. "I got another dick pic! Delete it! Please!".

Shaking his head, Jensen picks up my phone, deletes the pic, and blocks the user.

While we wait for Grayson to arrive, we do a few test runs of "Cowboy Casanova" by Carrie Underwood, the cover we planned to do. We've just finished our third run-through when I hear the front bell ring.

"I got it!" I holler as I sprint through the house, my boots slapping on the floor. I hear the game on the living room TV and know the boys wouldn't have gotten up anyway.

I throw open the door and the guy standing in front of me is handsome in every way you could imagine. He has sandy-blonde hair and slate-gray eyes. I'm pulled up short by his intense level of scrutiny. I realize I'm staring. I shake my head while he cocks an eyebrow and answers my grin with one of his own.

"Hi, I'm Delilah. You must be Grayson?" I reach out, offering my hand. I'm surprised when he passes me his phone instead. Looking down, I notice that he has his notes app open so I quickly skim the words on his screen.

Hi, I'm Grayson. You must be Delilah. It is exciting to meet you. I want to let you know that I am deaf, but I can read your

lips if you face me and enunciate clearly. Speaking louder will not help. I still won't be able to hear you. I know this is probably not what you expected, but I am an excellent drummer and cannot wait to try out for you!

I read the note a second time before I meet his eyes again. Tilting my head to the side, I gesture behind me. "Let's meet Jensen. He's my bassist and best friend. He's in the studio. Follow me." I travel down the hall, stopping to stick my head into the living room. "James, I'm trying out a drummer. It's going to be loud. Deal with it."

I stick out my tongue when he grumbles but continue down the hall anyway. I open the door and once again gesture for Grayson to go ahead. I make sure to face him before speaking up.

"Jenner, this is Grayson, the drummer who messaged us about auditioning. He's deaf, so always face him when you're talking and enunciate clearly. I'm excited to see what he's got!"

Jensen's mouth drops open. "He's deaf?" he exclaims, and I shoot him a dirty look. "How can he be a drummer and deaf?" Then he throws his hands in the air.

"He can read your lips, you know, you asshole! He's deaf, not dumb!" I punch Jensen in the shoulder, and he hisses, stepping back from me in fear of more retaliation.

Grayson doesn't appear to be upset by my best friend's lack of manners; he grins before grabbing his phone and tapping out a quick message for us to read.

Like this.

He quickly sets up his travel kit and twirls the sticks before starting on the epic drum solo from Led Zeppelin's song "Moby

Dick." The rolls are flawless, and the beat is spot on. He plays like he was born with sticks in his hands.

He's pure talent. Grayson finishes out the solo before grinning at our shocked faces. Moving his sticks to one hand, he shrugs his shoulders at us as if to say, "Well?"

"I think we have our drummer." I nod.

"No shit," Jensen grunts in reply.

"Guys, what if we do this song instead?" I set up the recording equipment before picking up my guitar, sliding on my new strap, and grabbing my favorite sparkling purple guitar pick. I show my phone to the guys, and they smile at me. "Ready? One. Two. One, two, three, FOUR!"

The opening riffs of "Three Small Words" by the Pixie Chicks fill the air, the drums loud and in front. By the song's end, we're all sweating, my fingers are numb, and I'm confident my hair is plastered to my head. I have never felt more energized in my LIFE.

"What do you think? You want to join Wild Child Reckless?"

Grayson makes a sign with his hands, and even with my limited—more like *no* knowledge of sign language—it appears to be optimistic. I attempt to copy the movement, and he corrects my finger placement and repeats it back to me. Then he hands me his phone with the words "hell yeah" typed out on the screen.

I grin, return his phone, and give signing another try. "Hell yeah."

Chapter 3
Alexander

I turn and watch Delilah lead some random guy from the door back to her studio. Nudging James's shoulder, I toss my head in their direction. "What's up with that?"

James shrugs. "You heard what Delilah said. He's a drummer here for an audition. What's the big deal?"

"What's the big deal? *What's the big deal?* Your baby sister just took a guy you've never met into a back room with no chaperone! Did you even know she was looking for a drummer?"

"Okay, Miss Post. Delilah is fine. She has Jensen with her, and besides, he's a South Elgin West student in their music program."

"How do you know that?"

"He messaged her over on her VidReel account. I saw the messages."

"Does she know you have the log-in for her VidReel account?"

"Jensen and I both have it. And, yes, Delilah knows. There have been a lot of jackasses out there being gross. We try to keep her from seeing as much of it as possible. She should be able to post what she wants online without some idiot sending inappropriate pictures to her. Jesus, she's still just a kid, and some of these creeps are old enough to be her dad." James takes another swig of his soda before picking up the bowl of chips.

Well, fuck. If her brother is okay with it, I can't say anything. No matter how much I may not like the situation. I'm shocked to hear about the messages she's been getting, though. It truly is vile.

In the years since the death of their father, James has been more of a hands-off kind of brother. To some extent, that changed when Delilah hit puberty, and he realized that boys like him at that age would be coming around. Then James started to take notice. Better late than never, I guess. But at fourteen, Delilah no longer needs the handholding or protectiveness of an older brother.

"Look, I wanted to talk to you about something, but you can't mention it to Delilah. Okay?" James's tone has me sitting up straighter. He never uses that tone. And on the rare occasion that he does, it's never for anything good. He takes a deep breath. "I'm going to enlist."

The words feel like a punch to the stomach. It takes everything I have left in me not to jump up and yell at him. James was so angry after his dad died overseas during a tour. It took years for him to get over it. In some ways, he never really did; now, he wants to follow in those footsteps. It's hard to wrap my brain around this news.

I shake my head and sigh. "You haven't told Delilah yet, have you?"

"I haven't even told my mom yet. There're some things I have to get in order before I officially sign up, but I wanted you to be the first to know. I need you to be here when I can't and to watch over Delilah and Mom while I'm gone. You're the only person in my life I can trust with this. I know you're supposed to be leaving for college soon. But you're just going to Havenbrook University and still planning to live at home?" At my nod of agreement, he continues, "So you'll watch out for them, right? You'll help Mom with the house and ensure Delilah stays safe. You've got to promise me, Alex. Promise."

"Tell me why, James. I'm trying to understand. You were so mad when your dad passed and left you guys all alone. Why would you be willing to go and follow in his footsteps? You *are* going Army, aren't you?" The look he gives me confirms my suspicions. "Which means you're voluntarily leaving them alone and breaking their hearts all at once. You could die and do to them what your dad did twice over. So please, tell me what brought this idea into your head and made you think it was a good one!"

James takes a deep breath, holding the air in his lungs before slowly releasing it. Then he drops his head between his knees. "Alex, you know me. You know my grades. I'm not going to get into any decent college. Not even Havenbrook. That isn't the future for me. If I enlist, I can make something of myself, something more than I could ever be in this small, backward Texas town."

The sudden silence, as the music coming from down the hall dies down, is nearly as shocking as the bomb James just dropped on my lap. I swallow roughly while my heart feels like it's lodged in my throat, hindering my ability to speak, so I nod. "Okay. Yeah. I can watch out for them. I *will* watch out for them, James. I'll be there and do whatever it takes to ensure they have everything they need."

He claps me on the shoulder and pulls me into a hug.

"When are you going to tell your mom and Delilah?"

"Tell me what?"

I look up and spot Delilah standing in the doorway with Jensen and the drummer. I turn to James, my guilty expression meeting his frown.

"About the recording time I booked you at a real studio as the rest of your birthday present. I was going to wait until dinner tonight to give it to you, but I guess the cat is out of the bag." James probably intended to hold off on this gift until he told Delilah about enlisting, and the fact that he had to pull it out now means he'll have nothing to distract her from the news later.

Delilah tackles her brother over the back of the couch, squealing in glee. I narrowly miss a foot to the face. As I dodge her flailing limbs, I see Jensen tapping out a message on his phone. The guys high-five before texting back and forth furiously. Delilah tugs James around the couch and introduces him to the drummer, named Grayson, and a certain word catches my ear. My jaw hits my knees when I realize that her drummer is deaf *and* kick-ass, from what we could hear anyway.

Tugging on one of her curls to get her attention, I tease, "What was that noise coming from the studio? Since when do you like anything other than country?"

Delilah rolls her eyes, props a hand on her hip, and flicks at my fist still holding her hair. "Not that you would know, since you haven't even played a song with me in *years*."

The way that last part is stressed makes me wince as the well-placed barb hits its mark. It's true. I haven't played guitar with her in years. But Delilah Callahan is my kryptonite, and for both our sakes, I need to stay far, far away.

"For your information, Alexander, we play a lot of different genres now. If you followed our VidReel page, you would know that. Excuse us. We have some songs to pick out!"

I wince again when she turns on her heel and the door slams shut.

Alexander. Delilah never calls me Alexander. I've always been X. Ever since that day when she was six years old and misheard my name.

The last year was tough for me, and I pulled back. What else are you supposed to do when you start to dream about your best friend's kid sister?

I'm here now, though, and if James wants me to keep an eye on her, then keep an eye on her I will. She better be ready because, unlike her brother, who gives her way too much leniency, X is on the job now. And it's a job I plan to take very, very seriously.

Later that night in bed, I scroll through VidReel. I watch the band's progression from when they first started posting to now. I have to admit they are getting better. Many of her videos have thousands of likes and comments. The one they posted today with Grayson already has 150,000 likes with almost as many comments—people wondering who the new addition is or asking about Jensen and if he's single.

Most of the remarks about Delilah have me clenching my teeth. How anyone thinks it's okay to say shit like that about someone is beyond me. I call James, and he answers on the third ring.

"Dude, do you know what time it is?" His voice is rough with sleep.

"Yeah, I know what time it is. The better question is... do *you* know what people are saying about Delilah on this stupid app? How can you let her continue to post videos? Most of the guys commenting are at least twice her age! It's disgusting!"

"I know."

"Excuse me?" I have to force myself to not march over there and kick his ass. "James, you knew about this. How could you know about this and not do something about it? She's your sister!"

James sighs down the line. "Look, I already told you. Jensen and I both have the log-in info. We keep it from getting out of hand. Is it disgusting? Yes. Believe me, I know it is. It's my sister. However, I can assure you that those comments have nothing on the ones we delete and ban before she sees them. I can also assure you she is as safe as possible, never goes to any events alone, and always has her pepper spray and taser. I've made her aware of where the threats are and how to watch out for them the best she can. You think I need to pay more attention to Delilah. I get that. Still, you know I love my sister and have done my best to ensure she stays safe while pursuing her dream."

"I'm sorry. You're right. I do know you love her. I've never doubted that, but I don't know." I suck in a long breath. "After today... knowing that you want me to watch her... You know I love you both. You're the best part of my extended family. At the same time, you're about to go away to do something dangerous, and seeing all the comments made me lose my cool. I can't stand the thought of losing you any more than I can stand the thought of something happening to her."

"Look, I know you've had a rough year. Especially after blowing out your knee just before the playoffs, then dealing with the therapy that came with it. It's been hard, but you still have your academic scholarship. You still know what you want to do with your life. You still have a dream that you can achieve. Do you know how lucky you are even with everything you've been through?"

"Yeah, I know. Okay. I can't lose you. You're the brother I never had. You have to promise me that you'll be safer than safe." I wait before I hear his voice come down the line.

"I promise."

Chapter 4
Delilah

James wanted to take me out for my birthday, so there was only one obvious choice: The Texas Rose. I smooth down my skirt as we're escorted to our table.

"So, Delilah, what plans do you have this summer? Anything exciting before starting high school next year?" Mom always tries to keep up with our lives, even when working double shifts.

"I don't have any plans besides playing with the band, recording the two songs that James bought me, and getting ready to start high school. There isn't much else to do. I was going to see about getting a job at the drive-in, but James said he would rather I wait. So, I didn't apply when they were hiring summer help."

This must be news to my mom because she focuses all her patented mom stare on my brother. "James? You were always talking about the need to be responsible. Why wouldn't you want your sister to get a job this summer? I think a summer job is what she needs."

Before James can answer, our waitress approaches the table. "Hey, James, Mrs. Callahan. How are you this evening?"

It doesn't escape my notice that she doesn't greet me. Her eyes never leave my brother; Jeanie has always been a bitch. She's also been trying to corner James for years, but he never gives her the time of day. I roll my eyes before opening my menu, like I don't already know what's on it since we've been coming here since I was born.

"Hey, Jeanie, just out for Delilah's birthday." My brother's tone makes it known that overlooking me will not be tolerated.

"Happy Birthday, Delilah." Jeanie turns her glare on me, and the fake cheerfulness makes my teeth hurt. "Do ya'll know what you want this evening?"

While James orders for us, I glance at our VidReel account. The video we posted this afternoon is blowing up. So I start a group chat with Grayson and Jensen and send them the screenshot. I'm so busy sharing the good news with the boys that I miss what James says at first.

"Delilah, did you hear me?"

"Huh? Oh, no, sorry. I missed it. What did you say?"

"I said I need to speak with you and Mom."

"Well, speak, Ubu, speak," I reply, sticking my tongue out at him, and he returns the gesture.

"Children! Settle down!" Mom sighs. "James, what did you want to tell us?"

"I'm enlisting."

Mom and I both stop and just look at him. *He's enlisting.* He's going away to fight and die and didn't even give me—us—the courtesy of being a part of this decision. It takes me a second to realize no one has said anything. The silence grows as he looks at each of us in turn.

I shake my head, then shake it again. I swear I must be halluci-nating. I pick up my glass, examining it closely for contamination.

What is in this water?

"Delilah, what are you doing? What is wrong with your water?" James reaches to take the glass from me.

"I think there must be something in it ʼcause if there isn't, you just told us you were enlisting. Since I know that can't be happening, the most logical answer is that I'm hallucinating. And the only way I could be hallucinating is if Jeanie put something in my water."

Sighing as if I am the problem with this dinner, James returns my cup. "Delilah, stop being dramatic. Yes, I said I'm enlisting."

"Dramatic? Me? You want *me* to stop being dramatic?"

"Yes. I want you to stop being dramatic."

I can feel the eyes of the other diners on me, but I'm beyond caring. "You take us out for my birthday and then drop a bomb like this? What were you thinking? Were *you* thinking? Did you think about what this would do to Mom? *To me?* Did you think about anything other than yourself when you made this decision? You know what happened when Dad died. Now you want to follow in his footsteps and leave us just like he did!"

I stand from the table so quickly my chair falls to the floor. I gesture pointedly to Mom, who still hasn't moved or said a word since James's announcement, her face now white as a sheet.

"If you don't want to be part of this family anymore, just leave. You don't have to go away and die. You can just go! We don't want you here anyway! Leave!" Storming away from the table, I head for the door, shoving my way past James as he tries to stop me.

When I reach the sidewalk, I stop and take a deep breath. I can't think. I'm pacing in front of the restaurant when the door opens, and James walks out. Without thinking, I stride up to him and swing my fist, just like Dad taught me, connecting with his jaw and making him step back to steady himself with the force of the blow.

I curse under my breath while shaking out my wrist. I think I broke my hand. "Fucking HELL, that HURT!"

"Goddamn it, Delilah! What the fuck!" James rubs his jaw, his eyes wide with shock.

"Don't *damn it, Delilah* me, you asshole! What the hell were you thinking! Enlisting! You couldn't think of anything better to do with your life than to just throw it away?" I'm working up another head of steam, so I move to swing again, but my brother steps out of the way.

"You get one, Delilah. That's it. No more. Now, will you shut up and listen, or will you just continue to run your mouth?"

I back up until I hit the brick wall; then I slide down so I can sit on the sidewalk. "Why?" I whisper. "Can you please just tell me why?"

James lowers himself next to me with a sigh. "Because."

"Because?"

"Because I love you. I love Mom. I haven't always shown it, but I love you more than you could ever know. I need to learn a skill, a trade, a way to earn a living that I can be proud of. Something more than I can do working a farm in this town. I need to be able to provide for you and her. I need to prove myself." James sighs again. "I need to do this, Dee. Please."

"I don't know how to do this without you. I can't lose you too. I won't survive it."

"You won't lose me. I know you don't believe me right now, but I promise I will come home. I promise."

I lay my head against his shoulder, the concrete rough under my thighs, and James rests his head against mine. We sit silently while people walk past us.

"Hey, guys, what are you doing out here? Sorry I'm late. I just got off work. Are we not going to dinner anymore?"

I look up and see X walking toward us.

I shake my head and push to my feet. "No. We're not going out to dinner anymore. I'll see you guys at home." I turn and stalk away, ignoring the sound of my name being called after me.

I text Jensen and wait for him a few blocks over from the restaurant, brushing off his questions and heading to my treehouse as soon as he drops me home.

Lying on my back, I stare at the ceiling, trying to wrap my head around James leaving, going to war, and the very real possibility he could die.

When I hear a noise outside, I don't bother looking to see who it is. "Go away, Jensen. I'll talk to you tomorrow. Promise."

"It isn't Jensen."

I turn to see X climbing through the door.

"Move over. There isn't as much room as there used to be."

I scoot to the side, but we still end up shoulder to shoulder. Sighing, he settles in next to me. We are silent for several minutes before I give in.

"What are you doing here, X?"

"Me? I'm just lying here listening to the frogs. What about you? You hiding up here?"

"I am not hiding!"

"Yeah, okay. You're right. You're not hiding. You're pouting."

"I'm not pouting either!"

X rolls on to his side and faces me. "Look. I know you aren't happy about this. I'm sure you're scared, mad, sad, probably a rainbow of emotions. Have you taken even a second to stop and think about how James feels? Your Mom?"

"I'm going to lose him, X. He's going to go away, and I'll never see him again. He's my big brother, my James, my world. I've never had to do this life without him. Losing Dad... I mean, you were there. It almost destroyed us. Losing James? It *will*." I stare at the ceiling to keep the tears from falling from my eyes.

"I know it feels that way now. You don't know what the future holds, and that's scary. But let me tell you what I do know. You're braver than you could ever believe and stronger than you know. Lean on me. If something does happen, I will be there. I'll always be there when you need me."

"You totally stole that, you thief."

"Sue me, Lil Bit. Just because I stole it doesn't mean it isn't true."

I finally turn to look at him. All I can see on his face is sincerity and affection, and that breaks my hold on my emotions. Tears stream down my face, and I can't stop them.

"Happy birthday to me."

X pulls me into his chest as my sobs fill the air. I cry until I can't cry anymore. Until I'm drained and empty. I feel myself drifting off to sleep when X murmurs, "Happy Birthday, Delilah."

Chapter 5
Alexander

My best friend's decision to break the news the way he did officially put him on my shit list. To make myself feel better, I picture all the different ways I would like to kick his ass while I hold Delilah as she cries herself to sleep.

When I'm sure she's knocked out, I pull a blanket from the chest we keep up here in the treehouse, cover her up, and climb down. Then I make my way inside in search of James. He's sitting on the couch with a beer, staring at the carpet between his feet. It takes him a minute to notice me. I've never seen him look so depressed.

"How is she?"

"She isn't good. Jesus, James. Why would you pick tonight of all nights? I mean, her birthday? Then you just blurt it out like that? No warning?"

"I know. I know. I just... I couldn't keep the secret anymore. I was going to break it to them gently. I was going to talk about my reasons. I wanted to tell them how it was a hard decision for me to make, and how I thought it was best for everyone. I planned on doing it gently, have a reasonable conversation, and answer all their questions. Then I was sitting there, and Delilah and Mom were looking at me, and I panicked. I couldn't hold it in anymore, and it just happened! We graduate soon, really soon, and I'll be signing those enlistment papers. I need them to know now, not later. But I could have handled it better. I know that."

Fuck this night.

Running my hands over my face, I reach out to grab a beer from the pack, sit back on the sofa next to James, and sip quietly. "You need to apologize to her."

"Christ, Alex, don't you think I know that? I don't know how to get her to talk to me when she's like this. You know how stubborn she is!"

"You could always let her hit you again." I smirk at him, knowing he must be livid that Delilah got the drop on him like that.

"Oh, fuck you, Stephenson. She isn't getting another chance to clean my clock."

"Let me think about it. I'll talk to Delilah too. You know she doesn't take change well. She cried herself to sleep in the treehouse tonight. Which means she's going to be extra cranky when she wakes up. If I were you, I'd have some extra strong coffee and French toast waiting. You know she can't stay mad at your stupid face when you make your dad's French toast."

"The two things she loves most in the morning." James chuckles. "You're not wrong. At this point, it can only help my case. So I'll use my sign-on bonus to pay off the final bit of the mortgage and the taxes the insurance money didn't cover."

The front door bursts open, hitting the wall behind it and bouncing so hard it almost closes again. "Delilah isn't answering her phone!" Jensen strides up to James. "Where is she?"

"Calm down. She's asleep in the treehouse," I tell him and can see Jensen physically deflate.

"Thank God. She wouldn't tell me what happened when I brought her home. She barely said a word. Someone needs to tell me what happened! The last I heard, you were taking her out for her birthday."

"I'm enlisting." James sounds resigned by this point, his jaw set tight and his shoulders dropping.

"Oh, fuck." Jensen plops down next to me. "You told her. You told her that you're enlisting and doing the same thing that killed your father. You did THAT on her BIRTHDAY. Are you completely insane?" Jensen shoots back up and starts yelling at James, who groans and stands, his hands on his hips and his head tilted to look at the ceiling.

"I know, okay. I know. I'm already trying to figure out how to get her to forgive me."

"That's simple. Don't do it."

"It isn't that simple. There are reasons I have to do this, and I sure as shit don't owe them to you."

"That is my best friend out there. You damn well do owe me the reasons."

"James?" Mrs. Callahan calls out a few seconds before walking in on the drama that's unfolding in the middle of her living room. "Is everything okay in here, boys?"

"It's fine, Mama. Nothing's wrong. Isn't that right, Jensen?"

"It's fine, Mrs. C. I promise. I'm going to go home. Please tell Dee to text me as soon as she wakes up." Jensen kisses Mrs. Callahan on her cheek, his fight seeming to dwindle as soon as Delilah's mom walks in. Though that doesn't stop him from shooting James a glare on his way out the front door.

Mrs. Callahan watches him leave before turning to us again. It's then I notice she has her arms behind her back. James must notice the same thing because he walks closer with a palm thrown out in her direction.

"Mama. That's Dad's go bag. Where did you get that?" James takes the bag from his mom's hand and pulls it close.

Mrs. Callahan draws in a deep breath before slowly releasing it. "After…" She pauses and swallows. "They returned his belongings. This was part of the box they gave me. James, I never wanted this life for you, but if you feel this is something you have to do, then I already know nothing I can say will change your mind. You have too much of your daddy in you, and I won't waste my time. I do want you to know that I love you. I will always be here when you need somewhere to go. This will always be your home." Tears run down her face.

James sets the bag on the couch before pulling his mom in for a tight hug, and I take this as my cue to leave.

From the front of the house, I can barely make out the silhouette of the treehouse in the distance. I get to the end of the driveway before something has me stopping and looking back. I can see James and Mrs. Callahan on the couch talking and can't help but wonder what my life would have been like if we never moved here and met this family. Years of good and bad memories play through my mind—more good than bad, to be honest. I can't imagine my life without these people in it.

James walks out the front door an hour later. I lean back against the hood of his truck as he hands me another beer. "They're going to be okay, right?" he asks me.

"I don't know. They're still fragile, even all these years later. I understand that people love the phrase 'time heals all wounds,' but that's complete shit. Some hurt never heals, and losing a loved one is the main kind."

We sip our drinks in the dark with the lightning bugs illuminating the sky and the frogs interrupting the quiet night. The heat is oppressive, but the silence is easy.

Finally, James pushes off the truck. "I won't apologize for making this decision. To apologize would mean I've done something wrong, but I still believe with all my heart that joining the Army is the right choice. That being said, I didn't go about it right, and I do owe several apologies for that. The first is to you, Alex. You've been my best friend, and I put you in an awkward position with Delilah and my mom."

We clap hands and side hug.

"Thanks, man, I appreciate it. I won't begin to say I understand what prompted you to make your decision, but you're right. You are and will always be my best friend."

"Same, Alex." With a wave, James heads inside, and I pivot toward my house, feeling both lighter and heavier about the way things turned out tonight.

Chapter 6
Delilah

I wake up to the sound of the Warrens' rooster crowing. Sitting up, I push my hair out of my face and let the blanket fall onto my lap. I shiver in the morning chill as the smell of the dew tickles my nose. If it's 6 a.m., I will eat my shoes. But this works in my favor. I can sneak back into my room, and with any luck, no one will realize I didn't officially come inside last night.

Looking out the window, I see that the sun has barely breached the horizon, and I groan just as the rooster crows again.

"Shut the fuck up, Jeffrey, you whore!" I yell, not in the mood for his particular brand of morning cheer.

He crows in response.

I groan again and roll onto my knees before folding the blanket and throwing my hair into a messy bun. I slowly climb down from the treehouse. As I sneak across the yard, the grass is wet and slick under my feet. I reach the back steps and creep up, skipping the intermediate board that creaks. I walk onto the patio. Slide open and then close the back door. I remove my shoes so they don't squeak on the linoleum. I get as far as the hallway before I hear a throat clear from the living room.

"Oh, Jesus Christ!" I jump in surprise.

"No, your brother, James," he replies, his tone dry and his expression seemingly amused. "I see you finally decided to come inside. Please shower, get ready, and meet me in the kitchen. Let's talk."

I watch my brother's back as he heads into the kitchen. I contemplate not doing a damn thing he says, when the aroma of coffee fills the air, followed closely by bacon. That bastard knows I would do almost anything for a cup of coffee—they could keep the Klondike bars—and he used it to his advantage. Cursing quietly under my breath, I head to my room to get cleaned up.

Forty-five minutes later, I walk into the kitchenette with my hair dripping down my back. James meets me at the door with a cup of coffee and a plate full of French toast and bacon. I admire the spread laid out in front of me. James must feel like shit to pull out the big guns. I don't forgive him, not in the least, but he is the only one who has been able to cook Dad's French toast, and I'll never pass up the chance to have it.

We both take our usual seats at the table. I inhale the sweet, sweet nectar of the gods, before taking a long gulp of the coffee while savoring the vanilla flavor. But my enjoyment is cut short when I hear James clear his throat, a sure sign of his nervousness.

"Dee, I want you to know I am so sorry for what happened last night. It was never my intention to ruin your birthday—"

I stop him. "No. We are not doing that now. I never got my dinner. I am starving, and my head is killing me. We are eating breakfast. That is what we are doing now. If you want to talk after, we can, but we are eating breakfast right now. Got it?"

James nods, picks up his fork, and starts eating. The only sound is the clinking of silverware and my mom's grandfather clock beside the mantel. We eat in silence.

I stand up when I'm finished and set my plate in the sink when something on the counter catches my eye. "Is that..." I pause because the words might as well be boulders in my throat, and the French toast turns to lead in my stomach. I think I'm going to be sick.

Following my line of sight, James nods. "Yeah, Mom gave it to me. We talked for a while about the whole thing. I realize what I did last night..." I can hear him audibly swallow. "...wasn't in the best of form. However, please listen. I can explain it and apologize to you simultaneously."

"You think you can just spout some words, and I'll forgive you? Will it be that easy? Do you even comprehend what you did wrong? Does it mean anything to you that you're single-handedly ruining this family again?"

"Delilah, I know I ruined your birthday, and I am sorry, but if you will just—"

I cut him off again. "You listen here, you self-centered son of a bitch. I am not some child upset that my birthday didn't go the way I planned. Does it suck that you picked that particular dinner? Yes, but that's not *why* I'm upset. I'm upset because you made this decision without us. We are a family. We discuss things that affect this family. *Together*. But, then, suddenly you go out on your own and decide, all alone, that our feelings don't matter. You've been talking to a recruiter for months now, right?"

James nods and I throw my hands into the air,

"Did you ever think that we might have wanted to support you all those months? That we could have had questions too? While we may have needed time to adjust to the thought of you being gone, that we would have supported you? No, you didn't give us the courtesy of those months. You gave us two weeks, James. *Two. Weeks.* It takes me longer to decide on a hairstyle, but I'm just supposed to be okay with losing my big brother because he *says so*?"

Slamming my coffee cup onto the counter, I shake my head in disgust.

"Do you think so little of us? Of this family? Damn it, James, don't you know that we only want you to be happy? Do you honestly believe we wouldn't support you if you needed this to be fully happy and fulfilled? Do you have so little faith in our love for you?" I can feel the tears forming in my eyes again before I angrily swipe them away. "You're my big brother. You've been the most important person in my world since I can remember. The fact that you thought I wouldn't support you breaks my heart."

I sigh and walk past him to the doorway.

"I love you, James. I will always love you. However, I have to be honest. I don't like you very much right now. One of these days, I'll be able to forgive you. I just don't think that day is today." I sweep out of the room and head to my studio. I need to be alone, and I need to find myself. I need my music. It's my constant. It's always there, and it'll never disappoint me. I'm desperate for the peace I feel with my guitar.

I check my phone and notice it's only 8 a.m. While I know it's too early to bring the group over, there's still time for a little solo with just me and my guitar, and I already know the song.

A knock on the door has me sitting upright. My back protests the movements, as do my neck and shoulders. Groaning, I look at the time and see it's almost noon. I've been playing for hours and didn't realize it. The door opens and in walks Jensen. I can tell he's worried. The lines between his eyebrows are deep and the twitch under his left eye is jumping.

"Julie Roberts, Fergie, and Jessica Andrews? You're upset. You want to tell me what's going on?"

Placing my guitar on its stand, I try to work the kinks out of my back. "Nothing much to tell. My brother is a horse's ass. He decided that the best time to drop a nuclear bomb on our family was during my birthday dinner. I could give a rat's ass about the dinner. Still, the fact that he would consider a life-changing decision without discussing it with us cheeses my grits."

Jensen flops onto the couch with a groan. "You know how much I hate it when you use that backcountry slang! Just speak English!"

I intentionally make my twang more pronounced, knowing it'll irritate him. The fact that he hates it makes me chuckle. I toss a throw pillow at him. "It pisses me off. He cheeses my grits means he pisses me off. Jesus, get some learning, will you?"

Jensen throws his head back on another groan. "Look… Full disclosure? I may have come over last night and almost kicked James's ass until he told me what was happening." He pretends he doesn't see my glare. "I'm not going to defend him. That's a Callahan conversation, but you should know that Grayson will be here in ten minutes to jam ' cause I know you need it."

I fall on the couch and lay my head on Jensen's shoulder. "Thank you. I do need it, but also, thank you for being my best friend, for being there for me whenever I need someone. My life would completely suck without you."

"Ditto, Dee. Ditto."

Chapter 7
Alexander

Graduation day is a rite of passage where we officially become adults in the eyes of the world. Or so I've been told.

But right now, all I can think about is how the cheap rayon gown is sticking to my skin, while I'm sitting in the small wooden chair waiting for my name to be called. I swear it is a million degrees in this auditorium. James has already been called to the podium and is back in his seat, waiting for the pageantry to end. He told me that he signed the papers with the recruiter yesterday; and in two weeks, he leaves for basic training, just like his dad.

Delilah still hasn't forgiven him. While she isn't entirely ignoring his existence, their everyday interactions are icier than a slushy from the corner store.

My row gets called to come up to the steps leading to the stage, and I stand at the bottom. I can admit, if only to myself, that this is bittersweet. If you asked me a year ago, I would have told you my future was set in stone. I was supposed to be getting ready to attend Notre Dame on a football scholarship. I was going to get out of this town. I was going to see the world. Growing up, you think you're invincible. I found out the hard way you're not.

I pull myself out of my reflection when I hear my name called. Shaking Principal Tudyk's hand, I take the rolled-up piece of paper that is the placeholder for my diploma. The spotlights are bright and hot as I walk off the other side of the stage. I can hear my family and friends cheering me on. Waving into the darkness past the spotlights, I exit the stage and retake my seat.

It isn't long before the list reaches its end and we are officially announced as this year's graduating class. Another cheer rings out in the auditorium, and we are done.

Thank fuck.

Exiting the building, I find Mom, Dad, and Mrs. Callahan just outside the door. Delilah is talking to Jensen. Their conversation is heated and animated before Jensen throws up his hand and stalks away. From what I can tell, Delilah has yet to acknowledge her brother. I slide next to her when Jensen leaves and tug a copper curl.

"Still upset, huh, Lil Bit?"

"I have no idea what you referring to, X. I am simply enjoying the graduation and waiting for my mom to be ready to go home." Her stiff and slightly formal tone has me grinning. On days when she has that tone, annoying her is as easy as pushing a button.

"I am referring to the fact that your brother signed a letter of intent with a recruiter yesterday. I am referring to the fact that you are avoiding him like you owe him money. I am also referring to the fact that even though I know he's apologized, you still have yet to forgive him. Why is that, Lil Bit, hm? Oh, c'mon. Do tell. We are dying to know." I sidle closer and twist my tone to a cartoonish style, knowing the reaction I'll get. I know I'm not wrong when she shoulder-checks me and grins.

"You are so annoying, X." Her tone is anything but annoyed. Leaning against the side of the building, she hangs her head and heaves a sigh. "You're not wrong, you know? He did apologize. I should forgive him but not for the reasons you think." Her voice is barely above a whisper, and I have to lean close to hear her.

"What reasons do you think *I* think?"

"That I'm selfish," she whispers. "I'm a spoiled little girl upset that James ruined my birthday. Because he broke Mom's heart and is throwing his life away. I'm jealous. James is getting out of this town but leaving us here. That he will leave us like Dad did." She chuckles, but it is mirthless. "Take your pick, X. Which one do you think describes me best?" Her words hitch at the end with a sadness I haven't heard since her father's funeral.

"Delilah, no. No one would believe that about you. No one would ever doubt how much you love James. How much we love you. Everyone is confused about why you've been hanging on to your anger for so long. I would be surprised if you didn't hold a grudge, but this feels excessive."

A riot of red curls obscures her tilted face as she stares at the ground while scuffing the toe of her boot. I lean back against the sun-warmed bricks, determined to wait her out. She may be young, but she's already a force to be reckoned with. You can't rush her; you must let her reach her conclusions. The one thing that Delilah Rose Callahan hates more than chunky peanut butter is being told what to do.

"Lil Bit?" I tread cautiously.

She sighs before lifting her eyes to the night sky. "It's a lie. That's my problem. One big, fat lie. I won't be gone for long. I'll be safe.

I'll be home soon. You have nothing to worry about." The more she says, the more bitter she sounds, and I don't like it. She angrily kicks the ground in front of her. "I'm sick and tired of the men in my life lying to me." She throws her hands up and pushes off the wall. I barely manage to dodge out of the way. "Everyone! Every single one of them has lied to me! Dad! James! Jensen! YOU!"

My head snaps back as if she struck me. "*Me?* Delilah Rose Callahan, when have I lied to you?"

"You left! You just woke up one day and decided I wasn't good enough to hang around, to practice with. You went so far as to stop playing guitar! Why else would you give up something you loved if not because of me?"

"Delilah! No, I just..." I start to say, and she interrupts me.

"No. Just forget it. You wanted to know why I haven't been able to forgive James? Now you know." With that, she runs over to her mom, whispers something in her ear, and then disappears into the night.

I stand there stunned for a minute before shaking it off and heading toward James. Grabbing his arm, I lean close. "We need to talk. Meet me at the Warrens South 15."

Forty-five minutes later, James and I are sitting on the tailgate of his pickup with a couple of beers. I explained what Delilah told me about why she's upset, and he looked genuinely hurt.

"I never realized she felt that way. How would I? I was young when Dad passed, but she was younger. I know she was distraught, but I never realized that she felt like he'd lied and betrayed her. That she *feels* that way about me now." He rubs his hands down his face with a groan. "She is never going to forgive me, is she, Alex?"

I clap him on the shoulder. "She will. You'll have to be extra careful where you're going and make it back in one piece, but she will forgive you. It may take longer than we both initially anticipated because, let's face it, your sister is the most stubborn girl we've ever met."

He chuckles while nodding his agreement. We clink our bottles together before finishing them up.

"C'mon. Let's head to your house. Your mom mentioned ordering pizza, which means Delilah will try to eat all the stuffed crust just to be mean."

James groans as he shuts the tailgate, and we head back home.

The radio starts on the local station as he cranks the car, and the headlights illuminate the field. They're advertising a local show barn auction coming up. Apparently, Wild Child Reckless will be performing.

"The band is really taking off, right?" I gesture at the radio as I snap my seat belt into place.

"Yeah, I've had a couple of labels reach out to me about signing them. Jensen's dad, Grayson's parents, and I all sat down and discussed it. I only agreed to something once they graduated. They're open to the kids doing whatever they want with the band, but graduating is nonnegotiable." James sounds both proud and scared at the same time.

I let out a low whistle. I knew they were getting popular, but I didn't realize it was on that level.

"Are you okay with her jetting off to who knows where and signing with some record label?" If she were my sister, I wouldn't be. However, I keep my opinion to myself.

"Delilah and I have had several conversations about labels and contracts and what to look out for. Grayson's dad—Mr. Stone—will handle all negotiations if they sign with a label. It's already been paid for by Jensen's dad. He wants to keep them both safe and apparently has a family lawyer on retainer. She knows that anything she wants must be in writing, and I trust him to follow not only Delilah's wishes but mine regarding the terms of the contract." James's nonchalance surprises me.

"I didn't realize you supported the band that much."

"Delilah can do anything she sets her mind to. I prefer to be prepared for all eventualities."

We pull up to the house, and I swear every light is on. A crowd is milling around and chatting while kids are running in the yard. I grin at the look of dismay on James's face as soon as he realizes our parents are throwing him a graduation/going away party.

"C'mon, Callahan. Let's go." I slap my buddy on the shoulder before opening my door and exiting.

James follows closely behind me, accepting hugs and hand-shakes from people as we pass by. Everyone congratulates him for his service and me for graduating. We finally make it to the porch, and I see James watching Maisie. She's sitting on the porch swing, sipping on what appears to be a lemonade.

I nudge his shoulder in her direction. We may only have two weeks before he ships out, but I'll ensure they're weeks to remember.

Chapter 8
Delilah

The last two weeks have been hell. Every night, I toss and turn to dreams about my dad begging me to forgive him. Telling me he loves me and that what James is doing is brave and honorable. Every morning, I wake up more tired than the night before. I haven't touched my guitar since the graduation party. Just like my brother, my music has left me. After another fitful night of trying to sleep, I give up and get up.

I pad into the kitchen and start the coffeemaker. There is not enough espresso in the world to make this day more palatable. James leaves for basic training today, and my life changes again. Forever. My head is pounding, so I rub my forehead while praying it'll help ease some of the tension. On top of the endless dreams of Dad, Mom has been on my case all week as well. She wants me to talk to James, to forgive him. If she only knew that I already did...

I set my forehead against the table and bang it softly. *Why am I so stubborn?*

"Delilah?"

When I peer up, I see James standing, visibly hesitant, in the doorway to the kitchen with his go bag at his feet. I don't think I ever noticed just how much he resembles our father until now: the same curly red hair, our shared green eyes, and his chin. With the go bag at his feet, he could pass for a younger Dad headed off to basic training with my mom waiting for him to come home. He always came home. Until he didn't.

Will history repeat itself with James? Will I lose my brother, who looks so much like our father, in the same way we lost him? Will we survive the burial of another Callahan man if we did?

I think decidedly not. That would be the crack that breaks the foundation of our family.

I look up at my brother with tears in my eyes that match his. Force out a huff of air, stand up, and move to him. James reaches out and takes my hand before tugging me closer. Then we both sink to our knees and embrace as the tears fall. That's how Mom finds us. She kneels at our backs and wraps her arms around us. Pressing a kiss to our heads, she whispers that it's time to go. I push myself off the floor and scrub my face with my sleeve, while James picks up his go bag.

We already decided that he would take the bus to his basic training station. He didn't want us making the drive and being caught out after dark.

I pull him in for another hug and bury my face in his chest. "I love you," I manage to choke out as the tears fall onto his shirt this time. "I will only forgive you if you come home in one piece. Promise me... promise me this and never break it." I hold up my pinkie and wait until he joins mine with his.

"I love you, Dee. I love you so much. Never forget how much. I will be back. I will watch over you no matter where I am. If things go sideways, you can always call me. Promise me that you will always call me," he says, his voice rough and more demanding than it usually is.

I choke on a sob as I nod my head in agreement.

James looks between Mom and me before adding, "I'm paying off the taxes and the mortgage when I get my enlistment bonus. I don't want you to worry while I am gone, Mom. Dee, I asked Alex to keep an eye on you since he's going to Havenbrook. You need anything, you go to him first, but always call me." Then, with another hug for each of us, he walks out the door.

Just like that, I'm truly alone for the first time.

I look around the house, which somehow remains the same. You would think when your world crumbles, there would be debris left in the aftermath, but you look around and somehow everything is the same. When I turn my head, I see Mom standing in the kitchen doorway, her eyes still on the front door, her mouth moving but no words coming out. I know that prayer. I've been saying the same one for two weeks now.

Something about the heaviness in my chest reignites my urge to play. Hurrying down the hall to my studio, I grab my guitar from the stand, but the room feels claustrophobic. My fingers twitch, and I catch a few song notes in my head before I turn and run out of the house. Swinging the guitar to my back, I climb into the tree house and settle on the cushions as my fingers strum the strings. I play for several bars before finding my voice.

"I can't stand this empty house.

The memories haunt me.

Some days I feel I may drown.

Even though you're gone,

Being without you here breaks me.
Some days are only rain.
I can't pretend that I'm okay,
The way others want me to be.
I'm standing here so lost,
The end of everything so close.
I have so much I want to say,
But you just walked away.
You left me knowing
Who I could've been, if you had stayed,
Breaking all that I had, trusting you.
Is that what you were trying to do?"

My head whips up when another set of strings joins in, and I see X sitting across from me, his guitar in place. He plays as if he never stopped—maybe he never did—and then we're weaving harmonies together once again.

"I'm still here, living with my regret.
Why can't we do it over?
I would trade a single day
For all the words that I had saved,
That I left unspoken.
I'm standing here,
But you're not.
I have so much I want to say,
But you just walked away.
You left me knowing
Who I could've been, if you had stayed,
Breaking all that I had, trusting you.

Is that what you were trying to do?"

As the final notes die off, we sit in silence. I startle when I feel X's hand on my shoulder.

"Dee?" he says, his voice soft. "Honey, we need to go inside. C'mon." Then he takes my guitar before helping me down the ladder and into the house.

I follow him into my room. He sits me on my bed and removes my shoes before laying me back on the pillows. He tucks my legs up before draping a throw over me.

"He's gone, X. He's gone, and he won't be back." My words are nothing more than a whisper in the silence.

"No, Dee. No. He will be back. He promised, remember? James never breaks his promises, especially not to you." X seems to emanate a confidence I don't yet feel.

"Why did he do it? I know all the *whys* he gave us, but I want to know the real reason." I can hear the tears that clog my throat, threatening to cut off my ability to think.

X walks back to my bed and bends down. "You," he whispers.

Not another word is spoken as he kisses my forehead and cuts off my bedside lamp. He doesn't look back as he walks to the bedroom door and shuts it behind him, and I can finally open the floodgates on everything I've been holding inside for weeks. I sob, scream into my pillow, curse, and pray. And when it's all said and done, I sleep. For the first time in weeks. I don't have a single dream.

When I wake up the following day, it's to a text on my phone.

James: I love you, baby sister. I've loved you every second of every day since you entered our family. I love your heart and

your smile, and your snark. I will not break my promise. You will see me again. I will come home. You are my world. Never forget.

I clutch my phone to my chest and refuse to cry anymore tears. *If James can be brave, then why can't I?*

I throw on my lounging clothes and walk into the hallway. I smell coffee coming from the kitchen and quickly check the time on my phone, 7 a.m. It's too early for Mom to be home.

So who's in my house?

I hurry to the kitchen, only to stop in the doorway when I see X cooking breakfast at the stove. "X? What are you doing here this early?"

"I never left. I slept on the sectional. I didn't want you to be alone if you needed something in the middle of the night. I figured you wouldn't feel your best when you woke up, and I wanted to help. French toast and extra strong espresso, just what the doctor ordered."

I have to snort. "No doctor would order that. It's extremely unhealthy." I eagerly take the plate, cutting off a piece of toast, shoving it in my mouth, and groaning in relief at the sweet sugary goodness that coats my tongue.

"Well, if the doctor knew what was good for him, he would. No one gets between you and French toast." X chuckles before picking up his cup of coffee and taking a sip. "I know your mom should be home soon. I made a plate for her too. It's in the microwave. I'm going to finish this and then head home."

I walk up behind X, as he sets his cup in the sink, and wrap my arms around his waist. He freezes and I lean in and squeeze him tighter, taking comfort in his warmth. "Thank you for everything. I don't know what promises James made you or what he made you promise in return, but I know that no one could have loved him more and been there for him but you. So, thank you. For everything you have done and that you're going to do." My voice is barely above a murmur, but X hears me and turns in my embrace to hug me back.

"Anything, Dee, anything at all, I'm here. Just say the word."

I sigh in relief and squeeze him tighter. "You want to watch a movie? I think there's a couple of new releases streaming right now." I pick up my cup of coffee and head for the couch.

X follows behind me but steals the remote from my hand. He grins as he turns on the TV. "I'll pick. Your taste in movies sucks."

Throwing a pillow at him, I get comfortable. Maybe the crack in my heart won't last forever after all.

Chapter 9
Alexander

It was an adjustment, not having James around. Delilah initially refused to go to James's basic training graduation. It took two weeks for us to convince her to go.

Finally, her mom put her foot down and told her she needed to grow up and that she would go and be a supportive sister, or she would answer to her. Delilah looked so shattered I quickly suggested that we all go. It could be a road trip.

We watch the graduation from the grass while sweating in the summer sun. When James is called, Mom and Ms. Callahan cry, their hands to their mouths to help muffle the sounds. Even Delilah has tears in her eyes as she watches her brother. James walks up to us after the ceremony ends and even his walk is different.

"Hey there, Callahan. I almost didn't recognize you with that snazzy new haircut."

James and I clap hands and hug as he approaches our group. "Yeah, well, you look like you could use one yourself, hippie." He flips my bangs up and over, and I swat his hand and shove his shoulder.

"James?" Delilah's voice is hesitant and quiet, and damn if I don't hate it.

I almost stop breathing as my heart races, waiting to see what my best friend will say when he finally sees his sister again. James turns quickly, pulling her into a hug, which she returns before the tears start to fall. He holds Delilah for a while, refusing to let her go, not that she tries that hard to escape.

This trip wasn't about me and my feelings; it was about Delilah. I may be an only child, but I've never seen a bond like that of the Callahan children. They whisper for several minutes, and I let them keep their sibling secrets. By the time they break apart, our group has no more dry eyes. We all hug, and the parents discuss where to go to lunch.

I pull James to the side. "So what's next for you after this? You've made it this far." I bump his shoulder, but he refuses to meet my eyes.

"Well, I have a couple of options open to me. I haven't really made a decision." His evasiveness has the hair on the back of my neck standing up.

"What do you mean you haven't made a decision? Are you even allowed to do that?"

This guy has planned everything since we were sixteen and wanted to hook up with the Markson twins. James shrugs, refusing to comment, and I realize how much he's changed. I almost don't recognize my best friend. He has a discipline, a hardness about him that was missing before.

"Callahan. C'mon. Don't be like that. What's going on?" I place a hand on his shoulder, shaking slightly.

He sighs and tilts his head back before finally meeting my eyes. "I can't tell you."

"What the fuck do you mean you can't tell me?" I try to keep my tone even and fail… miserably.

"I can't tell you because then you'll have to lie to Delilah and my mom. I can't tell you because I was told I couldn't tell anyone. And I can't tell you because you'll try to talk me out of it, and it's already done." He drops his eyes to his boots, and my jaw joins them.

"James, what have you done?" I whisper, not wanting anyone to overhear.

"What I had to do, Alex. What I had to." He claps a hand on my shoulder this time before joining our families in discussing where to go for lunch. I try to get him alone again, but he ensures it doesn't happen.

Before we know it, the day is over, and we're heading home. Delilah seems to be in better spirits, and while I'm still worried, I'm happy that she appears to be out of whatever funk was holding her down.

"Aren't you glad you went now?" I tease, tugging on one of her copper curls.

Delilah swats my hand away and tries to give me a grumpy face before laughing. "Yes, thank you. I'm glad I went. It was good to see James and to talk to him. To know he was safe, see it with my own two eyes." She turns slightly to meet my gaze. "I'm serious. Thank you." The smile is small and somewhat sad but still there, and that's all that matters.

"You're welcome, Lil Bit. You're welcome." I pull her close, and she sighs before putting her head on my shoulder, where she promptly passes out.

I spend the remainder of the ride home with her soft breath on my neck, her hair tickling my arm, and the press of her body against mine slowly driving me crazy. I close my eyes and lean my head back on the seat, willing my body not to react. To remember this is James's baby sister and she's only fifteen to my eighteen. Then Delilah mumbles in her sleep before cuddling closer and laying an arm across my chest.

This is going to be a long ride.

***

Wild Child Reckless is recording more videos than ever this summer. And Delilah is more herself even when she isn't singing. However, she still owns every stage she steps on. The hot Texas summer quickly ends, and a new adventure awaits. I'm starting my freshman year at Havenbrook, and Delilah is starting hers at Havenbrook Academy.

I spend longer than intended searching for a parking spot. I was supposed to take Delilah to her first day of school. She didn't answer my messages this morning, and when I saw Jensen pull up, I gave up expecting an answer, hopped into my Chevy, and cranked the AC on as cold as possible. It may only be 8 a.m., but it's already going to be a scorcher.

I trudge up the steps with a groan, sipping on the coffee in my hand as my messenger bag bangs back and forth against my hip, and make my way to my first class of the day. Literature. Why they had a sports medicine major studying this crap is beyond me, but seeing as it's a requirement, I don't have much of a choice.

Walking into the classroom, I make eye contact with a pretty blonde standing at the front of the room with a stack of papers. I walk up to her with a smile.

"Hi, my name is Megan. I'm Professor Daniel's TA. If you ever need anything..." She leans forward, letting me glance down the front of her shirt. "...just let me know," she practically purrs as she hands me a syllabus.

Taking the paper from her hand, I murmur my thanks and sit in the middle row. Other students mill around. Chatting. Many with cups of coffee like mine. I get the feeling of eyes on me and glance up from my syllabus to see Megan staring my way with a gleam in her brown eyes. When she catches me returning her glare, she runs her tongue over her bottom lip and winks. I arch my brow at her.

Maybe Havenbrook U is just the distraction I need.

The rest of the day is a wearisome jumble of new classes, new buildings, some old friends, and a disturbing lack of parking spaces. Pulling up in my drive, I'm relieved to see the light on at Delilah's house. So I head over and knock on her door. I listen to the crickets and tree frogs arguing in the dark. Lightning bugs flicker in the inky night, and the smell of magnolias is everywhere. I'm about to call it a lost cause and head home when Dee opens the door. She leans against the frame, partially-ly blocking my view of her.

"Good evening, Alexander. How nice of you to stop by. What can I do for you this fine Texas evening?" her tone is formal, but her body language is tired.

"I came to check on you and to hear about your first day of school. I noticed you had Jensen pick you up this morning, instead of returning my text. I was supposed to give you a ride, or did you forget?" I'm irritated at best, but I know that won't last long. I was already suspicious about why she didn't want to ride with me this morning. She thinks I haven't noticed the way she's been watching me, but the jokes on her, because I am *always* watching her too.

"Listen... I'm sorry I didn't text you back. After everything that's happened lately, I just needed an easy morning. It would be better to just catch a ride with Jensen since you had to make it to Havenbrook U, and I was in the other direction. You understand, right?"

"I completely understand. However, you know that I am here for you, right? If you ever need anything, I want you to call me, text me, do whatever you must to get me. Now let me in. I'm going to order food."

She opens the door wider, and I wander in before closing it behind me. Following her into the living room, I can't help but notice that her long red curls are brushing the waistband of her black yoga pants. Her steps are fluid, moving with a grace that comes naturally after years of dance and being on stage. Reaching out, I grab a curl and she pulls up short, turning to face me. I refuse to let go, so my arm brushes her arms and the side of her breast. Big green eyes look up into mine as her breath catches and time seems to stand still.

"Let's order some food, huh?" I almost whisper.

The spell is broken, and Delilah quickly moves around to the side of the sectional, settling with one leg pulled up under her rear. I can't take my eyes off her.

"Hello?" She snaps her fingers at me. "Earth to X. Come in, X."

"Brat."

"You love it."

"Keep telling yourself that, doll."

Lord, never let this woman find out how much she has me wrapped around her finger.

Settling on the main portion of the sectional, I pull out my phone and order the pizza. "So... Food will be here in thirty. You wanna hear about my first day at college? Buckle up, buttercup, ' cause it was a doozy." I regale her with tales of classes, buildings, and the hunt for the almighty parking space. By the end, I have Delilah laughing and we are piled up on each other on the sofa.

I manage to get a few stories out of her while we wait for the pizza as well as a promise to be able to give her a ride tomorrow. When she cuddles up close to me on the couch and the smell of her magnolia shampoo washes over me, I clench my jaw, doing my best not to react as she chatters happily while picking out a movie. I try every trick in the book: reciting times tables, thinking of old people naked, envisioning taking a cold shower. It's no use. I'm officially and unequivocally attracted to my best friend's little sister.

Going home that evening, I resolve myself to ignoring this attraction while doing my best to keep things platonic with Delilah.

The school year drags on, seasons pass, and I start spending more time with Megan, who seems more than happy to entertain me. Despite the number of nights that Delilah's truck is home alone, I keep to my side of the fence. Which also means I don't see Delilah as much as I should, and when James texts me, I always tell him she's doing fine even if I haven't heard from or seen her in several days. After all, Delilah promised to let me know if she needed me, so I take no news as good news.

I was wrong.

When I finally get a call from James, I'm driving home, the windows down and the warm breeze blowing through my truck. I answer using my hands-free, and my best friend's pissed-off voice reverberates in the small space.

"Where the fuck are you right now?"

Surprised by his harsh tone, it takes me a minute to respond. "I'm headed home from class," I snap back. "What the fuck is wrong with you?"

"What the fuck is wrong with me? What the fuck is wrong with *you*? I just got a call from Mom. Delilah's in the hospital. She flipped the truck. I told Mom getting her that hardship license was a bad idea, but Delilah begged and pleaded, since she was tired of having to bum rides. She said she tried call-ing *you* before the ambulance arrived. YOU weren't answering YOUR PHONE!"

My heart is in my throat as I pull an illegal U-turn in the middle of the farm-to-market road. My bookbag flies across the bench seat and onto the floorboard but I ignore it, pressing down on the gas pedal as I head toward Mercy General.

"Listen, I was in class and didn't check my phone before getting into my truck. It connected to my Bluetooth automatically or I wouldn't even be on this call, because my phone's still in my bag." I sigh. "Tell me what happened."

By the time I reach the hospital, James has filled me in. Why Delilah would swerve to miss a dog is anyone's guess, but according to the last update, there're no significant injuries. That said, she *will* be in a walking boot for the final three weeks of school. Something I have no doubt she isn't going to be happy about.

Rushing into the ER entrance, I see her mom at the nurses' station waving me over. "Alexander! How nice of you to come. She's over here."

I head that way, not that I need help finding her. I can hear Delilah cursing up a storm from the desk. Mrs. Callahan groans and shows me over to the curtained area.

I walk in and stop short. Delilah is covered in blood, and her pants have been cut off at the knee on her left side, where the doctor has already wrapped and booted her ankle. However, the reason for her clear displeasure seems to be the nurse presently trying to do her best to clean up the various scrapes and bruises.

Delilah glares and tries to sit up, and I can already tell this isn't the first time, because the nurse places a hand on her chest and pushes her back onto the bed. "You have to let me finish cleaning these. Sit. Still." The nurse meets Delilah's glare with one of her own, and finally, the pissed-off redhead settles on the spot.

"Delilah! Listen to Christy! Please!" Mrs. Callahan's exasperated tone has me hiding a grin. Apparently, this has been going on for a while.

"I am FINE, Mom! Someone needs to go check on the dog! He just ran out of nowhere! I didn't hit him, did I?"

"There was no report of a canine on the scene and the only blood found was inside the truck with you. Now sit down and let Christy clean those cuts, young lady!"

Delilah came by her temper honest, and it *honestly* came from Mrs. Callahan, who could be scary in her own right when necessary.

***

Three hours later, I help a booted Delilah into the living room. Groaning in frustration, she makes it to the sectional and does her best to sit down without bumping her foot. Mrs. C follows behind us, fussing like a mother hen, with Delilah's belongings from her truck. As I get Delilah settled, Mrs. C. hands me the bag of meds, a water bottle, and the TV remote.

"I will call Principal Tudyk, let him know what happened and that you'll be back in a few weeks. Try to get some rest while you can. Then I have to call your brother. That boy has been blowing up my phone for the past hour." Mrs. Callahan kisses her daughter's forehead and leaves to make her phone calls.

Delilah looks up from her spot on the couch. "What are you doing here?" she asks, her eyes widening as I walk around and sit down next to her.

"I've been here since the hospital. Dee, I am so sorry I didn't answer when you called. My phone was in my bag on silent during class but that's no excuse. I haven't been here like I promised I would be and that's unacceptable. I want you to know I'm here now. You are going to get so sick of seeing me by the time I'm done. I'm here to entertain you. To be at your beck and call, fetch whatever you want. Direct me, O' invalid one." My over-the-top tone earns me a pillow to the face. I catch and shove it behind my back before I steal the remote.

I'm flipping through the takeout menus when my phone rings. Megan. I swipe to ignore the call and go back to our food order. Delilah opens her mouth to comment when my phone starts ringing. Megan again. I once again swipe the call.

"Where's the fire, Alexander? You standing up a hot date or something?" Delilah's tone is teasing, but I don't buy it.

"Nope. No date tonight. However, I may end up having to take this call." I frown when Megan calls for a third time, so I shoot her a text to let her know that I'm dealing with an emergency and will text her later. Then I find the menu for a popular Thai place in town and start reading it off. "How do you feel about Thai?"

Delilah chews on her bottom lip as texts come through, blowing up my phone one after the other in rapid succession.

"I don't mind Thai, but I'm allergic to mushrooms, remember? So you have to be careful. They don't always list them."

"Well, we're not going to take that chance. Italian it is. I already know you like the three cheese tortellini Rosa. Do you want extra bread?" I silence my phone so we don't have to hear the dings and call to place our order for delivery.

I glance at the texts. *Something about me and Wild Child Reckless?* What is Megan on about? I'm confused but I can answer her later. Right now, Delilah is my focus. I've ignored her for far too long for my own selfish reasons. That isn't happening again. She could have died and I would have been the last to know.

"Fifty-two minutes. Do you need help going to the bathroom? A bottle of water? A pain pill? Maybe a blanket?" I grab the throw from the back of the couch and move to put it on her.

"Whoa. Slow down. What's going on? Not that I don't appreciate the company and the help. But you've never been this attentive. I haven't seen you for the better part of a year. What's the deal?" Delilah takes the blanket, but the look she shoots me says she isn't buying my bullshit.

Sighing, I sit down and turn slightly to face her. "I feel guilty that I haven't been over to check on you as much as I should have. So, the least I can do to make it up to you is ensure I'm always here when you need me now."

"That's really sweet. Honest. You do know I'll be stuck in this thing for at least three to six weeks, right?" She gestures at the clunky boot with a scowl.

"Yup. I know, and I'll be here as much as possible. At the same time, you try to heal. Never fear, Alexander is here!" I strike a superhero pose and take a pillow to the face, but hearing her laugh is worth it.

Over the next few nights, we play guitar and sing. I even guest star in a couple of her videos. The more time I spend with Delilah, the more I realize the remarkable woman she has become, one I almost missed out on getting to know.

Megan has been a total fan girl, begging me to be introduced, but I still haven't brought her around. I'm not sure what's stopping me but I'm hesitant to introduce her to Delilah.

By the time the boot comes off, I can honestly say that I'm in love with Delilah Rose Callahan, no matter how wrong, no matter how certain I am that her brother will kick my ass.

I love her and she can never, ever know.

Chapter 10
Delilah

Summer came around again, and X kept his word. We spent almost every day together for the five weeks I was stuck in that awful contraption. He was always bringing me something to eat and drink from the kitchen. He brought my assignments to and from school until I could return. When I got stir-crazy, he took me on rides in the pasture to get me out of the house, to the drive-in and the local Sonic. Jensen would pick me up after school and we would go to see his abuela, who fussed over me and made me my favorite tamales and clucked over how skinny I was.

Wild Child Reckless is more popular than ever. We have over four million followers and play at almost every sporting event, rodeo, fair, and rally in three counties. It's almost too good to be true.

I finally got my boot off yesterday and am making my way out of the kitchen, when X strolls in from class, and I swear he almost looks disappointed to see the damn thing gone. I thought he would have been pleased to not have to wait on me hand and foot anymore. The doctor cautioned me not to overdo it, but I can already tell that's exactly what I'm going to do. I'm going to perform all summer. I'm going to go viral, and I'm going to put Wild Child Reckless on the map!

"So you got the boot off finally?" X asks while leaning his back against the sectional.

"Yes! Thank goodness! I couldn't take one more day in it!" I slide on my flip-flops, relishing the feeling of freedom. Pulling my hair up into a messy bun, I step off my porch and stand in the summer sun as the rays warm my skin. I'm so distracted by the beautiful day and the ability to walk normally I don't hear X come up behind me.

"Boo!"

I screech and jump, turning to see him laughing at my expense. I lose my balance, and he sprints forward to catch me before pulling me back against his chest. I breathe in the warm smell of sunshine, green grass, and cologne that always seems to come from him. Laying my head against his chest, I can hear his heart racing. Arms slide around my waist and I swear he pulls me closer.

"You okay, Dee?" His voice rumbles right next to my ear.

My words catch in my throat as I turn to meet his eyes. "Y-yeah. I'm okay. You startled me." I can feel his breath on my cheek as he holds me but doesn't move to put me down.

"I didn't mean to make you fall," he whispers.

"I'm okay. No harm, no foul." I meet his eyes stare for stare while fighting the urge to blink.

The sound of a truck pulling into the drive breaks the spell. X sets me on my feet and takes several steps back. I can see his chest rising and falling with each rough breath and feel mine doing the same. We stand here, silent, until Jensen puts his truck in park.

The sound of his door opening has X turning and walking back toward his house.

"What's up with him?" Jensen asks as he makes his way to my side.

"He scared me and almost made me fall. He's just upset at himself. That's all. Are you ready to go?" I climb into the cab of Jensen's truck, but my eyes track back to the house next door. Where X is standing. Watching as we pull away.

I swear Wild Child Reckless ends up spending all summer going from gig to gig to gig. We make more money than we've ever made and put it back into buying better equipment.

I haven't seen X in weeks. Sometimes we would arrive at our respective homes at the same time, and once again I would feel him watching me. Our eyes would meet, but he never crossed back into my yard and I never crossed into his.

Before I realize it, it's time for the new school year to start. Mom is discussing getting me a truck for my birthday since I wrecked the last one. She doesn't want me driving hers anymore. Not that I blame her. For now, though, I'll continue to ride with Jensen since X has yet to do more than text me and check in weekly.

The first day of school dawned bright and early. I wake up more than ready to start the day. Jensen honks from the drive, so I grab my bag and run out. Grayson is in the back seat, having transferred from South Elgin West over the summer. I sign a quick hello, which he returns. Ever since Grayson joined the band, Jensen and I have gotten an ASL crash course. We have become relatively fluent, when it comes to general communication at least.

Pulling up to Havenbrook Academy, we see all the sparkling trucks in the parking lot. Jensen stops at the end of a row. We all pile out and walk up to the door before waving at our classmates standing around chatting before the first period. I bite my lip to hide my grin. I've been waiting all summer for this. I have a secret, and it's about to be discovered in the best possible way.

Summer Splash Carnival advertisements, Havenbrook Academy's most significant fundraiser, have been posted all over campus. The Summer Splash is the carnival our school hosts every year. It's really the event of the county, with vendors from all over the state vying to attend. There's no lot fee, and a fully refundable deposit holds your space, but 25% of all sales go to Havenbrook Academy. Which means lots sell out years in advance.

There's always one main event—the dunk tank. It usually features some high-profile person from the community. This year it's Jensen. I swallow a chuckle and end up snorting when I see the dunk tank poster come into view. I swear it's twice as large as any other year, with a picture of Jensen from our last performance. He's singing into the mic with sweat dripping down his face, and his white shirt is plastered to his chest. Objectively, I can say he looks hot as hell. However, we have never been more than friends. We like it that way.

I'm so busy trying not to laugh I don't notice that Jensen has stopped walking until I crash into his back. The look of horror on his face breaks me, and I cackle in response.

"Did you do this, Callahan?" He turns his hard-set glare on me, and I hide my face behind my hands as I laugh and nod.

I can hear him growl under his breath before he steps up to loom over me. The thing is, I trust Jensen entirely. Also, I never back down. I jump at him and he catches me out of reflex as I wrap my arm around his neck and tug him to the ground with me.

"Whatcha gonna do about it, Parker?" I'm grunting, trying to keep him down as we grapple. "Hmmm. Nothing, you're going to sit in that dunk tank like a good little bassist, and you're going to like it."

"Delilah Rose Callahan, Jensen Allen Parker!" Principal Tudyk comes flying down the stairs. When we continue wrestling, he pulls a foghorn from his pocket and blows three sharp blasts. "Stop this at ONCE!"

We break apart, panting and laughing hysterically on the ground. Grayson shakes his head at us before heading up the stairs to the front door. I lie here for a few more moments, my breath sawing in and out of my lungs and a massive smile on my face. Standing up, I dust off my jeans and grab my bag from the shrubs before heading for the stairs myself.

Principal Tudyk clears his throat, and I stop. My heart hits my feet, and I swear under my breath as I slowly turn to face him.

"Good Morning, Principal Tudyk. How was your summer?" I make my tone innocent and sweet, praying he doesn't decide to give me lunch detention. Jensen swipes his bag off the ground and bolts for the door, taking advantage of the distraction.

The rat bastard.

"Good Morning to you as well, Ms. Callahan. I'm sorry to delay your arrival to class, but I have an issue I was hoping you could help me resolve." He adjusts his glasses and straightens his tie. I'd swear he's nervous if I didn't know any better. This does not bode well for me.

Stifling a groan, I force a smile on my face. "Of COURSE! What can I do for you, sir?"

"Fantastic. You see, Havenbrook Academy is getting a very prestigious new student. The governor's daughter will be attending for the duration of her high school career. I need you to please show her a great big Wolverine Welcome and make sure she's comfortable here. I don't need to tell you what a great boon for our dear academy this will be." His tone has a slight warning to it, and I can read between the lines.

We want this girl to like it here.

Nodding my head, I reply, "Of course! That's no problem, Principal Tudyk. Where can I find her?" I look around and notice that we're one of the last few people at the front of the school. First bell must be ringing soon. I adjust my backpack over my shoulder, and the strap digs into my skin.

Why couldn't we have had this conversation at my locker? My back is going to hurt like a bitch all day.

"Ah, here she is!" Principal Tudyk fixes his tie again, smoothing a hand over his balding head.

I turn and smile at the girl walking toward us. She's tiny, smaller than my 5'4", and looks like a porcelain doll. My expression is wide and welcoming as I meet her halfway. "Hello! Welcome to Havenbrook Academy. I'm Delilah, but you can call me Dee. We are so glad to have you here!"

"Hello, my name is Lillian DuPont. It's very nice to meet you, Delilah." Her voice is soft with a faint accent that I can't quite place but know isn't local.

Turning, I gesture to the front of the school. "C'mon, Lillian, let's get your schedule, huh?" With one last smile at Principal Tudyk, I head to the double doors when Jensen bursts through.

"Dee, where are you? The final bell has rung, and Mr. Pendle—" Jensen stops abruptly and blinks at us.

"Uh, Jensen? Are you okay there, Parker?" I wave my hand in front of his face, and he doesn't move or blink. I turn and see that Lillian appears to be equally fascinated. "Jensen, this is Lillian DuPont. She just moved here and will be starting at Havenbrook."

All color drains from his face so fast I grab his arm, afraid he might fall. He shakes off my hand, spins abruptly, and stalks back into the school. I slowly pivot to face Lillian, and her face has fallen. She looks like she's about to cry. Running a hand through my curls, I blow out a frustrated breath.

What the fuck just happened?

Deciding to deal with one problem at a time, I gesture to the school again. "I'm not even going to pretend to know what that was. However, we'll be discussing this another time. Let's get your schedule, Lillian. We've already missed the final bell."

I missed homeroom completely while getting Lillian set up with a schedule. She ended up on B block, which is on the opposite end of campus at the start of my A block, until after lunch when our schedules merge. She was quiet and unfailingly polite the entire morning.

It's very suspicious.

I grab my books from my locker and sit next to Jensen in second period. I jab my elbow into his side as hard as possible. "What the hell was that this morning, huh? You looked like you had an aneurysm over the new girl! Do you want me to let her get lost or something?"

I wouldn't actually do that. It would be like kicking a puppy. I don't know this girl's story but starting a new school is hard enough, and there's no way I would make it harder on her than it already is.

However, I get the reaction I was going for when Jensen jumps up like his ass is on fire and gets right in my face. "You even think about doing anything to her, Delilah, and believe me, girl or not, we will be going rounds."

This isn't the Jensen I know. This isn't my best friend. This is someone else entirely, and I'm unsure what to do with this person. I eye his angry frame up and down before pulling him back into his seat.

"You're my best friend, and I love you more than life itself, but this is a line, Delilah Rose Callahan, and I dare you to cross it," he hisses.

"Okay, seriously, what the ever-loving FUCK!" My voice is louder than I realize, and the entire class goes quiet and stares at us. Jensen slumps slightly over his knees with his head in his hands. I set a palm on his shoulder. "You know I would never do that, right? I'm not that person. I was messing with you to get a reaction. And I definitely got one. So you better start talking. Now."

"You remember how I told you my dad met someone and has been seeing her for a year? And remember how he just sprung it on me that they were only dating, but now they were getting married?"

This was right after graduation. I was still mad at James then, but I do remember the conversation. "Yeah, I remember. You told me the lady was supposed to be coming down over the summer but got delayed and would be here soon. What does that have to do with the price of peas in China, Jensen? Did she show up? Has she been mean to you?"

"No, she's been fine. She showed up last weekend, and that's when I discovered she has a daughter. No one mentioned it before because she lived with her dad then. But now she's living here... *with us!*"

Obviously, I'm missing something. "Okay, I get how that could be upsetting, but it doesn't explain what happened this morning."

"You remember how we went to the Thompson twins' party at Mathison's place and I told you about the girl I met?"

"Yeah, I remember that too. You said she was the most gorgeous girl you ever saw and she slipped away before you could get her number. What does that have to do with..." My voice trails off as the reality of what he's saying sinks in.

"My new stepsister's name is Lillian DuPont, and she's the girl from the party."

I can barely hear him as he mumbles his confession, his face in his hands, but when the words register, I sit ramrod straight in my chair. "Oh. Fuck."

Chapter 11
Delilah

I'm sitting in science class when the call comes over the intercom.

"Delilah Callahan, please report to the auditorium. Delilah Callahan, to the auditorium."

I gather my books, giving the teacher a shrug as I leave class and head in that direction. When I push through the doors, the first thing I notice are the twenty girls dressed in workout clothes, stretching. I'm about to turn around and leave when one of them spots me. She lets out a loud squeal as she runs up to me, and I cringe at the sound.

Grabbing my arms, she starts to talk animatedly, and it takes a second for her words to register. When they do, my jaw drops while she continues to prattle on. "I was so excited when I saw your name on the sign-up sheet! The lead singer of Wild Child Reckless wants to join OUR dance team. Of course, you don't have to try out. I mean, we've all seen you perform. It was a no-brainer to add you to our team. Did you forget practice was today? Where are my manners? My name's Christi. I'm the dance captain and thrilled you've joined us!"

Her grin is perky as she drags me over to the other girls.

She claps her hands to get everyone's attention as she places me between her and the rest of the team. "Ladies, this is Delilah Callahan, if you didn't already know. She's decided to join us this year. Let's give her a big Dazzling Dancers welcome!"

The girls cheer and whistle, bouncing up and down like neurotic yo-yos. Christi turns back to me with a smile.

"I know you're just joining the team, so if you want to sit with the other recruits, we can show you the routine we're working on. Then we are going to start breaking it down to teach. Do you mind holding this?" Christi passes me her clipboard before pointing to the bleachers where three other girls are seated.

I stumble over and lower myself down in a daze while the music is cued up. I glance down at the clipboard and notice it has the sign-up sheet on top. At the bottom is my name, but that isn't my handwriting. The more I look at it, the more I recognize the scribbled writing.

"That son of a bitch!" I snarl, earning myself a look from the girls next to me. Rolling my eyes, I debate leaving but decide that dance really could only help me at this point.

At the same time, that doesn't mean I'll let this slide. Vengeance will be mine! So I settle in to watch the routine before we get called up to join.

I walk into the cafeteria forty-five minutes later, my core muscles screaming. I thought I was in shape. By the time I'm done, it's abundantly clear I don't know the meaning of the word. How anyone can do those routines for as long as they do is beyond me. Dance girls are beasts.

Jensen sees me hobbling into the cafeteria and bursts out laughing. I flip him the bird and go grab my tray. When I return to our table, I sit across from Lillian, who has been eating lunch with us lately. She's watching us with wide eyes. The girl's quiet and overly polite but seems naturally sweet. Jensen likes to ruffle her feathers, a fact I find amusing.

He rolls his eyes, but I get an idea and feel my smile widen as I point my fork in my friend's direction. "Just keep laughing, bass boy. The dunk tank is calling your name! The carnival is this weekend, or have you forgotten?" Then I hoist myself up on the table and face the cafeteria full of students. "Ladies, this weekend only, the one you've been waiting for: Mr. Jensen Parker, bassist for Wild Child Reckless, will be the feature star of the Summer Splash dunk tank! Save up your dollars. He won't come cheap!"

Girls start cheering, a few boys too, and when I sit back down, Jensen's face is positively murderous. I cackle in glee. Jensen has a lot to learn about payback. James was the master, and I was his willing pupil. A blush stains Lillian's cheeks, but I don't think Jensen notices.

I decide to ease her into conversation. "So, Lillian. You're coming to the Summer Splash Carnival this weekend, right? It's the biggest summer event in Havenbrook. There's so much to do! Rides, food vendors, a silent auction, raffles, plus all the local artisans set up stalls. I love the magnolia and honey bar from Soaps and Ropes. They're a local dude ranch but they specialize in making handmade goat milk soaps that smell divine!" I pick up a french fry and swirl it in my ketchup.

Lillian looks down at her hands before sighing. "I don't know. I may have to attend some event with my dad this weekend. I hope I'll be able to go to the carnival instead though." She doesn't look thrilled at the thought of hanging out with her dad and a bunch of stuffy politicians.

"Well, I hope you get to go. I'll text you, and we can ride together if you can come." I smile at her encouragingly. Jensen slams his soda can down, drawing our attention his way as he stands up, dumps his tray on the sideboard, and stalks outside.

Lillian glances over to me, her eyes wide with shock, and I shrug before returning to my lunch.

After the final bell, I'm heading to the parking lot when my phone chimes with a text. I pull my cell from my pocket and see a message from Christi, informing me that this evening's practice will be moved to the football field since they are waxing the gymnasium. I throw my head back on a groan as I shuffle in that direction, mentally preparing myself for the fresh hell I know is in store for me.

I'm definitely going to kill Jensen.

It is the Summer Splash Carnival, and the town square is packed. I walk around the booths, checking out the offerings. I smell the different food vendors, and my stomach begins to rumble. So I head straight to the funnel cake. And, sure enough, I'm first in line. The girl knows my order by heart, but she still recites it twice to make sure. I'm standing at the window waiting with my plasticware and napkins when I hear someone call out behind me.

"Hey, save some for the rest of us! Other people are hungry too."

I don't recognize the voice, so I turn and look but don't see anyone. Whoever it is, they're making an effort to not be seen. Which puts me on high alert. I take my plate, move around, and see X crouching in line. I shove his shoulder, and the people around us laugh.

"Listen. It's not my fault you were late for the party." I bite the warm, delicious treat, not caring that I now have powdered sugar everywhere. "You know the first funnel cake of the weekend has to be mine!"

X chuckles and taps my nose. "Yeah, I know. Trust me, you've dragged James and me here enough times for me to have it memorized: extra crispy, powdered sugar, chocolate syrup, and strawberries. I swear you are the only person in town who eats funnel cake that way, and they still stock the ingredients every year."

I take another big bite. "Yup!" I grin, and X smiles back.

"I've been texting you to see how you are doing, but you haven't answered. Is everything okay?"

"Yeah, sorry. I suck I know. This year is going to be super busy."

"Is everything okay?"

"Well, it's interesting if nothing else."

X laughs and I join him before taking another bite from my plate.

"Well, I have to get going. We have to perform after this, and then Jensen is on the dunk tank. Make sure you stop by and dunk him for me. You know I can't hit the broad side of a barn. Also, you're not blocked but I was ignoring you. You were being a twat."

X hums noncommittally, rocking back on his heels. "If you say so, Dee. I'll meet you at the stage in a bit. You need help setting up?"

"Nope, we got it. Thanks. We had help from the football team this morning before the stalls opened. I just have to grab my guitar from the truck." I take another big bite, not caring that my cheeks are puffing out like a chipmunk.

X chuckles and wipes some chocolate off my chin, and our eyes meet. Time seems to stop, the carnival noises fade, and I find myself holding my breath. All I can see are his sky-blue eyes. Then X clears his throat, and just like that, the sound comes roaring back. I can feel myself gasping for air, which makes me choke on powdered sugar. He slaps me on the back, and the moment, if we even had one, is gone.

I straighten up and motion toward the stage. "Maybe I'll see you later?"

X nods, and I take that as an excuse to dash away, dumping my trash in a nearby can. A hand lands on my shoulder, and I jump and let out a shriek.

Grayson backs away, his palms raised in surrender. He signs quickly. *"I was just coming to tell you that we are getting ready. We couldn't get you on your phone, so Jensen sent me to find you."*

Sighing, I sign, *"Sorry. I didn't hear you walk up. I'm just grabbing my guitar. I'll meet you there."*

Grayson tilts his head and looks me up and down. *"What did Alexander do?"*

"Alexander? He didn't do anything. Why would you say that?" I keep my face free of any emotion. Grayson can read even the most minute facial expressions like no one's business, and what happened between X and me isn't up for discussion. I'm not even sure what it is, if it's anything at all.

"Yeah. Okay. See you on stage." Grayson pivots on his heel, twirling his drumsticks as he goes, and I sigh in relief.

I make it to the stage just in time for the warm-up. People are milling around in front of us, a few are taking pictures, but the night is young. And I know from experience that the crowd will grow.

Picking up my guitar, I slide it on, cinch the strap, and strum a few notes. Then I tilt my head and sign the song number before walking up to the mic while listening to the crowd cheer. "Hello, Havenbrook! How do you love the carnival so far?"

Several people shout their replies.

"I already got the first funnel cake of the season, so you missed out! Don't worry, Maisie will make her delicious treats all weekend!"

The crowd is playing along, laughing with Jensen and Grayson. I see X walk up to the side stage and feel nervous for the first time. I swallow roughly, trying to focus my attention on our set. When the first strains of music come over the speakers, I finally relax.

I got this.

We play for three hours straight, and when we finally stop, X is right where he was when we started. The final chord drifts away, and the crowd starts chanting for an encore.

I step back up to the mic and swipe at the sweat dripping down my face. "Don't worry, folks, we'll be back tomorrow. However, remember that Wild Child Reckless's own Jensen Parker is up next for the dunk tank! One dollar a throw, and it's all for a good cause!"

The ladies in the crowd cheer. Jensen gives a short wave, and I swear his cheeks match the red of my hair.

It doesn't take long for us to break down our equipment before the dunk tank attendees escort Jensen off the stage. X walks up, takes my guitar, and hands me a water bottle. I open it and greedily gulp down half the contents. I swear this is the best water I have ever tasted. He tosses one to Grayson as well.

"You've improved a lot. I'm impressed," X says, and I preen under his praise.

"We've put a lot of practice into this particular set. I know a lot of videos from the show will be posted online, so it needed to be flawless." I shrug as I down the second half of the bottle, and X hands me another.

"Well, you succeeded. I can't think of a single thing I would have changed." He starts stacking amps and coiling cords.

"I have to go to the mall tomorrow, but Mom needs the truck. Can you give me a ride?" I close my guitar case before standing back up.

"Yeah, I got you, Dee. Don't worry." X grabs the equipment and loads it all into Jensen's truck. "Let's go watch your band-mate get drenched, Lil Bit."

The line for the dunk tank wraps around the square while Jensen sits on his small seat, glaring at me. I'm doubled over with laughter. Signing him up for the dunk tank is the best prank ever.

It takes several tries before someone finally nails the bullseye, and Jensen drops with a shout. He erupts from the tank and sprays water all over X and me. We laugh as we wring out our clothes. Then Jensen uses both hands to drench us again. I attempt to turn and run away but end up slipping in the mud. My arms flail, and Jensen half jumps over the rim to try to help, but it's someone else who catches me.

Suddenly, I find myself face-to-face with X, our noses mere inches apart and our clothes drenched. We stand like this for several heartbeats before he blinks. And for the second time today, the spell is broken.

"Here now, Dee. Be careful." He sets me on my feet, and I step back, pulling my shirt out and twisting the water loose.

"Yeah. Sorry. Um, I'm going to head home. Will I see you tomorrow? I was hoping to go around eleven?" I concentrate on getting the water out of my shirt, instead of looking at him.

"Eleven is fine. I'll text you when I'm ready. You're going to answer me this time though, right?"

I know his tone is teasing, so I roll my eyes. "Yes. I'll answer this time. Thanks, X." I stick out my tongue, hoping he doesn't see how weird I'm feeling, then briskly head for my truck as I avoid looking at Jensen for all I'm worth. He's seething at me from the dunk tank, and I know that if looks could kill, I would be very much dead where I stand.

There's a time and a place to unpack this thing with me and X, and here and now is not it. In fact, we could move it to the attic for a century, and I would be happy.

Chapter 12
Alexander

I text Delilah when I'm ready to head out the following morning, and she meets me at the truck. We chat casually back and forth about the carnival, and she shows me some of the videos that have been posted. Their VidReel account now has over four million followers.

She's Havenbrook royalty.

I pull into the mall and throw my truck into park. Delilah unclips her belt before opening her door. Then she hops down and looks back at me over one shoulder. "I'm supposed to meet Jensen and Grayson. Can you wait to see if they show?"

I unclip my belt and kill the engine. "I'll come in with you for a bit. There's some stuff I wanted to get while I'm out, and I can do that just as well here as I can at the boot and buckles."

Delilah shrugs and waits for me to join her before we head inside.

"I need a few more pairs of jeans and a new pair of boots. Mom got everything else last week but forgot to pick them up." Dee lists off her shopping list. I ruffle her curls, and she swipes at my hand.

Laughing, we stroll into the clothing store. Delilah heads right for the sale racks, flipping through the selections before piling items on her arm and heading to the back of the store. I wander around, quietly browsing, but nothing catches my eye.

Until I spot a chick in the mirrored changing area, her back facing me as she tries on a few store items. I desperately want her to turn around because I can't see her face from here, but her body has certainly caught my attention. Her hair is bundled up on the top of her head under a plaid cap that matches the short skirt. She's wearing a tight black tank top while her long, tanned legs are covered in a pair of knee-high socks I suddenly want to peel down with my teeth. Her shit-kicker black Docs are the icing on an already tempting cupcake.

I can feel my cock hardening behind the zipper of my jeans and hide behind a clothing rack as I surreptitiously adjust myself. I watch her intently, silently begging her to turn around. She doesn't appear to hear my wordless pleas as she continues to consider the outfit she's wearing while slowly killing me.

Then she removes the cap, and red curls fall down her back in a messy wave. I bite my knuckle to keep myself from striding up to her and doing something I genuinely wouldn't regret but that *would* more than likely get me kicked out of the mall.

I stalk around the racks, trying to see her reflection in the mirror. I know she's perfect, but I need to see her face more than I need my next breath. Warning bells are ringing, but my dick doesn't listen. He wants her, and he doesn't give a damn about the consequences.

The girl's head jerks up, and she waves at someone to her left before picking up her phone and bringing it to her ear. And for a moment, I'm awestruck. That is until my heart hits my boots as

I peer down and see my cell ringing in my hand. Swallowing the knot in my throat, I answer and croak out a weak hello.

"Hey, X! Grayson and Jensen are here, so I'll pay for my clothes and hitch a ride with them. That okay?"

I feel like I was just doused with a bucket of ice water. I press my thumbs into my eyes, willing the vision of Delilah out of my head. It doesn't work. I'm standing here with a raging hard-on for my best friend's little sister. I'm going to hell... because James is going to kill me.

Rubbing a hand over my face, I throw my head back, trying to will my throbbing cock to deflate. Holy. Fucking. Shit. There are so many different ways this is inappropriate.

"Yeah, Dee, that's fine." I keep my tone as normal as possible. "I'll see you next week?"

"You okay, X? You sound kinda funny."

I see Delilah gathering her bags off the floor before pulling the tags off the outfit she's wearing and handing them to a sales associate with her credit card. She's going to buy it. She's going to buy it, and she's going to wear it OUT OF THE STORE!

I can't stop myself from growling. *Over my dead body.* That outfit is entirely too revealing for her. I adjust my cock again—clearly he hasn't gotten the memo that he's not supposed to be this interested in Delilah—and stalk in her direction. "Dee, look up."

She glances around, finally spotting me. She smiles and waves, and fuck if it doesn't make my dick ten times harder.

Using another rack to hide the evidence, I gesture her over to me. "Delilah Rose Callahan, what the FUCK are you wearing?" I'm aware my tone is snappier than it should be, but she also shouldn't look like every guy's wet dream in public. I'll end up having to kill half the male population of Havenbrook.

Delilah peers down at herself before her glare lands on me again. "I'm wearing clothes, X. What did you think I was wearing?" She raises a defiant eyebrow at me. The problem with Delilah is that her five-foot-four frame comes with a ten-foot-tall temper.

Clenching my teeth, I try to rein in my emotions. And fail miserably. "What would James think if he saw you dressed like this? You're..." I splutter over my words. "You're just a kid!"

Her jaw drops while spots of color glow high on her ivory cheeks.

Oh, fuck.

Delilah takes a few swaying steps toward me, and I involuntarily take a step back. Her smile is sweet and deadly as she leans a forearm on the clothes rack between us. "If my brother wanted to have an opinion on what I was wearing, he shouldn't have signed his life away and left. But even if he were here, he would tell me that I'm allowed to wear what I want when I want as long as I don't hurt anyone."

She shoves off the rack, pushing it straight into my crotch, and I grunt with the effort of not reacting.

"If by chance he did have an issue, my darling Alexander," she continues, her tone saccharine and dark while the use of my full name is meant to emphasize how much shit I'm in. "I would tell him exactly what I'm going to tell you. Fuck off. It's my body—it's my choice."

With that, Delilah turns and walks off, and I can't stop myself from staring at her ass as she goes. When she's out of sight, I sigh and rub a hand down my face again. I've never had a reaction to Delilah like this before. Heck, I've never reacted to any woman like this before.

How did this happen? How did this day go so very off track?

I hang my head on a loud groan, startling a nearby shopper before raising a hand in apology. Then I slowly make my way to the front of the store. I can see out into the parking lot and spot Delilah and her crew standing at the back of Jensen's F150. When she notices my exit, she turns on her heels and flounces toward the front of the truck, conveying in no uncertain terms that I'm still on her shit list. Which means I'll have to keep my distance from her until whatever this is works itself out of my system.

That's it! That's what I'll do. I'll busy myself with college. She'll busy herself with high school. And we'll hardly ever see each other. This arrangement could work out perfectly!

Delilah gives me one more glare before slamming the truck door, and I rub the back of my neck. I'm so fucked.

I start to head to my own truck when my phone goes off again. Glancing down, I see a text from Megan inviting me out to eat. I don't have a good reason to say no, but at the same time, I'm not sure I want to say yes.

When I peer up again, I see Jensen's F150 pulling out of the parking lot. Delilah is sitting in the passenger seat with that plaid hat perched on her long red curls. She and Jensen must be arguing, if her animated hand gestures are anything to go by. Alternatively, she could just be complaining to him about me. Either way, I feel sorry for the kid.

I return my attention to my phone and type out a quick text to Megan.

Me: Sure. I can pick you up in twenty. Where do you wanna go?

She must've been waiting for me, because her reply pops up almost instantly.

Megan: Do you wanna go to The Lunchbox? I know the square will be crowded with the carnival, but we should still be able to get a table?

Me: Sure. What's your address? I can pick you up. I'm at the mall now.

Megan: 3428 Wisteria Lane. It's the red brick house on the corner. You'll see the camper next to the garage. See you in twenty!

When I pull up to the address she gave me about fifteen minutes later, the front door opens, and Megan bounces down the stairs. I get out of my truck and meet her on the passenger side, opening the door for her. She kisses me on the cheek, murmuring a quiet hello, as I offer her a hand up into the truck before going back around and heading for The Lunchbox.

Megan keeps up a steady stream of chatter as we drive the ten minutes to the square, and I'm left to wonder if she ever takes a breath. I hop out of the truck once we park and go back around to help her out. She accepts my hand with thanks and another kiss on the cheek. I hear a choked noise and see Delilah and Grayson unloading Jensen's truck. Grayson signs something to Delilah, and she responds before ignoring me entirely and heading to the stage.

Megan stares after her, before her gaze bounces between Delilah and me.

"That was Delilah. She's the lead singer of Wild Child Reckless."

"Yeah. It was. You a fan?" I place a hand on Megan's back to get her moving. I don't want to be here if Delilah turns back around.

"I mean, I wouldn't say a die-hard fan, but I do follow her VidReel page, and I've been to a few of her shows. They're good. Do you know her?"

I'm not sure why she's asking. I'm certain we've had this conversation before. But I'm too out of sorts to question it, as I feel myself starting to sweat under Megan's scrutiny. "I'm friends with her brother, James. He joined the Army recently." I open the door of The Lunchbox for Megan to step in front of me, and she slips under my arm.

Then I slide into the opposite side of the booth she picks and immediately regret my decision when I see that I have an unobstructed view of the stage, and Delilah is still wearing the outfit from the mall. I mentally slap myself while refocusing my attention on my date.

Conversation flows with Megan, and before long, I realize she seems to be more interested in who I know than who I am. She chatters on about her friends, where they are from and who they are related to, while intermittently asking me about my family, my connections, and my involvement with Wild Child Reckless. When I tell her that I really have more to do with James than the band itself, I can see her visibly deflate.

"Do you think you can?" Megan asks out of the blue while picking at her salad.

"Do I think I can what?"

"Introduce me."

"To who?"

"Delilah and the band, of course. I really think she could benefit from a makeover—and I *am* somewhat of a genius when it comes to fashion. Obviously."

At the mention of Delilah, I look out the window to see her jumping around on the stage, trying to energize the audience. My dick immediately takes notice, and I want to punch myself in the nuts to get him to behave.

As soon as the riff starts, I recognize their signature song "Wild Child Reckless," and I have to grin. I know these lyrics 'cause they're about Delilah. James helped write them a few summers ago. When my favorite verse comes up, I find myself singing along under my breath.

"Oh, they got their hands full.

You can't tame a pistol,

All fire and freckles.

Make you wish you were dead.

Clotheslines make a tightrope,

Daddy's little daredevil.

Mama had high hopes.

You'll raise a little hell

When you raise a redhead.

Now tell us how it is, uh-hum.

Always has a sunburn,

Not gonna compromise!

Daddy's belt couldn't break the temper.

Bull in a china shop, but rose-colored reckless.

Gonna always do it anyway; trouble loves a redhead!"

Megan smiles. "That was amazing. You must have heard that one a lot. It was on the local radio station for months when it first dropped."

I hum noncommittally and gesture at her salad. "Are you done?"

She nods, and I motion to the waitress for the check. Time to get out of here before I say or do something I regret. With one last look at the stage, I guide Megan to my truck.

She kisses my cheek again when we return to her house and invites me in, but I decline. I promise to text her later, but my mind is anywhere but on the girl I was with as I head home.

Chapter 13
Delilah

I'm still so mad at Alexander that I refuse his texted offer to drive me to school the following day, opting to ride with Jensen instead.

I mean, who does he think he is anyway?

I saw him with that blonde at The Lunchbox. I've never actually seen him with anyone before, and while I know he dates, it's different to see him taking her to our spot.

I run a frustrated hand through my curls, shaking them out. I'm beyond ready for this school year. Something to focus on besides Alexander and his sudden assholish behavior.

Jensen takes one look at my face when I hop in the cab of his truck and wisely remains silent on the ride to school. I make it through the day and am ready to go to practice. I need to burn off all this restless energy I have building up inside me. I thought joining the dance squad would be easy, but all it did was highlight how unfit I am.

After a long, two-hour practice, I trudge up the front steps of my house. All I want to do is take a hot shower and die. Though I have to admit it worked. My mind is blissfully blank as I dig around in my purse for my keys. Until someone calls my name. Turning around, I see X standing behind me with a pizza box in his hands.

"Hey, Dee. I was wondering where you were."

I glare at him as I continue to root for my keys while refusing to answer.

X sighs. "Still mad at me, I see. I know your mom is at work tonight, so I brought stuffed-crust pizza. "

I eye the box as my stomach grumbles, causing X to grin. I roll my eyes with an exaggerated sigh. "Fine. I forgive you. Bring the pizza." I finally manage to find my keys and unlock the house. "I need a shower. Pick a movie. I'll be back in a bit."

When I've thoroughly washed the day away, I walk back into the living room to see the pizza on the coffee table. I collapse next to X with a groan, grab a piece, and take a big bite.

"God, this is so good," I moan around a mouthful of food. Then I take another big bite, sit there, and chew. I'm so tired I feel like I could pass out on the spot.

We eat in silence for several minutes before X clears his throat. "So, you were home late today. Did the band have a gig?"

Reaching for another slice of pizza, I shake my head before sinking my teeth into more of the cheese than I can likely fit in my mouth. "No, we don't have anything lined up now," I force out between bites. "I had dance practice, and I'm telling you it kicked my ass." I take a swig from the bottle of water X got me and lean back, stretching my spine against the couch.

"Dance practice? How do you have dance practice?" X closes the pizza box and stacks our dirty plates on top.

"Jensen got pissy that I signed him up for the dunk tank, so to even the score, he signed me up for dance squad. Joke's on him, though. 'Cause I made the team, and we had practice tonight.

Those girls are intense, but they are good. I think I'm going to learn a lot. I still have to buy a uniform, which means I need to talk to Mom." I sigh at the ceiling, leaning my head back. "It's just a lot right now, but I know it'll be worth it." I pick up the remote and open the streaming app. "What do you want to watch?"

X looks on as I scroll through options until we get to the latest thriller. "What about that one? I've heard good things... So you're on the dance squad too, huh? That sounds like fun, but do you really have time? Don't dance squads like usually compete and stuff?"

Since I don't care what we watch, I push play and settle back into the couch. "Yeah, we compete, but we know the schedule ahead of time, even the events we may not qualify for. So I can mark off the dates and ensure there're no conflicts with the band. Besides, it's going really well. The routines are fun and they pick some great songs. We're going to be performing at all the halftime shows." I stretch my back over the couch again, groaning in relief when I hear my spine pop. "I saw you with that little blonde at The Lunchbox, by the way. There something you need to tell me?" I shove X's shoulder.

He doesn't budge, just looks at me funny.

I grab a napkin and run it over my mouth. "What? Do I have pizza on my face?"

X chuckles. "No, you don't. And, yes, you did see me. That was Megan, the TA for one of my professors. She texted and asked if I wanted to go out. She picked the spot, not me."

"Hmm. Sure, if you say so."

"She also asked me if I knew you."

"What did you tell her?"

"That I was friends with your brother." X shrugs like it's no big deal.

I suck in a breath because his nonchalance hurts. "Well, at least it wasn't a lie." We sit in silence for several minutes before I find myself asking, "What did you think of it?"

"Think of what?"

"The performance."

"It was good. The song's come a long way. You're doing really well for yourselves. I know James is proud."

It takes everything I have not to ask: *what about you?*

Seems like a waste of breath. If X was proud, he would say as much, right?

I move a bunch of pillows around, getting comfortable, and then do my best to concentrate on the TV. X reaches behind me, grabs the throw off the back of the sofa, and tosses it over my legs. We both settle in to watch the movie, but before I realize it, I'm fast asleep.

***

The light on my face wakes me, but I don't want to get up. I'm so warm. I try to snuggle into the heat, but it moves. My eyes fly open to see a chest under my cheek. I close and reopen my eyes, but it doesn't change the scene in front of me. X is holding me against his chest with our legs entwined as he snores softly. The scent of his aftershave tickles my nose and I lie here, doing my best to force myself awake.

As the cobwebs slowly clear out of my head, I realize that my alarm is going off. I sit up with a gasp while shuffling to grab my phone. His arms tighten momentarily before they loosen enough to let me sit upright.

X snorts and jerks awake. "Wha-what? What's going on? What happened? Delilah? What are you...? What am I...? What?"

"I'm late!" I squeal and dash for my room.

"Delilah?"

"X, I'm going to be late for school!"

I hear X calling out my name from the living room but I can't stop. I have to get ready. Jensen will be here any minute. I throw my hair into a messy bun and jump up and down to get my favorite pair of skinny jeans over my hips. I've just opened my dresser drawer when I hear Jensen honk from the drive. I fist a pair of socks and slam the drawer, grabbing my bookbag and boots on the way to the door.

"Delilah..." X tries again, but I cut him off.

"I have to go! Lock the house behind you! Talk to you later! Text me!" I hop into the truck's cab, throw my bag into the back, and bend over to shove my feet into my socks.

"Um, Delilah, why is Alexander Stephenson standing in your doorway?" Jensen says, and I look up to see X eyeing us from the front porch.

"We fell asleep last night watching a movie. Can we go now? We're going to be late for school!" I force my feet into my boots, stomping against the floorboard to set them in place.

"Yeah. We can go, but we will be talking about this later."

"About what? There's nothing to talk about. Let's go!"

Jensen snorts. "Yeah. Okay. Sure."

"Jenner—"

"Oh, don't Jenner me," he says. I growl at him and he laughs. "Growl all you want, babe. I'm not the one who spent the night with my brother's best friend."

"I didn't spend the night—"

"Did you wake up with Alexander Stephenson?"

"Well, I mean, *technically,* yes."

"Point made."

I groan in frustration as we pull into the school parking lot. I look around and realize someone's missing. "Where's Lily?"

"She drove herself today. Her dad bought her a car for her birthday."

I scan the parking lot before I see her blonde curls exiting a bright-blue Mini Cooper. "Oh, there she is!" I point, and Jensen follows my finger as Chad Walters appears to be approaching her car.

The captain of the football team thinks he's God's gift to women—if that were the case, the return queue would be miles long. He set his sights on me last year but James and Jensen shut it down. Now, it seems Lily is his new target.

"Looks like Chad wants to try his luck." I nod my head to Lily, and Jensen's jaw turns to steel.

He slams the truck into park and storms across the lot, pushing the football player out of the way. I can't tell what's being said in the distance but Lily starts backing up. Which tells me the girl is scared.

When Chad shoves at Jensen's chest, I hop down from the truck and call out, "Lily! Get over here!"

She hurries to my side, and we watch as the resource officer arrives and breaks up the brewing fight. Jensen glares in our direction before striding into the school.

"Lil, you okay?" I ask. She appears a little shaken but nods her head. I loop an arm around her shoulders and tug her close. "C'mon. Let's get to class. Forget those losers."

Chapter 14
Alexander

I watch Jensen's truck pull out of the drive, sigh, and rub a hand over my face before shutting the door. Then I pull out my phone to check the time, see three missed calls and a handful of texts from Megan. And groan.

Deciding to deal with her later, I toss out our trash from last night and wipe down the coffee table before gathering my shoes and locking the door behind me. I may not have class, but I still cannot hang around all day waiting for Delilah to get home.

I cross the yard, trudge in through the front door, and head straight for my en suite. I turn the shower up as hot as possible, tossing my dirty clothes into the hamper, and step under the spray. I let the water wash over me. Which helps soothe the aches from sleeping on Delilah's couch. Leaning one hand against the tile wall, I palm my hard cock and slowly move my hand up and down my shaft.

I speed up and then curse as I catch the scent of magnolia drifting on the steam. I bite my bottom lip as a flash of red hair and green eyes flits through my brain, and I come harder than I think I have ever come in my life. By the time I'm finished, I'm gasping for air, and my knees feel weak. When my vision clears, I realize what I did, and my stomach drops. I wash any evidence down the drain and turn the tap to cold.

Stepping out of the shower, I wrap a towel around my waist and point a finger at my reflection. Using it as the slap in the face I need. "You will not go there. You will not be that guy. You will distance yourself from Delilah. She's your best friend's little sister and deserves better, you asshole."

The creep in the mirror nods back at me before I push off the sink and go to get dressed. I spy my phone on my desk and grab it. I'll text Megan back too.

***

A few hours later, I find myself at lunch with Megan and I can't stop thinking…

Was her laugh always this shrill?

I can feel the beginnings of a migraine when I hear my phone chirp. I check my notifications and see a message from Delilah.

Dee: Sorry to dash out this morning! I have dance practice tonight until eight. See you for dinner? We can try to finish the movie again if you want?

I clutch the phone so tight it creaks.

"Who's that?" Megan asks between breaths of air. She rambles on so long I'm surprised any oxygen makes it to her lungs.

"Oh, it's Delilah—she's got practice tonight."

"Wild Child Reckless?" Megan perks up, and I shoot her a glare.

"Noooo. Dance."

"Oh, so then why's she texting you?" Her gaze sharpens and I sigh.

"She wanted to know if we were going to grab dinner. Since her mother works nights, I usually bring something over on weekdays."

"Hmm," Megan hums noncommittally.

I gesture for the check, leaving some cash on the table before escorting her back to my truck.

"Do you think I could come?"

The question catches me off guard. "Come where?"

"To a practice with the band. Get a behind-the-scenes look. Maybe I can film it for my channel?"

"I—um—I'm not sure. I'd have to ask the group. I'll let you know." I rub the back of my neck, already knowing the answer while also knowing that if I don't ask I may very well not hear the end of it.

Megan kisses me before heading inside. I promise to message her later, the unanswered text from Delilah still at the forefront of my mind. I want to reply and agree to come over. I want to tell her I'll pick up Thai and guarantee a mushroom never comes within feet of her food, but I can't. I can't be around her again like that. I'm no saint.

I wait until I get home to shoot her a message.

Me: Sorry, Dee. I can't tonight. I have plans with Megan. Maybe next time?

I keep it vague but unbreakable. Her text comes back quickly.

Dee: That's okay. I'll see what the guys are doing! Talk to you later!

I have to do this.

I suck in a deep breath and bang my head against the front door for both of us. It's going to be a long night.

***

I manage to avoid seeing Delilah, alone, for a whole six months. In all that time, I've attended four different Wild Child Reckless practices with Megan. Delilah agreed to let her tag along, and I know it was only because I asked.

How do I know this you may wonder?

Well, if looks could kill, I'd be deader than a doorknob every time Megan starts going on about Delilah's "look" and suggesting a makeover. All live on her channel, of course. To date, Delilah has yet to take her up on the offer.

Tonight I'm standing on the sidelines at the Wolverines' game, shadowing Coach Michaels. They're up seven to three when halftime comes around. The cheerleaders and dance squad take the field as the players leave. The music starts, and I find myself choking on my tongue the moment I spot Delilah.

Her curly red hair makes her easy to pinpoint, but the fact that her uniform—if you want to call it that—barely exists means I'm once again ready to blind every man in a five-mile radius for daring to look at her. I can feel a rough growl slipping out as I watch her move, her ass jiggling in the too-tiny shorts and the crop top begging for relief as it tries to contain her breasts. Delilah jumps, kicks, dips, and sways with her teammates in time to the music, and I bite my tongue, willing my cock to settle down.

I must have done something terrible in another life to be punished this way.

I'm trying to discreetly adjust myself when I see a blonde pony-tail heading my way. Megan. For once, I'm happy to see her. Nothing will kill my hard-on faster. I find myself zoning out while Megan prattles on.

Before I realize it, the music has stopped, and Delilah is bouncing across the field in my direction. "Hey! Hey, Megan! How are things?"

"Who did your makeup?" Megan's tone is sharp, and Delilah and I both blink at her in confusion.

"Oh, um, one of the girls on the dance team. I don't typically wear it but it's required for the performance so…" Delilah trails off.

"Next time, text me and I'll do it. You look like a clown."

"You look gorgeous," I bark out while glaring at Megan, who doesn't notice the hurt now shadowing Delilah's green eyes.

"Alex, honey! I'm just saying—"

"I think we all know what you're saying, Megan. Why don't you go see if you can get us something from the concession stand? I'll meet you at the fifty-yard line after halftime." I hold out a twenty-dollar bill, hoping she gets the hint.

Megan narrows her eyes before snatching the money from my hand and flouncing off toward the boosters.

"Wow. What a catch. Is she the reason you haven't been around much lately, X?" Delilah asks, her eyes still wide with hurt.

I swallow the sudden onslaught of guilt. Reach out a hand and tug a curl like I always do. "I'm sorry, Dee. I promise I'll do better. You mad at me?" I play with the coil, running the silky strands through my fingertips.

"Yup. I am. You'll have to bring me a stuffed-crust pizza to make it up to me."

"Let me guess... extra cheese too?" I'll gladly buy her a hundred pizzas if it means she doesn't have that look on her face because of me.

"Yup!" Delilah pops the P before quickly rejoining her teammates.

I'm so going to hell, but from the looks of it, I'll have plenty of company, seeing as I'm not the only one who watches her ass as she walks away.

***

I find myself on Delilah's doorstep forty-five minutes after the game ends with a Wolverine win. I'm clutching a pizza box in my hands, stuffed crust with extra cheese, ready to beg for her forgiveness if necessary. It wasn't right how I treated Delilah the past few months; however, I couldn't, and still can't, figure out any other way to be around her and not ...*react*.

Delilah opens the door, and my jaw drops. She's in a tank top and sleep shorts with her wet hair hanging down her back in loose curls. Swallowing roughly, I hold out the pizza since no saliva is left in my mouth.

"You brought the pizza! Score!" Delilah grabs the box before heading into the living room. Usually, I would sit next to her on the couch. But I'm not a masochist, so I pick the recliner. It's safer for both my sanity and my libido. If Delilah notices, she doesn't mention it as she digs into her first slice of many.

This routine becomes the new normal for us when we do hang out. I only see Delilah two days a week. So far, that keeps me in her good graces *and* my honor intact. I still attend all the perfor-mances I can, and it doesn't escape my notice that Delilah has started incorporating her newly learned dance moves into the band's routine. I didn't think Wild Child Reckless could get more popular, but they do.

However, the nights that I wake up harder than steel with wisps of dreams of her drifting away are more and more frequent as the months go on. Before I realize it, Delilah is about to graduate high school. I'm about to do the same with college. And James is coming home to celebrate with us.

If I knew that life as I knew it was about to end, I would have done things very differently in the coming days...

Chapter 15
Delilah

"OMG, yesssss!" I step out of Jensen's F150 and stretch my arms to the sky to pull the kinks out of my back. The ride to this pasture is long and bumpy but also the most secluded, which is part of the charm. I smooth out my shorts and grab my guitar case, only to have Grayson take it from me and walk away. Shrugging my shoulders, I head toward the bonfire. I notice twice as many trucks as usual and have to grin. Word must have gotten around that we were performing tonight.

"Yo, Delilah! You're here! I was starting to get worried, babe." Travis Mitchell walks up, throwing an arm around my shoulders, and accidentally spills some beer down my shirt.

I shrug out of his grip and force a grin to lessen the blow. "Yeah, I wasn't sure we could make it, but then we thought *why not?* Who wants to miss the party of the year? Plus a chance to play? That's always a good time."

I see Lillian sitting on a bale of hay arranged around the fire and head her way, waving a quick goodbye to Travis.

"Hey, girlie! I didn't expect you to be here! Have you gotten a drink yet?"

"Yeah, Jensen invited me, and since the year is almost over, there was no way I would miss this. Besides, I never miss a chance to see you guys perform."

I grab her arm and tug her to her feet. "Yeah. I know, girl. Let's go get something to drink. I think the Thompson twins managed to swipe some kegs from their dad's store again. C'mon."

Grabbing a couple of red solo cups, we fill them to the brim and walk around the fire, visiting with everyone. The night is in full swing. Someone is playing music from the cab of their truck, with couples dancing around the fire. I've missed nights like this, relishing the ability to let go and just... be. I can feel myself starting to relax the more I drink.

"So, why this pasture? I didn't think I was ever going to find it. I would have missed it if it weren't for the bonfire." Lillian sips her beer, wrinkling her nose at the taste.

I chug down another gulp before replying. "Because the Warrens have a half barn, which is nothing more than a few stalls, a tack, and a feed room. But it has a flat concrete pad, and..." I wiggle my brows. "...it has electricity, which is all we need. Otherwise, it would be a very one-sided show."

Lillian nods before she looks over my shoulder. Following her gaze, I see that Jensen is tuning his bass.

"Oh shit. Gotta go. Grab me a refill?" I hand my cup to Lillian and grab my guitar off the stand.

Then I quickly check to ensure the bumpy ride into the field didn't throw it out of tune. I notice Lillian step back up and set my cup on the amp, and I quickly reach over to grab it. Holding it up in a salute to say thanks.

Satisfied with what I hear, I turn and grip the mic next. "What's going on, motherfuckers?"

I'm answered with a loud "woo-hoo" by entirely too many drunk teenagers in a country field. *Good times.*

"Hell yeah! Let's get started! Grab your girl or guy if you haven't already and let's have fun!"

We launch into our favorite dance sets with a shared laugh, playing a mix of country, rock, and pop, only stopping for the occasional refreshment. And before I realize it, we've been playing for hours, and I'm more than a little tipsy.

We've just finished another song when I noticed Lillian gesturing frantically from the side of our makeshift stage. "Delilah! Word is some guys from Havenbrook University are coming!"

At first, it doesn't click. When it finally does, I go pale. "Why does that matte—oh, shit. Alexander."

"Yes! We have to leave!"

Fueled by too much alcohol, I shake my head. "Nope. He's not the boss of me. And after all the stuff they did when they were our age, he can fuck right off. I'm not leaving. In fact... try this on for size." I whisper my plan in her ear, and her eyes get bigger and bigger with every word.

"Delilah, no! You can't! Please. Let's just go." She tries to tug me away, but I dig my feet in harder.

"Nope. I refuse to let them ruin my good time, Lillian." I stomp back on stage. Turn to Jensen and Grayson, and sign the name of the song.

"Delilah, are you sure? We still need to polish that one. Look, let's just pack up. It's getting late anyway. I'll stop and get us stuffed-crust pizza on the way home," Jensen tries to reason with me.

"No. C'mon." I sign the words as I say them. "Let's do this."

Grayson shrugs at Jensen, who sighs but goes back to his microphone. We play the opening riffs as a few new trucks pull up and their doors open. I see the headlights of additional vehicles coming down the path.

As the crowd of college boys heads our way, I see X conversing at the back of the group with a girl in jean shorts and a tiny tank top, her blonde hair pulled high on her head.

Megan. Jealousy and rage run hot through my body, and I'm shocked by its intensity.

So that's how he wants to play? Well, then, game on.

I find myself belting lyrics like it's my last performance and the song has personally wronged me.

"Who are you trying to fuck now?

Who is this other girl?

I bet she's dyin' to fuck ya.

How dare she try to rock your world.

You know I'm not that dumb though.

Never gonna be a silly blonde,

 'Cause I'm not what you truly wanted.

Yeah, not what you wanted, right?

Not the girl who does it all for you.

You never think it's your fault.

Someone else is always callin',

For your brand of charmin'.

So why is there a kiss next to her name?

Who the fuck is she?

Is she the other girl?

I bet she's tryin' to keep ya,

And you're her entire world.

I'm sick and tired of waitin',

Sittin' at home, waiting on you to phone.

When I see her name, and you don't explain.

Who the fuck do you think you are? Oh!"

By the time the song ends, everyone is going crazy. Alexander has gotten a drink and is watching the stage but still talking to Megan.

Irrationally pissed at his indifference, I swivel on my heel and head back up to the mic. "Did ya'll like that?"

The volume of drunk cheers doubles.

"Well, if you liked that one, I'm sure you'll love this even more! Boys?" I turn and signal for the next song.

Jensen immediately grabs my arm. "Delilah, no. C'mon, let's go."

I shake him off, swipe up my cup, and down the rest of the drink before setting my guitar back on the stand. "No. We're doing this. C'mon."

"Afterward, we leave. Promise me, Delilah, or I will pack up right now and drive off without you." His tone is serious, but something tells me he's bluffing.

"Fine. Yes. After this, if you want, we can leave. Promise." I can see Lillian watching us with worry plastered on her face. I do my best to reassure her with a smile and fail miserably if the look she's giving me is anything to go by.

Jensen sighs before striking the opening chords. I grab the mic and arch my back against one of the poles.

"Every night I dream about you,

But you don't notice me, so I'm about to

Make sure I stand out from the crowd.

God can't save me, oh, no.

I'm frustrated.

I want to get you naked,

And my thoughts are so unholy.

But, Lord, I need you... only you.

The more I push, the more you move away.

And the more I don't want to play this game.

The more I want you.

I dream about you in my bed, in my shower, every hour.

If you don't notice me, I'm about to make you.

You're my own special brand of hell.

I want you to think about me as well, oh."

I dance around using the barn poles, knowing I'm putting on more of a show than usual. Determined not to be ignored, I change my moves. I shimmy, sway, and shake my ass for all I'm worth while working the stage like it owes me money.

Guys are whooping and hollering with their phones out. And finally, X looks up. Megan tries to get his attention again, but his eyes never leave mine. I smirk in challenge and continue to sing. And just like the lyrics say, the more I sing and dance, the redder his face gets. As soon as the final note dies, X is up on the stage, dragging me back to the feed room, his grip rough on my wrist.

"X, what the fuck!" I can feel the anger radiating off him in waves, and my own anger flares in response.

How dare he!

He slams the door behind us before he sits me on the feed bin. Shoving both hands through his hair, he paces while muttering to himself. I try to stand, and he forces me back down.

Finally, he pivots to face me. "What the hell were you thinking, Delilah? Did you see all those guys with their phones out? How could you be so stupid? So reckless?"

"You know the name of my band, right? Jesus, Alexander, what's your problem? It's a show. I was performing. You act like you've never seen anyone in the history of the world dance like that." I wave a dismissive hand and pretend to inspect my cuticles. In reality, I'm jumping with glee.

Suck it, Barbie! If he's here with me, he's not there with her.

Alexander leans over, his nostrils flaring in agitation. "I know James has always allowed you to do whatever you want, but he's not here now." The look on his face is intense, as his voice drops to almost a growl. "I am. He asked me to look after you! I told your brother I would watch over you. Keep you safe. And here you are, acting like a Baby Dolls' stripper on dollar draft night in the middle of a fucking cow pasture!"

I feel my spine stiffening before I push to my feet and shove a finger into his face. "You listen to me, Alexander Brian Stephenson. I am not and have never been your responsibility. I am seventeen years old! I can make my own decisions! I'm not a child!" I'm so mad I can feel the tears clogging the back of my throat.

X turns away, throwing his hands in the air before rounding on me, as he grits out through clenched teeth, "Then you need to stop acting like a child! Grow up!" He might as well have slapped me.

My gasp is audible despite the music still playing outside. Standing my ground, I move into his space. "You know, you're being a little self-righteous right now. Remember, I know all about what you and James used to get up to in this exact same pasture. If you have an issue with what I do, I suggest you get over it. I don't answer to you." Turning on my heel, I reach for the door.

X grabs my arm, pulling me close to him. "You listen to me, Lil Bit. You may think you're grown, but you're not. You're just a little girl playing pretend. Time's up. You better start growing up and fast."

I refuse to let him see how much his words hurt me. I will not cry. Instead, I grab my anger and pull it around me like a blanket. "You think I don't know that James isn't here? And that you would rather be doing literally anything else than once again being stuck babysitting his kid sister? Yes. I know. Trust me, I know. You've made that abundantly clear over the last few years. Well, the joke's on you. Because I'm no longer your responsibility. I turn eighteen in two months. We graduate in three. On top of all that, the band and I signed a contract with a producer last week. We leave the day after graduation."

With that last blow, I slam out of the feed room. Throw a quick sign at the boys, grab Lillian, and head straight for the keg. I plan on getting my buzz back.

Alexander Stephenson can go straight to hell!

Chapter 16
Alexander

My lips curl into a snarl as I punch the wall several times before I lean my head against it in defeat. "FUCK!"

They've signed a contract. *Why did no one tell me?*

I'm pacing the feed room, the sound of the door slamming lingering in the air. I've tried so hard, kept my distance, and shut her down whenever she wanted to hang out, and this is how I'm repaid? Is Delilah just going to up and leave?

I stomp out of the tack room behind her, intent on giving her a piece of my mind. Only to stop in my tracks when I don't see her. I take a deep breath. I need to calm down.

I grab a cup and head to the keg. I'll get a drink, tamp down my temper, and then we can discuss all these issues like rational people. It's the perfect plan.

Six drinks later, I still haven't found Delilah, let alone managed to get her alone for a conversation. I sit down on a hay bale that is positioned between two trucks and take another sip from my cup before settling in to keep watch. I see a flash of red from the other side of the fire and push to my feet. She's there talking to that blonde who's always hanging around Jensen. They appear to be arguing. I'm in the process of going over to confront her when someone steps in front of me.

"Hey there. I've been looking for you all night. You just dis-appeared on me." Megan runs a hand down my arm, and it's all I can do not to fling it off me.

"Yeah, sorry about that. I had to take care of something."

"Have you talked to Dee about letting me make over the band? Did you see what she was wearing?" Megan wrinkles her nose, but I know I'll be seeing those jean shorts Delilah was wearing on stage in my dreams very soon.

"Oh, well, no. I haven't mentioned it to her."

"I heard they signed a recording contract. That's so exciting. I can definitely help her with her image before she leaves. I'm going to go find her and talk to her."

I grab Megan's hand when she turns to walk off and she falls back against me. She cards her hand through my hair. The world spins, and I tumble back onto a hay bale.

Guess I'm much drunker than I thought.

Megan takes the opportunity to straddle my lap, her lips heading for mine. My eyes flick behind her, over to where Delilah is watching us across the fire, her green eyes shining in the orange flames. She shakes her head, turns, and stalks away, the blonde following close behind her. I stand and shove Megan off me; her screech as she hits the ground has people looking our way.

But the alcohol has dulled my senses enough that I don't care if I have an audience.

I dash around the fire to see Jensen's truck pulling out of the field. Frustrated, I kick the tire of the nearest truck. I'm too drunk to drive, and by the time I sober up, she'll have shut me out again.

So I turn back toward the bonfire and find a hay bale and a bottle of water. It's going to be a long night.

***

It's dawn before I find myself pulling up in my drive. The lights in the house are on, but Mom's truck is gone. I step inside and my eyes immediately bounce around the room. It looks like we've been robbed. Furniture is shoved over, magazines litter the floor, and remnants from last night's dinner are still sitting on the table. Mom would never leave dishes out overnight. I can feel fear sliding down my spine like an icy finger.

Pulling out my cell phone, I see Mom has been calling for hours. I curse and quickly call her back. "Alexander, there you are! I couldn't find you. Where have you been? I'm at Mercy General. It's your father..." she says in one long breath.

I drop to my knees, my cell phone sliding from my grasp without even realizing it. When the shock starts to wear off and the panic sets in, I rush from the house, jump back into my truck, and crank it up. The gas pedal hits the floor, as the engine roars to life, and I speed down the street, desperate to reach the hospital.

Mrs. Callahan is standing at the nurses' station when I arrive, and she points to a side corridor. "Neuro wing!"

I don't slow down as I make the turn. I reach the end of the hallway and end up at a second nurses' station. I lean over, gasping, while I try to catch my breath.

"Alexander!"

My head snaps in the direction of my name to see my mom leaning against the doorway to the waiting room. "Mom, what happened? Where's Dad?"

"We were having dinner. Your father arrived home late from that big job over in Dayton and felt a little more rundown than usual. The next thing I knew, he told me to call 9-1-1 before he collapsed to the floor. Dr. Albright has already stopped by to check in with us. They're not sure what it is yet, but your father's stable… for now."

I throw myself into the small plastic chair. The waiting room is cold and smells like disinfectant. I can hear the TV in the corner advertising some cookware. Mom sits down next to me, putting her arm around my shoulder. I lean against her, and we wait. Until, what feels like days later, the doctor finally comes out and sits down across from us.

"Hey, Peggy, Alex. How are you holding up?"

"I'd be doing better, Dr. Albright, if you would tell me how my husband is doing." My mom's voice is shaky but determined.

Dr. Albright sighs. "Let's start with the good news. John is resting right now. We still have more tests to run, but he's alive, and we are hopeful for a complete recovery; however, time will be the true test. He has a lot of changes he has to make, and for someone of his age and disposition, it can prove to be tough."

Mom collapses against me and sobs. I hold her close while saying a silent prayer of thanks.

"Now for the bad news," Dr. Albright continues. "He suffered a pretty severe stroke. We're unsure of the extent of the damage. But in all likelihood, he will require extensive physical and occupational therapy."

"Of course, we'll get him whatever he needs," Mom says, and I can see her already making lists in her head. "When do you think John will be released?"

"We'd like to keep him for a bit longer to make sure there are no additional complications as well as to get him evaluated to see the level of care he may require. So I can't give you a definitive date. It'll depend on the test results."

"Can I see him?" My mom looks hopeful as she smiles at Dr. Albright.

"Sure, Peggy, you can see him. No more than a few minutes, okay? Let's go. John needs all the rest he can get."

I watch Mom follow the doctor down the hall before scrubbing my face with my hands. What time is it? I'm exhausted. I stand and stretch out my back, thinking about getting something to eat, when I sense movement on my right.

Delilah approaches me, holding a brown bag and a drink tray with coffee cups. Her smile is dim, and her eyes are sad. "Hey," she whispers. "Mom called and told me your dad was rushed in. I'm betting you guys could use some coffee and something to eat by now. Have you heard anything?"

I take the tray, setting it on a side table before pulling her into my arms. She sighs and drops her hands to my waist. My reasons for being upset with her seem so trivial now.

"He's going to be okay. It was a stroke. We've been telling him he needs to slow down for years. Now he'll have no choice. Dr. Albright was just in." My voice cracks, so I quickly clear my throat. "He's alive, though, Dee. I thought I lost him. That's all I could think on the drive over. That I lost him. And it was like I couldn't breathe."

"I hate that feeling." If she weren't pressed so close to me, I wouldn't have caught those words, but she was, and I did. And my heart cracks a little more.

"Lil Bit." My chest aches with the need to protect her from anything and anyone. The take-no-shit, no-holds-barred girl next door, so strong—the life of the party—is still infinitely fragile.

Damn, this girl.

She sighs deeply. "I'm glad he'll be okay. Will you let me know if you need anything? We're here for you. You know that, right?"

I breathe in the magnolia scent of her hair and feel my pulse settle. "Yeah, Dee. I know. Look, we need to talk about some things soon. I need you to trust me for a few more months. Just bear with me, okay? Can you do that for me?"

"O-okay. Yeah, X, I can do that. I'm going to go find my mom and then get out of here." Delilah hitches her thumb toward the emergency entrance, and I nod.

"Yeah, you head home and get some rest. I'll text you soon." I hug her closer and take another deep breath of her sweet scent.

She turns to walk down the hall, giving me a little wave, and I watch her walk away until she turns the corner.

I glance down when my phone goes off. I have two text messages. One's from James, letting me know he is thinking about me and to keep him updated. I'm tapping out a reply when I see a flash of something in my periphery. No one's there when I glance that way, though, so I return to my phone while heading back into the waiting room.

I drop into one of the chairs and pull the bag of food Dee brought onto my lap. After I take a grateful sip of the coffee and devour a breakfast taco, I almost feel human. Until my phone starts to beep again and a slew of messages comes pouring in.

Megan.

I shake my head and block her number. I'm so over her. Maybe if I ghost her, she'll get the hint. I may not know my entire future, but I do know one thing.

Megan isn't it. Not by a long shot.

Chapter 17
Delilah

I was already home when Mom called to tell me about Mr. Stephenson. At first, I was paralyzed. Unable to move, act. The feelings were overwhelming and frightening. All I could think was that he was dead and I would lose the only other father figure I had in my life.

When I shook off the initial shock and made it to the hospital, Mrs. Stephenson and X were already in the waiting room. And I was glad I grabbed something from the drive-through next door. They probably hadn't had anything to eat or drink in hours, and I needed to do something to feel useful.

Right now, my shoes squeak on the tile floors loudly in the hallway's silence. I shiver in the forced air. For once, I'm unsure if my presence is welcome. X wasn't exactly happy with me today. And, frankly, in the early light of day, I feel a little ashamed of how I acted, the way I pushed him.

He's sitting in a chair in the waiting room, his head in his hands, when I approach the door. But the relief I see on his face as soon as he looks up makes my heart beat faster.

I hold out the fast food like a peace offering. "Hey, Mom called and told me your dad was rushed in. I'm betting you guys could use some coffee and something to eat by now. Have you heard anything?"

***

I can feel my heart stuttering at how close we were to losing Mr. Stephenson. Before I can catch myself, I whisper, "I hate that feeling," and bury my face into X's chest, because this isn't about me. It's about him.

"Lil Bit."

I take a big breath and release it slowly. "I'm glad he'll be okay. Will you let me know if you need anything? We're here for you. You know that, right?"

X presses his face into my hair, breathes deeply, and seems to draw upon an incredible peace. I like being that for him, a little bit of relaxation on a night when I know he could use it. "Yeah, Dee. I know. Look, we need to talk about some things soon. I need you to trust me for a few more months. Just bear with me, okay? Can you do that for me?"

I look up at him in confusion, hoping to find the answers I need in his gaze, but all I see is exhaustion and stress. "O-okay. Yeah, X, I can do that. I'm going to go find my mom and then get out of here." I gesture back toward the nurses' station where Mom is standing, and he nods at me.

"Yeah, you head home and get some rest. I'll text you soon." He pulls me close, taking another deep breath and holding it in before slowly releasing it.

I turn and walk back down the hall as I wave goodbye to X, my heart lighter. Until I round the cardiac nurses' station and see Megan.

"I hope you know your little plan won't work. Alexander is mine. We *will* be getting married. He knows we're Havenbrook's next power couple. Not. You." Her sharp nails poke me in my chest, and I bat her hand away. Megan crosses her arms and smirks. "You know we talk about you. How you're a silly little girl and how he tries to be nice to you because of your brother, but the truth is he can't wait to get rid of you."

I roll my eyes and go to stalk past her when her next words give me pause.

"I can prove it. I'll show you the messages. Then you'll see I'm telling the truth and stop trying so hard." The glee in her eyes has me second-guessing myself, but I take the top-of-the-line phone she hands me and start scrolling through the message thread. I reach the bottom when I notice it says that X is typing.

I walk down the hall, peek around the corner, and see X standing outside the waiting room. Typing on his phone before giving it a small shake and tucking it back into his pocket. I move back toward Megan and look down at the new message.

Alexander: I love you, sweet angel. I don't know what I'd do without you. I'll see you soon.

My stomach sinks. I'm such an idiot. I can't do this. I thought I could. I really did. But I can't. Thrusting Megan's phone back into her palm, I choke out some excuse and run out of the hospital like the hounds of hell are on my heels.

Then I dig my own phone out of my pocket and call Jensen. His voice is groggy when he finally answers. "Dee, what the hell? Are you okay?"

"Jensen, Operation *No Quitter* is a go. I'm hanging up with you and calling the label. I need you to get in touch with Grayson. So we can be on our way as soon as possible. I want to have tickets in my hand by this afternoon." The words hitch in my throat, and I interrupt him before he can start his questioning. "Jensen. This is not a drill. If you have ever been my friend, I need you now. We have to leave Havenbrook." I can feel the hot tears sliding down my cheeks, and I swipe them away, angry that Alexander has me crying again.

"Okay, Dee. I'll wake Grayson up. It'll be okay. I promise. Okay?" Jensen's tone is soft and comforting, like an old blanket you can't help but wrap around you. I know he has questions and I wish I had the answers for him. But right now, I don't.

I slide into my truck's front seat, banging my head against the steering wheel. "Thanks, Jenner, you're a savior. I love you. I'll call you when I get an answer about the tickets." I hang up and sob.

I sob for all the pieces of my broken heart and for every dream I have had that will never come true. When I don't think I could have any fluids left in my body, I wipe off my face with fast food napkins from the glove box. The rough texture is oddly refreshing.

The whole drive home, I'm haunted by a tune in my head. I don't recognize the chords. I'm humming the hook when I pull into my driveway. I park next to Jensen's F150, opening my door as the boys exit theirs. Jensen immediately wraps me in his arms, and I take comfort in the familiarity. I sense movement and notice that Lillian is here as well.

That's new.

"Lillian's gonna take us to the airport and drive my truck home. I didn't want to leave it in long-term parking until Dad could finally pick it up."

I dip my head in greeting before making my way inside. "I talked to the airline. A flight bound for LAX leaves in four hours. It'll take us about an hour to get to the airport. Martin, at the label, said not to worry about packing anything but some clothes. They'll send someone to pack the rest and move it for us. However, I'm taking my guitar! I don't trust anyone else with her."

Jensen nods before relaying the message to Grayson.

A couple of months ago, we were approached by a label from LA. The offer was everything we could have hoped for. Mr. Stone negotiated the contract, and the penalty for violating any of the terms is steep enough that the label won't dream of pulling any shenanigans. Our parents had approached Principal Tudyk about allowing us to graduate early. We already have all our credits, so missing the end of the school year isn't an issue. We won't be walking the stage, which is sad, but it's not worth missing this opportunity.

For half a second, my heart hoped that Alexander would admit he's just as crazy for me as I am for him. I'm not even sure when it happened, but one day he went from being my brother's best friend to becoming the one person I couldn't picture not seeing every day.

But I was wrong.

"There's one thing I want to do before we leave. Let's go to the studio. Jensen, I'm going to need your help. It's time to say goodbye."

As Jensen sets up the recording equipment, I settle on the stool with my guitar.

"Good morning, Havenbrook! We have some fantastic news that we were just given permission to share! It's Wild Child Reckless, coming at you with the tea. Are you ready?"

Grayson gives us a drumroll.

"We've signed with Revelation Records out of LA! That's right, your hometown favorites are going coastal! Yes, we may be leaving you, but we will always love you! Havenbrook will always be our home, and we are going to miss each and every one of you more than you know! To prove it, I have something for you all today. Something that's never been seen or heard. Get ready, Havenbrook."

The opening strands of music are almost melancholy compared to our previous songs but I strum along with a clear voice.

"You've already told me
What you think about me.
There's no need to argue.
I can't say I blame you.
You don't know I'm leaving.
Just know I have my reasons.
Our memories can't be replaced.
There's no smile on my face.
Call it bad timing, no future.
I wish he didn't love her.
I'm too late, no hope left.
I'm writing from the airport,
Songs about losing and failing.

It hurts to move; I'm broken now

And I'm found once again.

I turn to my friends,

My people who understand.

They get the master plan.

Not all hope is gone,

And I've been waiting for too long.

I don't need to face this on my own.

You said I needed to grow up.

Well, I guess this is growing up."

As the notes die away, I slide my guitar to the side. Look into the camera and address Havenbrook one last time.

"Thank you to everyone who's supported us over the years. We wouldn't be here without you. We love you. This is Wild Child Reckless, signing off. We'll see you on the other side."

Chapter 18
Delilah

As soon as I step off the plane, I'm immediately assaulted by a heat so intense it almost makes me homesick.

"I don't think we're in Kansas anymore." Jensen waves a hand in front of his face.

"Yeah, the smog is pretty bad," Grayson chimes in from my left.

"Good news is the record label already has a place for us to stay, and we're going there first. They want us to settle in and relax for a bit, and then we are supposed to meet up with them at three." I check my phone. "It's ten now, so we should have plenty of time."

We exit baggage claim and see a man holding a sign with my name on the front.

"Hi, I'm Delilah Callahan."

"Good morning, miss. My name is Gregory. I'm going to be your driver. Let me get those bags." He reaches for my guitar, and I quickly pull it back.

"No offense, Greggy. But no one carries this baby but me. You're welcome to help out with the rest of the luggage, but this one stays with me."

He gives me a wry salute and reaches for the case beside me.

When we exit the terminal, I spot a long, sleek, black car parked by the curb and suspect it's for us. Which is confirmed when Gregory sets our belongings into the trunk.

The sun is bright and shining, and the wind is refreshing as it comes in off the ocean and brushes my face. A part of me that was nervous about the change relaxes.

I did it. I'm following my dream.

A small voice in the back of my head whispers something about Alexander, and I shove it into a box and push it into a hole.

I'm jolted out of my musings by Jensen taking one hand and Grayson taking the other. "Do you wanna talk about it?" the former asks.

"No. I just wanna focus on us and this adventure."

Grayson hugs me before kissing my cheek. I shove him sideways and grin. He knew I would. Then we all pile into the waiting limo, ready to see what our future in LA holds.

Traffic is just as bad as all the stories I've heard, and it takes us two hours to reach the high-rise we'll be staying at. I'm glad I visited the powder room before we left the airport. Poor Jensen wasn't quite so lucky.

Gregory grabs a few of our bags, some porters carry the rest, and we all head up the elevator as he gives us a history of the building. "You will be staying in the Raleigh Room. It is a four-bedroom, four-bath condo. The spare room has already been set up as your practice space. Every apartment in this building is owned by Revelation Records and has been thoroughly soundproofed. There's maid service and a household manager. If you have any specific requests regarding food, please note them on the kitchen list, and the shopping service will facilitate your needs. I'm available between the hours of 7 a.m. and 10 p.m. Outside of those hours, we have an alternate car service at your disposal."

Jensen is looking at me, his eyes progressively widening with each word coming out of Gregory's mouth. Grayson taps my shoulder. *"Is he for real right now?"*

I gulp down my apprehension and nod my head. "Yeah. I think he is."

Gregory uses a card to open the front door as we exit the elevator. "You'll each have your own key card access and security team. You must swipe your cards to utilize the lift, which will only go to your floor, as well as to enter the apartment."

"Wait a minute, please." I turn to Grayson and summarize Gregory's spiel before turning back again. "In the future, please ensure you face Grayson and enunciate clearly for important updates. We can interpret most things but never want him to feel excluded. I would also like to have at least one person on the staff who knows sign language. I understand this isn't always feasible, so if you know someone willing to learn, that would be a helpful alternative."

"Of course, miss. As a matter of fact, your PA—you'll meet Madison later—came highly recommended and is currently attending classes to add ASL interpreter to her list of credentials. We'll get you in contact with her immediately." Gregory inclines his head toward the staff trailing behind him.

Grayson taps me on the shoulder. *"Did he say that our assistant is taking classes to be an interpreter?"*

"Yes, they added her to our staff when they found out. Could you help her like you helped us? You know, the more you use it, the faster you learn." I can't help but take in Grayson's huge smile.

"Of course. I'm impressed she's taking lessons. It can be challeng-ing. I also like that she wanted to learn before she knew she would work for us. That means she is doing it for the right reasons."

I match Grayson's pleased smile with one of my own, and we continue into the condo. Gregory gives us the rest of the tour, mindful to turn toward the group so that Grayson continues to feel included. I still interpret most of what's said so that nothing is missed.

Gregory finally leaves us but not before mentioning that he'll return at two to pick us up for our meeting. Jensen rushes off to the nearest bathroom, while I collapse onto the sofa with a sigh. The cool microfiber cloth feels good against my hot skin. This is all I wanted for years, and now that we have it, I find myself wishing for something else. Something I can never have.

Jensen sits down and pulls me against him. Grayson squeezes in on my other side, tucking in close. I try to stop the tears, but I can't. I sit and cry while my two best friends hold me together, and my world falls apart.

After my detour to Mini-Breakdownville, we get unpacked and eat some lunch. I've never seen such a stocked fridge in my life. They really did try to think of everything. I take a quick shower and change my clothes. I may not know what this meet-ing's going to entail, but I refuse to sit in some stuffy office for hours and be uncomfortable.

Just as he promised, Gregory returns promptly at two to collect us. And not long after, I'm standing in front of Revelation Records' headquarters building. I let out a low whistle. It has to be fifty stories tall with miles and miles of glass windows.

When we walk through the door, we are met by Mr. Concord's assistant, Levi. Mr. Concord is part owner of Revelation Records. He flew to Texas to speak to me after I threw Levi off my porch with a threat or two thrown in the mix.

Levi is a toad, if I say so myself.

"Levi." If my tone conveys that I smell something terrible, it's purely coincidental.

"Ms. Callahan, Mr. Parker, Mr. Stone. I'm pleased to inform you that Mr. Concord and Mr. Sterling are waiting in the sound booth. Please follow me." He turns and walks toward the elevator bank. Where he presses the button to call the lift and steps back. "The sound booths are all located on the thirty-second floor. You're in booth fourteen on the right-hand side." When the doors open, Levi walks away without another word.

We step inside, and I hit the button for floor thirty-two.

Grayson taps my shoulder. *"What was his problem? I'm deaf and could tell he had a stick up his ass."*

I shrug. "That's Levi. He's an assistant. He came to Texas to try to recruit us. I told him if he stepped foot on my porch again, I would feed him lead for breakfast."

Jensen and Grayson gawk at me. *"Why would you do that? Alternatively, why did we sign with this label if you wanted to shoot their assistant?"*

Blush creeps up my cheeks. "Levi made sexually suggestive comments about how he could help further my career. I may have made some about how I could end his. Needless to say, he doesn't like me anymore. Mr. Concord flew down and personally negotiated our contract. They gave us all our demands, plus a higher percentage than any other label. It seemed the best choice."

"Delilah Rose Callahan, did you use that man's abhorrent behavior to get us more money?"

Putting it simply... "Yes."

Jensen hugs me. "God, I love you."

We all laugh as the elevator doors open to an impressive corridor with a row of rooms stretching out on each side of us. We step forward, locate the door numbered fourteen, and knock before entering.

Mr. Concord immediately pushes up from the table to greet us. "Delilah! Jensen! Grayson! Welcome! We're so glad you're finally here!" The man is probably in his forties. He's wearing denim jeans and a bolo tie, and his face has copious laugh lines.

I liked him instantly when I met him. He also seems to be fair, and Mr. Stone said he didn't get flustered during negotiations or throw tantrums like some of the others, which I personally found a little disturbing. Besides Levi, I couldn't find a fault with the label so far, especially when Mr. Concord seemed excited to stay an extra two weeks after we signed so he could sightsee.

"Hi, Mr. Concord. No issues so far. Everyone has been love—" I choke on the last word as he wraps me in a hug that makes breathing difficult.

"Great! Great! Great! Love to hear it! Let me introduce you to my partner, Jerrod. We've been running this circus for so many years it's insane to think about." He pulls me after him, and I glance back at the boys, who are grinning like loons.

Assholes.

Mr. Sterling is a slight man with warm, golden-brown skin. His brown eyes are wreathed in similar laugh lines, and his black hair is still thick, despite being in his mid-to-late fifties. He's dressed impeccably in a sharply pressed gray suit, while his smile is tentative like he's used to his partner's antics but doesn't want to get in the line of fire. It's welcoming nonetheless.

He takes my hand, politely and pleasantly, and gives it a shake and a pat before greeting my bandmates. "I'm glad you could all make the trip." Mr. Sterling's accent is slightly different; though I can't place it. "If you are amenable, we have some decisions to make before we can start producing music. First and foremost is choosing your pianist and backup singer."

"I'm sorry... Our *what*?" Jensen interrupts.

"You just have to decide who's the best fit as your pianist." Mr. Sterling fans a stack of headshots on the table like we're selecting pictures for our Christmas cards. "Adding a pianist and some additional background vocals will help round out your sound. We have several profiles and samples here for you to look through."

I find myself sitting at the table and picking up picture after picture. "You just want us to pick someone? Like we're picking out a puppy at the pound? What if they can't play our sound, or don't gel with our vibe?" I shake my head.

This is far-fetched and miles away from what I thought we would be discussing in this meeting. Ever, in fact. I never even contemplated adding piano as an accompanying element to our sound.

Mr. Sterling laughs jovially, and Mr. Concord joins him. "Oh, heavens, no. It's really quite common in the industry. You can see their qualifications on the back. You pick out your favorites, then we have them audition for you. If you like them, they do a guest spot and play with you as a group. If you still approve, they join and sign with us."

I automatically translate as Mr. Sterling speaks. I know it helps Grayson, but I do so without thinking most days. I share a look with the guys, who shrug at me in return. "Well, come on, Barbie. Let's pick a bandmate then."

We spread the photos across the table. Unsure of what to do, we each grab a profile and dive in. I have no idea how this will actually turn out, seeing as it's sort of like getting married at first sight.

I mean, what could possibly go wrong?

Chapter 19
Alexander

I groan and stretch the kinks out of my shoulders. It's been two weeks since the stroke landed my dad in the hospital. Between the initial tests and evaluations, the results, getting him set up for full-time nursing care at home, physical and occupational therapy, and keeping the business he worked his whole life to build *afloat*, I'm more than a little dead.

Sighing, I pick up my phone. No new notifications. I haven't seen Delilah since that day at the hospital, and she hasn't answered any of my texts. However, I've been so busy I haven't even had time to walk next door, falling into bed at ungodly o'clock, only to get up at the crack of dawn and start all over again. I'm getting frustrated at her lack of communication. She's never ignored me. Even when she was the maddest she's ever been at me, she still texted me back and told me *in detail* what I could do to myself. This silence can't be good.

I waffle back and forth for a minute before I break and text James.

Me: Hey, man, I'm finally getting a chance to breathe. Life is a crazy town here lately. How are things with you? Sorry it's been a while, but with everything going on with dad, I haven't had a chance to catch up with Dee lately.

It takes a few minutes before I see the bubbles at the bottom of the screen, indicating he's writing back. I head toward the elevator, and it doesn't take long to decide I'm done with this day. It's Friday. There are no pressing jobs this weekend, and I want to see if I can catch Delilah at home. I've spotted her truck in the drive most nights, so I have a good chance, unless she's been riding with Jensen.

James: Dude, you're kidding me, right? I know you're not that stupid.

I scoff. *No, I'm not that stupid.*

But life has been a shitshow lately, so things have slipped, and I plan on telling him just that when another text comes flying in. It's a link. I click it, and it leads me to the Wild Child Reckless VidReel page.

I watch in growing horror as Delilah settles on the stool with her guitar and she starts to speak.

"Good morning, Havenbrook! We have some fantastic news that we were just given permission to share! It's Wild Child Reckless, coming at you with the tea. Are you ready?..."

I place a hand on the elevator wall as static fills my head and white-knuckle my phone as the video continues to play. Delilah starts to sing, but I can't hear anything over the thudding of my heart in my chest. I stumble into the lobby before falling to my knees. When the fog clears, I finally hear the end of the song she's playing. It's new.

"Well, I guess this is growing up..."

I wince as the lyrics hit their intended mark, and the words I hurled at her are returned to me. *Grow up.* That's what I told her she needed to do. I feel the bile rise in the back of my throat. They're in LA. I can't believe it.

I don't remember the ride home, but when I pull up to my house, I see her truck in the drive next to Mrs. Callahan's. The lights are on so I walk next door, but I might as well be walking to my doom. Each step is progressively more difficult than the last. Clearing my throat, I knock on the front door, and it isn't lost on me that out of all the hundreds of times I have done the same thing, this is the one that could break me.

"Alexander! Hi, sweetie! How are you? I saw that you brought your dad home last week. How's he doing?" Mrs. Callahan is wiping her hands on a dish towel, and I watch the motion.

"Is it true?" I hate that my voice cracks, but there's no stopping it. I still can't believe it's real even if I know in my heart that it is.

Mrs. Callahan sighs before opening the door enough for me to walk into the living room. "Yeah, honey, it's true. I was still deciding about the band leaving before Delilah's birthday and graduation. But you know how that girl is. Once she gets her mind set on something, there's no stopping her. She made some valid points, and it was discussed between all us parents, and we agreed."

I sink down on the couch. I can still smell her here. The scent of magnolia. And her sweater is still tossed over the arm of the sofa. There's no way she's really gone. This has to be some elaborate prank meant to get back at me for being absent.

I jump up to my feet and stride into her studio, swinging the door open wide. A bare room meets my gaze. I pull up short in disbelief.

Mrs. Callahan walks up behind me. "The label came by last week and packed everything up. The house is so quiet now that she's gone…" Her voice echoes in the empty space.

I walk in and turn in a slow circle. She did it. She really did it! She left. She left, and she didn't say goodbye.

Why wouldn't she say goodbye?

I go to walk out of the room, and something by the baseboard catches my eye. Bending down, I pick up Dee's lucky guitar pick. It's the one I gave her with her first guitar. I close the little piece of plastic in my fist and slip it into my pocket.

"You okay, sweetie?" Mrs. Callahan is waiting in the living room when I walk back out.

"Tell me what you can about the terms," I say as I plop myself down on the sofa.

Mrs. Callahan joins me. "Well. It's a one-year contract with mutual options to extend. This is common with new artists. I know this label had some initial issues, but they offered higher profits and met more of her demands."

I have to laugh at the last part. Saying no to Delilah is basically impossible. She's a pit bull when she gets an idea in her head.

"The label has a place to put the band up until they can decide if they want to buy, rent, or what have you. It's a perk for the first year of their initial contract, and if they remain after that, they can rent from the label at a discount." Mrs. C is ticking off the major points of the contract on her fingers.

Knowing Delilah, she negotiated the reduction. I smirk at the thought.

"The label wants them to hire a pianist/backup singer. They've been auditioning people for about a week now and have yet to find one that fits. She's starting to get frustrated. I feel bad for Mr. Concord. He's never seen Delilah as anything but accommodating. He's about to get a rude awakening."

Mrs. C shakes her head, and I have to join her. Having spent the last twelve years in Delilah's inner circle, I know for a fact that a frustrated Delilah is a wild card. She may do what you ask or she may burn it to the ground. You never really know. My chuckle is evil, because Mr. Concord *is* about to get a rude awakening.

I stand from the sofa, give Mrs. Callahan a hug for taking the time to speak with me, and then head outside. Where my previous steps were filled with dread, now they're filled with a renewed determination.

She can run but she can never hide. She's my muse, my angel, and my sole reason for living. I just realized it too late. I'm gonna get the girl. There's no other option.

When I reach my house, I open my laptop. I need to make a plan. A plan to get Delilah Callahan back in my life. Starting now.

Chapter 20
Delilah

I groan as the latest audition leaves. The sound guys throw down their headsets, and I lean forward with my head in my hands. They've all been talented artists. Talent isn't the issue. The issue is that they're all... cardboard. They have no life, no fire, no spark, no soul.

Where is the joy, the sass, the drive?

"Okay, we've been at this for hours. Obviously, we need to rethink our search parameters. Delilah? Why don't you and the boys head out for the night? We can meet back up in a few days with some new options." This comes from Cora.

She's our manager and beyond fantastic. She wasn't supposed to be our manager. Originally, it was some dick named Grant, but then I heard her giving another artist a dressing down, and I knew she was meant to be ours. Now Grant is in charge of that artist, and Cora has us. She, in my not-so-humble opinion, got the better end of the bargain.

"Deal." I throw down my pen, and Jensen rubs my shoulders.

The past three weeks have been hell. How is it this hard to find another band member in a city where you could throw a dart and hit fifteen musically inclined people?

We ride down the lift in silence, each of us lost in our thoughts. When we exit the building, the sun is just setting, and the wind is warm and pleasant.

I wave off Gregory and set off walking. "Let's go find something fun to do and some food. I don't want to go back to the condo."

Both boys agree with me, and we wander around. I can't believe we've spent our first three weeks in LA in the studio or the condo. The streets are bustling with people, and the smell of different types of food wafts in the breeze. My stomach rumbles, reminding me that the sandwich we ordered for lunch was hours ago and that my body is not a massive fan of skipping meals. As we get ready to turn the corner, I catch a melody and stop in my tracks.

Grayson runs me over, and we almost hit the ground.

"What the hell, Dee?" Jensen exclaims, but he stops when I hold up my hand. I point to a nondescript door with a sign over it that reads *Josephine's*. I listen intently...

There! I motion for the boys to follow me and walk up to the door. Which is worn with a small sign that says: *knock*. The small inset window opens when I do just that, and a pair of heavily kohled eyes stares at me.

"Password?"

"Oh. Um. I don't know. We're new to town. So..." I let my voice trail off, forcing myself to look confused.

The person on the other side of the door chuckles. "Virgins, huh? Check the VidReel page, my lovelies. Therein lies redemption." His deep baritone gives me chills in the best way.

Jensen already has his phone out and is typing. He scrolls for a few minutes before he raises his head. "Toto"

"Welcome, Dorothy. You're not in Kansas anymore!" the stranger crows, and the door swings open.

We head inside, immediately turning to the right and down the narrow stairs. The booths are plush red velvet, and the shelving holds so many liquor bottles the lighting casts a rainbow of colors over the bar. The cocktail waitresses are dressed in period wear, befitting the 1920s, while the bartenders are in vests and suspenders.

As we hit the central area, I gasp, "It's a speakeasy!"

One of the most beautiful women I may have ever seen is in a gorgeous emerald-green and blue dress on stage. Her long dark hair is curly with streaks of all different colors running through the masses, her tawny skin warm under the stage lights. She plays the piano, and her eyes are closed as she croons into the microphone. I don't recognize the song, but she projects so much feeling through the lyrics my stomach clenches in sympathy for the songwriter's plight.

"I wish I could hate you,

That I didn't want to be you.

Man, I wish you had never walked into this bar.

I hate that I see what he sees (you're perfect),

That you're everything I will never be (never be).

I wish I could get over him the way he has me,

And that seeing you here wasn't hard.

I hope life works out for you both (but I don't).

I kind of hope I finally let him go (but I won't).

But then again (maybe)

I don't."

I forcibly drag Grayson and Jensen to the table at the front. It's early for most people to be out, so we don't have to fight anyone for good seating. There's a sign on the stage in an elegant script that reads: *Mia's music and musings.*

"I want her." I turn to the boys and gesture over my shoulder.

"You want her? Did you switch teams, love?" Jensen's tone is teasing, but I'm dead serious.

"No, you idiot. I want her as our backup singer and pianist. She is what we've been looking for. She's the perfect addition! Tell me I'm wrong." I lay down the challenge, and my tone is so belligerent I'm almost glad Grayson is deaf, but I'm far from being able to be polite now. We've spent three weeks drudging through interviews, and the answer to our problems was three blocks down the road.

"I know I play drums, but I think she's hot! We should hire her so I can ask her for a good time or two." Grayson's grin is cheeky as he delivers his verdict.

I choke and gasp on the water I was sipping. We've met all of his girlfriends, but he's never been this blatantly crude before, and I know it's because we're the only ones who can understand him right now.

"Excuse me?" A hand taps my shoulder, and I turn. We must have been so wrapped up in our conversation we didn't realize that Mia finished her song, noticed us, and walked over.

She waves her hands to get Grayson's attention before responding in flawless sign. "My first cousin is deaf, you wankpuffin. It would help if you didn't assume that no one around you would understand because it's uncommon. Also, I wouldn't fuck you for practice, Bongo Boy." She gives a cheeky wave, shrugs, and walks toward the back room.

I burst out laughing at the look on Grayson's face. It's priceless. It takes a minute for me to get myself under control, and even Jensen chuckles.

"Okay, so band vote. What do we think of asking Mia to audition? My vote is obviously yes."

"Audition? Yes." Jensen has always been the most cautious of the group. But then again, he's been through a little more than the rest of us, so it's understandable.

His grandparents have resurfaced in his life, and he doesn't know how they've been getting the information they have. I know he went no contact with them after his mom died, but anytime anyone brings up that part of his life, he shuts down. For them to suddenly be getting the information has us all shook.

"I don't want to do an automatic yes to her joining the group, but I'm game to asking her to audition to see how she is with our sound."

"She's got my vote. It's been a while since someone other than Delilah put me in my place. Besides, I think I can turn her around." Grayson is grinning again.

"Well then, it's unanimous. Let's go get our girl." I stand from the table and follow Mia into the back room. It's dark, but there's a door with a sign that says *lounge* on it. It's a safe bet that she's back there.

I pass another cocktail waitress and stop her. "Hi, we're looking for Mia. Is she back here?" I give the girl my best and friendliest smile, which she happily returns.

"Mia? Yeah, doll, she's in the lounge. You just head on back." She smirks at Grayson as she sashays past, giving him a wink. He grins in return and follows her with his gaze.

I slap his chest. He winks at me, and I roll my eyes. *Boys. Ugh.*

I head back down the hall to the lounge door and knock. A chorus of voices tells me to enter. Walking in, I see that the lounge is more of a break room, with several employees sitting around on their phones. I see Mia in the far corner with a cup of something warm in her hands. She seems to be almost meditating, if the intense look of concentration on her face is anything to go by.

"Hi, excuse me. Do you have a minute?" I sit down across from her, while the boys end up spreading out behind me.

"Ah, it's Bongo Boy and his crew. Yes, I have, as you say, 'a' minute. How can I help you?" Her voice has a lyrical cadence that I immediately fall in love with. She's not from around here. That much is clear. Then again, neither are we. Truth is she could be from Mars and I would still want her in the band.

"I'm not going to beat around the bush. I want you to join our band. We need a pianist/backup singer, and I choose you." I meet her gaze without blinking.

Mia throws back her head laughing, the sound breaking through the air like butterflies. "I'm not a Pokémon!" She wipes the tears under her eyes without disturbing the heavy kohl lines. "Well, as much as I would love to join your little garage band, I have a full-time gig here and need something that pays. While I am sure you sound amazing in your bathroom, this is the real world, and I have bills to pay."

I take Cora's card from my wallet and slide it across the table. Mia picks it up and stares at it like it just might bite her. "Be there tomorrow at 3 p.m. Ask for Cora and tell her you spoke with Delilah and that you are there to audition." I stand and stare at her to show how serious I am. "I *will* see you tomorrow at three, won't I, Mia?"

***

I've been pacing the studio since two this afternoon. We've run through the latest song a couple of times, and it's as solid as it will be without our newest bandmate. When we left Josephine's, I immediately called Cora and told her the news. She wanted to run a background check on Mia for her credentials, and I told her in no uncertain terms that she wasn't to scare the girl away. Cora could run all the checks she wants but only after we get Mia in the studio. Even then, unless she's wanted for murder in six states, that girl *will* be touring with us.

I look at the clock. It's a quarter till three.

Jensen knocks my shoulder. "Jeez, Dee, you're so nervous you're about to jump out of your skin."

"I know, but what if she doesn't show? What if she does show up and says no? What if she—"

Jensen puts his hand over my mouth, and I hear the intercom. "I have a Mia down here. Says she is supposed to be auditioning with Delilah?" the front desk receptionist announces, and I squeak beneath Jensen's grip. He chuckles and drops his arm.

Cora hits the intercom and tells them to send Mia up before turning back to me. "Are you sure about this, Delilah? She's an unknown. So many things could go wrong."

"So was I until I wasn't. I'm so sure about this it's unreal. Mia's the one, Cora," I say just as the pianist in question walks in.

Mia's eyes widen as she takes in the sound booth, the techs waiting for us to do something and all of us just staring at her. "Bloody hell." Mia pulls up short. "You are *not* a garage band."

I shake my head and chuckle. "No. Definitely not anymore."

Cora comes up with a clipboard and clears her throat. "Sorry... I know Delilah is pretty set on you joining, but since we are still technically auditioning, I will need you to fill this out. It's a typical application form, permission to run a background check, and a standard NDA. You may be playing songs that have yet to be released. Just standard procedure."

Mia takes the clipboard while her eyes continue to bug out of her head. "I thought you were taking the piss last night. I would get here, and they would laugh at me, but you were serious. You were really serious."

"So incredibly serious, Mia." I grin at her, and she leans on a counter and begins filling out the forms. This is the first time I've seen someone complete the paperwork so fast. "Once you're finished with that..." I gesture to the clipboard. "...and Cora stops glaring at me, we can make some music."

Mia signs the last one with a flourish and hands the clipboard back to Cora, who reads the first page. "Amiri Biondi, twenty-three, from—"

Mia interrupts her. "Mia. I go by Mia now."

Cora nods. "Of course, Mia. Well, you've already met the group. Still, I must officially inform you that you are here to audition as a pianist/backup singer for Wild Child Reckless. Revelation Records will also employ you if you are chosen for the position. You will have to commit to all obligations that should come from that. You're okay with these terms?"

"Am I okay with giving up my two-bedroom flat and my four roommates? Yes. I'm so okay with this."

The rest of us chuckle. Even Mia lets out a small giggle, but I can sense she may not have been kidding as much as we thought.

I stand up and clap my hands. "Okay, now that that's all done, let's make some music!"

We move into the booth and gather at our respective instruments. I pick up the sheet music and hand it out.

"This song is going to be the first song on our EP. Let's go through it a couple of times, then we can try to record."

Everyone nods and gets to work.

We have a clean copy four hours later, and Mia has integrated into our group like she's always been here. Even Cora is smiling. "Yes! That's it! Got it!" she crows, her exuberance contagious. We all high-five.

"So, Mia. What do you think? Do you want to join Wild Child Reckless? There's a bedroom with your name on it."

Her laughter winds down, and she meets my grin. "I'm so there!"

And just like that, we gain our fourth band member.

"Fantastic! Let's pull out our next song, 'Wild Child Reckless,' and go over it. I bet we can get a clean copy before we stop for the night!"

We head back to our instruments as Grayson strikes out the beat and we all join in. It's nearly midnight by the time we finish, and we all head out to grab a bite to eat.

"I know you've not been in town long, but there's this place about six blocks down the road that makes the best chicken tikka masala... Do you guys wanna try it?" Mia hitches her bag higher on her shoulder, appearing a little nervous.

"Hell, yes, we do! Let's go, girl! I'm all about that naan life!"

She giggles at my enthusiasm. We head out the door, and I bump into someone coming in, knocking a stack of papers to the ground.

"Oh, I am so sorry. That was my fault! Are you okay?" I'm gathering up the papers when warm hands close over mine.

"*Tesorina*, do not worry. Nothing is harmed."

I look into warm brown eyes with a shock of dark hair falling across them. His smirk is sinful as he stares up and down my body. I can feel myself blushing as I quickly shove his papers back into his hand and push up to my feet.

"Again, I'm so sorry." I'm a sweaty mess! I shove my hair behind my ears, wishing I'd had a chance to shower after we closed up. "I wasn't watching where I was going."

"What is your name, *bella*?" The rough timbre of his voice washes over me, and I swear the temperature rises ten degrees.

"Dee—Delilah. My name is Delilah."

"What are you doing here at this time of night, Delilah?" He reaches out, grabs a piece of my hair, and plays with the ends.

I swallow roughly. "We just got done recording—" I gesture weakly to the others, all standing there watching the interaction with a variety of expressions gracing their faces. "We were heading to get something to eat."

He hums noncommittally. "Go get your dinner, *tesorina*. After all, it is very late. Maybe I will be seeing you soon, yes?" He turns and walks to the bank of elevators, and I feel like I can finally breathe again.

Mia immediately grabs my arm and drags me outside. "Do you know who that was? DO YOU KNOW WHO THAT WAS!"

Why is she shaking me?

I swing around to look, but he's already in the lift. "No. Who was that?" I can still feel his warm hand touching me.

"Delilah, that was Giovanni SANTORO. And just the hottest artist of the year. He's sold out shows up and down both coasts." She squeaks and covers her mouth. "He just lost his opening act. They split up. Delilah, what if he wants us to be his opening act?"

I laugh. "Chill, Mia. I just literally ran into the guy. I'm sure he has zero idea who we even are. We're so not there yet. We're still just getting started. There's no way someone as famous as you say Giovanni Santoro is would want Wild Child Reckless to open for him. Now, how about that food? I have a feeling some fresh roti is calling my name."

We head out of the building and down the sidewalk while part of my mind stays behind at the label.

Chapter 21
Delilah

Cora is waiting when we walk into the studio the following week. A brown-haired girl nervously shifting from foot to foot by our manager's side. Mia is on her phone, typing furiously while Grayson and Jensen each shoot me a look.

"Guys, this is Madison." Cora gestures to the newcomer. "She's your PA. She would have been here sooner but was finishing some certifications. Madison has been with Revelation Records for several years and will be your point of contact when you go on tour."

With a slight nod of her head and a clearing of her throat, Madison begins, "Hello, everyone. Like Cora said, my name is Madison, but you can call me Maddie." She signs as she speaks. I remember Gregory mentioning she was taking interpreter classes. I'd completely forgotten about it during the flurry of activity these past few days.

We each introduce ourselves, and Maddie responds with a welcoming smile.

"We are so excited to have you join our team, Maddie! Let's get going this morning!" I clap my hands before passing out sheet music. "I came up with this last night. If possible, I want to go over it today. I know it's rough, but if we work on it now, I'm sure we can polish it." I pick up my guitar while the others flip through the sheets.

"You wrote this last night?" Mia points to the pages in her hand.

"Yes. I wrote it last night." I refuse to meet her eyes, pretending to tune my guitar instead.

"Don't you sleep?" Jensen asks me, and I double down on busying my hands.

"Not lately."

"Dee..." he chastises me.

"Can we just practice it, please?" I see Grayson smiling at me and look in his direction.

"I love you, Dee."

"I love you too, G-man. Ready to rock?"

"Yeah, Dee. Let's rock," He snaps up his sticks and sounds the snare in rapid succession, beginning the intro to our newest song.

"Said you'd die for me, could die for me, would you die for me?

But you lied to me. Why'd you lie to me? Why'd you lie to me? Yeah.

Are your thoughts about me every time you touch her? (you lied).

I hope your new girl hears this song and she loves it (loves it).

Banging on the door and hanging on the line (no one's home).

I want an answer, but you be lyin'. You be lyin', yeah (you lie).

Anything the devil won't do

He's gonna send me to do.

You can't hide that you're dead inside, (so dead).

Never gonna see me cry (cry).

I'll spell it out; it's easy enough (so easy).

I was there; I followed my gut.

I don't play games; I saw her phone.

You can have all those girls; I'm never coming home.

Been a while since you heard from me.

Now I'm spinning; here is the verse, honey (the verse).

Turns out it shows ʼcause I'm selling out shows,

Selling copies of our break-up note.

You brought her into our lives, and you didn't respect my privacy.

I know all your secrets; they won't die with me (nope).

Thought you'd keep it on the low (the low).

Say I'm crazy, but I know (you know).

Nothing's changed though (nothing).

Said you'd take a bullet, that you'd die for me (lies).

I wish I knew then you'd been lyin' to me (to me).

We were everything, but you were playing with me (me).

Learned a lesson when you showed the truth; I see (I see).

Said you'd die for me, could die for me. Would you die for me? (would you).

But you lied to me. Why'd you lie to me? why'd you lie to me? Yeah.

You lied, and my heart died! (died).

As the last notes fade, I feel like the rubber band holding me together snaps, and I sink onto the floor, holding my guitar. Everyone shouts my name, but I can't bring myself to lift my head, and then I hear a different voice.

"*Tesoro mio stai bene?* Delilah? Move back! *Andare indietro!*"

Thick arms lift me up, and I'm cradled against a broad chest. I can smell the hint of smoke and sage with notes of coffee. I feel myself being lowered to the couch in the corner and my feet being raised. Warm hands move through my hair, and I turn into them, seeking the comfort they give freely.

My head is lifted, and glass is pressed to my lips as I hear a voice whisper in my ear, "*Per favore, bevi l'acqua, piccolo amore.*"

I open my mouth and drink the water greedily. I honestly don't remember the last time I drank anything. Did I have something at dinner last night?

"Delilah?" That's Jensen.

He's probably worried sick. I need to get up and push myself into a sitting position, but three different hands push me back down.

"Delilah, you need to lie down. The doctor is on the way. Please just lie there and wait." He sounds strained now, and I look around, trying to find him.

When I do finally spot him, he's behind the sofa with his hands tucked in his pockets, looking anywhere but at me. When a warm hand smooths my hair, I turn to meet the worried eyes of Giovanni Santoro.

"Wh-what are you doing here?" I croak out as he helps me raise the glass of water back to my mouth, silently encouraging me to take a sip.

"Well, I was here to ask you and your group to be my opening act for the rest of my tour. However, *il mio bel disastro*, I'm afraid that I'll have to rescind that offer if you do not take better care of yourself. Touring is hard work and very taxing on the body, even one as magnificent as yours. If you're not well, I'm afraid you cannot tour. No matter how much I would wish to have you."

"You-you want us to tour with you? As your opening act? Are you fucking kidding me right now?" Mia shrieks from the end of the sofa.

"I'm not, as you say, *fucking kidding you*. I have an eye for talent, and after hearing your group play, I know you will blow up. I want to be the one to help you spread your wings." His fingers are running through my hair, and I find the action relaxing.

As soon as the doctor bustles through the door, everyone makes room. He places various machines on me and takes different readings. Then he begins asking questions about my eating and sleeping habits, which I reluctantly admit could be better lately. With every answer, I feel the temperature in the room drop. By the end of the mini interrogation, no one in the room is happy with me, including the hotter-than-sin Giovanni.

"Ms. Callahan, you are rundown, you have lost weight, and you are not sleeping enough for your body to recover from the stress you put it through. You must take a break, reduce stress, and eat a minimum of three meals a day. I'm also going to recommend a daily vitamin and a brand of protein shakes I think will help until we get you back to fighting shape."

As the doctor closes his bag, Giovanni reaches out a hand and places it on the older man's shoulder. "If she rests and does as you say, will she be tour ready in a month?"

The older man's bushy eyebrows almost hit his hairline. He glances at me on the couch and then back to Giovanni. "She's not in great shape, but it could be worse. Touring is stressful on the body. I fear if someone isn't watching, she could end up in the hospital. She may be able to tour, but someone must ensure she cares for herself."

"Oh, I can guarantee she will be well looked after," Giovanni vows as he meets my eyes across the room.

"Well. Fuck," I mutter as I drop my head back down on the pillow.

Cora comes striding into the room after showing the doctor out, only to pull up short when she sees Giovanni. "Mr. Santoro, what are you doing here?"

"Ah, Ms. Fields, I'm just speaking with my new opening act for the second leg of my tour."

Everyone gasps while Gio continues to hold my gaze.

"Opening Act? Do you want Wild Child Reckless to be your new opening act? They've just signed with the label. We're still working on their EP," Cora stutters, clearly shocked at the sudden turn of events.

"Yes, yes." Giovanni waves a dismissive hand. "The second half of the tour starts on the east coast, but most will be west. They can still record for the label. But the stage experience will mature their sound as well as provide good publicity. Yes. It's decided." He stands and holds out his hand for me to take, which I reluctantly accept. He pulls me suddenly upright and against his chest. "*Tesorina*, you will take better care of yourself, or I will take care of you. Is that something you want?"

I shake my head, my brain a little foggy for more than one reason, while Gio clicks his tongue.

Mia sits next to me and whispers, "Delilah, that was Giovanni Santoro, and he wants us to tour with him."

I nod and turn to Cora. "Can he do that?"

"It seems he did," is her only reply.

***

It's 7:55 p.m. on a Wednesday, two weeks later, when Giovanni knocks on our door. I open it to see him in his pressed suit and designer tie with a bouquet of yellow daises in his hand, and my breath catches.

"*Tesorina*, you look splendid." His kiss on my cheek is warm, and I catch a whiff of his cologne, dark and bold notes with hints of orange. Sinful and sexy, just like the man in front of me.

I clear my throat and smile at him. "Thank you, although I will admit that I was slightly surprised by your invitation."

His hand at the small of my back urges me to the open elevator. He presses the button when we walk into the car before pulling me close to him. "Well, *tesorina*. I have a weakness for pretty things. Since you brushed me off last time, I've seen your green eyes haunting me, even in my sleep."

My jaw drops at his words, and I'm still trying to wrap my brain around what he said when he ushers me from the elevator into a waiting town car. At my questioning gaze, he tucks me under his arm.

"We are going to Providence. They have the best seafood in LA. We can talk about the tour, and I'll answer any questions you may have. However, you can be sure that I will closely monitor your health. What happened the other day will not happen again. If for no other reason than I'm here now." The arrogance in his tone shouldn't be a turn-on. But, heaven help me, it is. "Now, Delilah. What questions do you have about touring with me?"

"Actually, I have several." I speak firmly and proceed to pepper him with every question I can think of.

He answers them all, including some about logistics and even a few I didn't have. When he discloses our percentage of the show, he quotes an amount I know is well above the industry standard.

"Gio, you know that is too much. No other opening act gets that much on any contract. You're being unreasonable."

"Well, *cara mia*, it's in my contract to negotiate, so you will get the percentage I have set for you. It is nonnegotiable." He cocks his head and smiles at me, and I sigh.

"You are going to be trouble," I tell him, and he bursts out laughing.

The next day, we meet as a group at the label. It is almost too easy to mesh ourselves together for the tour. Logistics are hammered out, contracts signed, and we get our first official schedule of events.

The next four months are a whirlwind of concerts, dates with Giovanni, and lousy road food. Opening for him has made our fan base grow by leaps and bounds. The next thing I know, we are returning to the west coast, and I'm spending more nights with him than at home.

"*Tesorina?*"

I turn from the view of the LA morning skyline in Gio's apartment. Falling into a relationship with him has been like slipping into a warm bath. It's relaxing, comforting, and my favorite way to unwind after a stressful day. Giovanni is a charmer. He's funny, intelligent, and more than a little overwhelming. I've never met someone who dominates a room like he does. When I asked him when he decided he wanted me, he said he started courting me during our dinner at Providence but knew he had to work hard to earn my heart.

"Hmm?" I bring my coffee cup to my mouth as I pad over to him, my shirt falling off my shoulder. I let him pull me into his lap.

"You're thinking awfully hard. What is on that beautiful mind, *bella*?" He kisses my neck, and I lean back against his shoulder with a sigh.

"Gio…"

He rumbles his approval, which makes me laugh.

"Gio, I'm being serious here." I shove his hands aside from where they are traveling under my shirt.

"Fine. Yes, *amore*. What is so important that you must deny me access to my favorite playground?"

I know he's teasing, but still, I turn and face him. "You know they want us to go on our own tour after we finish opening for you, right?"

"Yes, we've talked about this, *amore*. You know that you are always welcome to continue to tour with me, though. I don't know what I would do without you in my arms every night."

"Gio, we won't just open for you forever. You knew that when you signed us." Whenever I bring up doing our tour, he tries to get us to agree to continue to open for him. I'm getting frustrated at being forced back into this same circular conversation. "Gio, you were already popular in Europe before you came to the States. You've been doing this for longer than we have, which means we are at vastly different places in our careers. Touring with you has been amazing. The past six months have been a dream come true.

This isn't where my dream ends, though. You know that, right?" I place both hands on his face and bring our foreheads together.

"*Non chiedermi di vivere senza di te,*" he whispers as he pulls me closer, catching my lips with his. As the fire blooms between us, a small voice in my brain keeps wondering if this is the flame that will burn away all we are.

Chapter 22
Alexander

It's been almost eight months since Delilah left for LA. I dream about her every night. And whenever I close my eyes, the dream plays out again like it's happening in real time.

Delilah is sitting on our wrap-around porch in the early morning light. She clutches a cup of coffee, her long red curls delightfully tousled from our nighttime exertions. She's sipping the coffee with her feet pulled up under her thighs. I walk up behind her and run my hand over her shoulder, where her sweater has slipped to reveal a sliver of warm skin. I remove the cup from her hand before pulling her up and against me.

Then I bring my lips to hers and devour her mouth. I kiss her as if my life depends on it, and her lips hold the sweet nectar of life. Pulling her against me, I lift her so her legs wrap around my waist, my aching cock brushing against the silken valley between her legs.

Time seems to slip, and we're back in our bed.

The sheets smell of magnolia, and I find myself pressing her down into them as I thrust against her warm heat. I release her mouth and slide my lips down to wrap around a hard nipple through her shirt. Delilah's moans urge me to thrust harder. I growl against her neck, frustrated at the clothing that separates us. I slide my hands down to her waist and push her tiny cotton sleep shorts down her legs—

And then I wake up. Harder than steel. It takes less than a dozen pumps of my hand before I'm coming so hard my abs are sore, and I'm left panting while staring at the ceiling in my darkened room.

I toss and turn for hours, trying to go back to sleep. But every time I close my eyes, I see her red hair sprawled out on my sheets and hear her moans in my ear. And I'm instantly hard again, unable to resist milking myself to her memory.

The sun is just moving over the horizon when I give up trying to sleep altogether and go for a punishing run instead, followed by an ice-cold shower. Walking into the office, I release a deep breath before sitting at my dad's massive mahogany desk. Things have been getting better slowly.

Dad is home, therapy is going well, and I'm still managing the family business. The stroke was his wake-up call to change his priorities. He isn't the only one to hear that call either. I had a different vision for the path my life would take, fighting with my dad for years about helping him out at the business—because, if I'm being honest, I was scared. I was afraid to take something my dad had built from scratch and run it into the ground. As my old man likes to say, though, those fears were unfounded. It turns out I'm a natural.

I lay my head against the back of my office chair, rubbing my irritated eyes. Something has got to give. I need to be able to sleep, but I don't want to give up my nightly dreams of Delilah.

Maybe I can catch a catnap on the sofa after my three o'clock meeting?

I'm sitting at my dad's desk reviewing inventory reports when I hear my receptionist squeal. I jump up and run out of the room, expecting to see a bug or maybe a mouse. Janelle has no tolerance for creepy crawlies of any kind, but she's at her desk with a newspaper. I'm distracted by the fact they still print newspapers before I realize she is screaming about something she's reading.

"Janelle, we have been over this. You keep giving me a heart attack. When you make noises like that, I think something's wrong!" I'm only mildly scolding the fifty-something woman who has worked for my dad for years. Truth is she probably knows this business better than he does. It's one of the things he warned me about when we first discussed me taking over for him.

Listen, Janelle has been with me for years. She probably knows the business better than I do, so don't try to micromanage her. She may look like she isn't doing much of anything, but she can work rings around anyone, including me.

He put this down on a typed-out note since he still has a slight slur and prefers communicating this way.

"You got it, Dad," I told him. "I won't run her off. You know that. I don't have a memory of your office that doesn't include Janelle."

And he clapped me on the back, and here we are.

He's been home for seven months, and I've been here learning and running the business he spent his life building.

I rub the back of my neck. Sometimes I just wish none of this had ever happened. I would still be on track to work in sports medicine, and Dad would be at his desk like he always was, but life is about learning to manage the hand you're dealt, and this is mine. Besides, if this proves anything, it's that I was made for the construction business.

"Why did you holler, Janelle?" I try to keep my tone steady, but even I can hear the irritation bleed through.

"Look!" She turns the paper around, and the first thing I see in bold letters is the title: *Indie Newcomer Joining Santoro Tour!*

Underneath is a picture of Delilah with her arm around the waist of Giovanni Santoro, who has her tucked close against his side. She's smiling up at him with obvious affection as she brushes a loose curl behind her ear. She looks happy.

My mouth drops open in surprise. I yank the paper from Janelle's hands to have a closer look. And my eyes quickly scan over the article.

Wild Child Reckless, a Texas Indie Band, hit the LA scene eight months ago with the release of their first single, a self-titled track. It broke records everywhere and continues to climb the charts. Mr. Santoro has taken a shine to the lovely Delilah—lead singer of WCR—and has invited them to open for the remainder of his west coast tour. Fans were shocked when his previous opener, Honey Bee, disbanded, citing irreconcilable differences. However, Mr. Santoro appears more than happy with the unexpected matchup!

I read the article twice, and the words don't change. I drop the paper on Janelle's desk before storming back into my office. Slamming open my laptop, and against my better judgment, I Google Delilah and Santoro, and what I see knocks me on my ass.

Story upon story about the pair, pictured up and down the west coast. Images of them out at dinner, Delilah in tiny dresses and smiling for the camera. Wild Child Reckless on stage, with some woman I don't recognize on the piano. Even more articles about the tour and the band making waves in the music industry. I collapse into my seat.

How did I miss this?

"Janelle. I'm going to head home for today. Please cancel my three o'clock. And call me if there are any issues. If you don't see me tomorrow, please ensure the Donaldson build gets that tile shipment on time." I grab my jacket and head to the door without waiting for her response.

I go directly to the airport. There's no way this is happening. I won't let it.

***

When the plane touches down in LA six hours later, I flag down a cab and head straight for Revelation Records. Traffic is backed up, so I pay the driver, hop out in the middle of the street, and hurry down the sidewalk. I can feel my shirt sticking to me. The humidity is oppressive. My heart is racing, and my stomach is rolling in waves.

I open the heavy glass door and see a petite brunette at the check-in desk. "Hello! Welcome to Revelation Records! How may I help you?" Her smile is wide and entirely too cheerful.

"Hi, I need to speak with—" My heart stops when I hear a voice call out from behind me.

"Alexander?"

I slowly turn, and there she is. A vision in the evening sun. Her hair is shorter and straighter, and her black dress stops above her knees and molds to her figure like a glove. Gone is the girl who ran in the fields and caught lightning bugs. In her place, there's a woman who makes my breath catch and my palms sweat.

"Delilah," I manage to choke out and move to hug her. But she steps back, and I freeze. When I meet her gaze, I realize her eyes have no smile or warmth. "Delilah?"

"Alexander, what are you doing here? Is it James? Is everything okay? Why didn't anyone call me?" She pulls her phone out of her small purse and frantically checks for texts or calls that aren't there.

"James? James is fine. He called last week. I'm here because of you, Delilah." My mouth is dry, and I can't catch a full breath. The woman in front of me may not resemble the girl I knew, but she's still mine.

Her head snaps up, and she meets my eyes. "Because of me? What about me? Alexander, you're not making any sense! Why. Are. You. Here?"

"Delilah, I—" I'm interrupted when the elevator dings. The door opens, revealing Giovanni Santoro. I can feel my chest rumbling in anger. This is the fool who thought he could steal my girl.

He saunters out, his suit jacket over his arm as he presents the very picture of nonchalant elegance and money. "*Tesorina*, there you are. I was starting to worry." He walks up to Delilah, pulling her close and kissing her forehead.

She curls into his body as if seeking protection, and it's a hammer between my eyes when I realize she may be doing just that—seeking safety in him, from me. I rub a hand over my heart, which is currently in pieces on the floor.

"Ciao! I'm Giovanni. Are you a friend of *mia bellissima cara*?" He holds out his hand as if to shake mine, and I reluctantly return the gesture.

Delilah clears her throat. "Gio, this is Alexander. He's my brother's best friend. Remember when I told you." She trails off, appearing nervous while refusing to meet my eyes as Gio nods in agreement.

"Ah, yes, now that you mention it, I do remember." His gaze turns thoughtful as he looks between me and Delilah. "Darling, we need to get going. I promised you seafood after the last show. So we have that reservation at Providence." Santoro threads her arm through his and turns, as if to walk off.

"Delilah! Please? Just give me five minutes. Please?" I may sound desperate, but I'm beyond caring at this point.

Delilah sighs, kisses Santoro on the cheek, then walks back to me. "What do you want, Alexander?" Her body language, more than her tone, sets me on edge.

"Delilah, you can't be... Tell me you're not... He's entirely too old for you!" My words stumble and trip, and when they finally land, I wish I'd kept my mouth shut. This isn't Delilah angry. No, I've seen her angry. This is something else, and whatever it is does not bode well for me.

"You flew all this way, and that's what you HAD to say to me? He's too old for me? What? Can't I want him? Or he can't want me?" Her voice trembles, and I swear I hear sirens going off. Delilah gets right in my face, poking my chest hard. "Yes, he might be older, but so what? He cares for me, treats me like I should be treated, and at least HE never lied to me or made me feel *less than* just because of my age." With a pointed look, she takes a step back. "Go home, Alexander. You're not my keeper anymore. You are relieved of your silly little burden."

For a moment, her eyes glimmer with tears before she pulls them back, straightens her shoulders, and leaves with Santoro. *Without* a backward glance in my direction. I look around in a daze.

What the hell just happened?

Chapter 23
Delilah

Walking into our condo, I'm shocked to see everyone up and waiting for me. I pause at the door.

"Hey, is everything okay?" I meet the eyes of each person I call my family, looking for a tell as to what might be happening.

Jensen clears his throat before standing and handing me his phone. I look at the screen to see it open to a popular gossip site.

Wild Child Reckless touring? Is the Princess of Pop about to make her very own debut?

I scan the article, which includes a picture of Gio and me entering Providence. There's a lot of speculation about Wild Child Reckless and Gio and my relationship and what the upcoming tour could mean for all of us.

I find myself laughing. "That man is a genius."

"Dee?" Mia stands and walks toward us. "Does this mean what I think it means? Not that opening for Giovanni hasn't been incredible, because it has. However, we were worried that with the..." She pauses before continuing. "...developing feelings between you two that we might be opening for him for a while longer." Since Mia has joined the band, she has grown comfortable with us, dropping some of her more formal speech pattern while integrating herself as if she's always been here.

"Well, I was coming home to talk to you guys about it. But I see that, once again, Gio was correct." I gesture to Jensen's phone. "He's the one who let it slip to the paps. He said news of the tour would make the gossip rags within the hour. Dinner this evening was spent planning, with your approval, our debut. Wild Child Reckless is officially headlining our own tour. Let me show you the preliminary itinerary we came up with, and then we can expand from there."

Glancing at my phone, I realize we were so lost in our discussion over dinner that it's almost two in the morning. We wrap up the meeting, all of us yawning despite the excitement we must be feeling. Heading back to my room, I fall face-first on the bed. Everyone is still chattering away in the living room. My eyes drift back to my phone and I see that there's a text notification waiting for me. I open it and my stomach hits my feet.

X: Dee, I wonder if you'll even get this. I know I haven't been there like I said I would, and you have no reason to believe me. I miss you. You're everything, Dee. I need to see you. Can you meet me? I'll be in LA for the rest of tonight before I fly out tomorrow. I would love to see you. Call whenever.

I throw myself back down on my bed with a groan. The last thing I want is to deal with Alexander at two in the morning. Why can't he return to Texas and his perfect life and leave me alone?

Rolling over, I pull my pillow over my face and scream. The sound of a throat clearing has me sitting up. "Is this a bad time?" Mia grins at me from the doorway, and I flop back down.

"You have no idea," I mutter.

"Boy troubles?"

"Emphasis on the BOY."

"Ah, so not Gio then. I will say he looked less than thrilled when he left. Trouble in paradise?"

I have to snort. "Paradise, huh?" I sit up with another loud sigh.

"When Gio and I were leaving for dinner, Alexander ambushed me in the lobby."

"That asshole was here? Why didn't you tell me? I would have come downstairs and stomped him a new one." Mia's anger makes me feel better.

It was one night not long after she joined the band when I broke down and told her everything that had happened. The whole sad little tale. Ever since then, she's been Team Delilah. Alternating between wanting to fly down to Texas to kick Alexanders ass herself and sic some of her friends on him.

"I didn't think about it. He said some pretty awful stuff, and I put him in his place. He thinks Gio is too old for me."

"Fuck what he thinks. Gio treats you like a princess, something that Alexander never did."

"Why would he? I'm his best friend's little sister."

Mia gives me a look that I know all too well. She thinks the reason Alexander is such an asshole to me is because he wants me. I will never admit it but deep down I hope that's true. However, Alexander is off-limits and I have to remember why.

"Yeah. That's the reason. Sure." I can hear the sarcasm in my own voice and roll my eyes. "Anywaaays," I draw out the words. "He caused a huge stink in the lobby, so I called him on his shit and walked out. Gio questioned me about him over dinner. I'm not so sure he's thrilled that Alexander's in town. I was supposed to spend the night at his place, but he dropped me off here instead. I'm pretty sure it's over now. He can't pull our contract, but I'm not sure he's Team Delilah anymore."

"Aw, hons, it will be okay." Mia curls up next to me in bed, putting an arm around my shoulder, which gives her a prime view of my phone still open on Alexander's message.

"He texted you!"

I wince at her yell. *My poor eardrums.* "Yeah, I'm not sure when. I just got it."

"Oh, he has balls—this one does. Let me text him back. I can tell him exactly what he can do with his *I miss you* and *you're everything.* He can go home to Little Miss Suzy Homemaker! My girl has history to make! She's gonna be famous, and she has no time for little fuckboys who can't make up their minds about what they want!"

By the time Mia reaches the end of her tirade, I've finally pulled my phone from her grasp. "Mia. I love you. You know that. However, I can handle this. I promise. Go to bed. It's gonna be a long day tomorrow, and you won't be a grump-a-saurus the whole day. Got me?"

She throws her hands in the air. "I got you. I got you. Let me know if you need me to put Alexander in his place. Have shit-kickers, will travel."

Shaking my head, I chuckle as she shuts my door. I lie on my bed for a moment, staring at his text while lost in memory. Then I force out a sigh and type out a response. Delete it and type it out again. I repeat this six times before I finally get the words right.

Me: Alexander, please go home. My life is here now, and yours is there. Please go live your life, and let me live mine. I wish you both the best.

I continue to stare at the lights from my window, thinking about a future I will never have. And when my phone goes off again, just a few minutes later, I groan before checking it. I glance outside, debating what to say. Then finally shoot off a text to Mia, letting her know where I'm going, and answer X's phone call.

I guess it's Alexander's lucky night. Let's get some coffee.

Chapter 24
Alexander

The LA nightlife is not something I'm sure I could ever get used to. The noise alone is enough to wake the dead. How anyone sleeps in this town is beyond me. That could be part of the problem—no one ever sleeps.

I'm staring at the ceiling of my hotel room when my phone lights up. I reach over the pillows to grab it while checking the time on the bedside clock—it's two in the morning. Unlocking my screen, I see I have a text from Delilah, and my throat goes dry.

Dee: Alexander, please go home. My life is here now, and yours is there. Please go live your life, and let me live mine. I wish you both the best.

I stare at the phone for a minute, thinking I must have read it wrong. Wish who the best? Does she not understand? Doesn't she know my life isn't worth living if she isn't in it? How could I possibly live my life without her?

I immediately hit dial on her contact, and the phone rings in my ear, amplified by the sound of my heart racing.

Please let her pick up.

When the line clicks over, I choke out, "Dee."

She sighs into the phone before she answers. "Hello, Alexander."

I close my eyes, soaking in the sound of a voice I wasn't sure I would hear again. "Dee, please. I need to talk to you. I need to see you. Please. I am begging you. Meet me for coffee, a taco, hell, a pretzel. I'm not above bribery. As long as you say you'll meet me, anything you want." I give zero shits that I sound desperate because this right here IS a desperate situation. I just need her to meet me, listen, and tell me what happened.

Another sigh whispers down the line, followed by a low groan. "Alexander... We're going on tour. It was decided tonight. We meet with the label tomorrow to begin the planning process. Then everything will be officially announced to the public."

"That is FANTASTIC, sweetheart! That's such a big deal!" I enthuse before a thought occurs to me, and I swallow past the lump in my throat. And, despite my better judgment, I ask the question I really do not want to know the answer to. "Are you going with him?"

"No." Dee chuckles softly into the phone before continuing. "We are not touring with Gio. He'll be in the middle of his own tour. This is just Wild Child Reckless! We'll need an opening act, but since we are new, it'll be something small before we come out on stage. Besides, Giovanni Santoro is no one's opening act."

I release a relieved breath.

"Alexander, I don't understand why you're here. I know that some things were said before the move, and I'm sorry for how I left things. I should have told you, and I should have said goodbye to everyone personally. I apologize for that and admit it wasn't the best way to handle the situation. I decided, given the circumstances, that I should not be there anymore, and the label had already wanted us to fly down early. It seemed like the best option for both of us."

I shake my head even though she can't see me. *How can this be best for anyone when she's not in my life anymore?*

"Delilah. You're wrong. Please. Meet me for coffee. There's a 24-hour diner just a few blocks from you. Please. I need to talk to you. Afterward, if you never want to hear from me again, so be it. Just give me this."

"I'm not even going to guess how you know that, but okay. Fine. Yes, I'll meet you for coffee. Give me half an hour, and I'll be there." Delilah's reluctance practically saturates the line.

I don't care. She said yes.

I jump out of bed and start swiping up my discarded clothes. Delilah is going to meet me for coffee and finally talk to me. I can tell her everything, and she'll listen. Coffee with Dee is just the break I need.

I walk into the diner with ten minutes to spare and find a table in the back. It isn't packed, but I want more privacy than something in the middle can provide.

The waitress promptly drops a menu in front of me. "What can I get you?" she asks, her voice reminding me of a bag of gravel and lending credence to the fact she's probably smoked five packs a day every day for the last forty years.

"I'll get a cup of coffee, cream and sugar, and a hot chocolate, extra marshmallows. I'm waiting for someone. We may order food in a bit. I'll let you know. Thanks." I keep the menu in front of me but don't even move my eyes off the entrance.

Delilah should be here any minute, and as if summoned by my thoughts, the bell chimes as she steps through the door. I suck in a breath and end up inhaling spit and choking when I see her in her jean shorts and white tank with a plaid overshirt. She must have worn this exact outfit every day in Texas. It never once looked this... provocative. And I am not the only one to think so, given the number of eyes on her as she scans the diner's interior.

I see the moment she notices me. Her eyes sparkle with warmth and affection before some thought appears to shut those emotions down. Determined to return that sparkle, I approach her with a hug.

"Dee." My voice cracks as I tug her against my chest, my head resting on her hair as I breathe in her magnolia scent and drag it deep into my lungs. I've missed this. The smell of her. I can feel myself start to settle. I may not know much, but I know I cannot lose this woman. I pull her closer, needing to feel her just a minute longer than is probably polite.

Right now, I'm beyond propriety.

"Hey, X," she whispers into my shirt, doubling my heart rate. She hasn't called me X in so long.

"C'mon, let's sit down. I've ordered you a hot chocolate because I know how you are about your coffee. I didn't figure this location would be up to snuff." I wait for her to settle into her chair before reclaiming mine.

"Did you get—"

"Extra marshmallows. Yes. I would never forget that." I chuckle, and she joins me. Those details, the little moments, are forever branded in my heart. A sign of my love for this woman.

Delilah smiles at the waitress when the mug is set on the table before cupping it in her hands and blowing gently. I stir in my cream and sugar, and we sit in slightly strained but somehow comfortable silence for a few minutes. I feel her eyes darting up to look at me, but no one says a word.

"Why did you—"

"Why are you—"

We both start and stop simultaneously, our eyes meeting from across the table before we end up laughing. I gesture for Delilah to go first.

She inhales deeply before steadying her glare in my direction. "Why are you here, Alexander?"

I flinch a little. I never thought I'd miss being X so much. But her question also pokes at a small part of me that's still furious with her for leaving like she did. "The only way to answer that question is to ask another one. Why wouldn't I be here? My life changed overnight, Dee. *Overnight.* You, of all people, should know how that feels. I needed time to get everything settled with my parents. I asked you to give me that, and you left the next day. Why wouldn't I fly halfway across the country for minutes with the girl I asked to wait for me? Why wouldn't I beg, borrow, steal, or lie for a chance to find out what was going on in her beautiful head that meant she couldn't wait a day for me?" My chest is heaving by the time I'm done, and I feel like I have run a six-minute mile.

Delilah's face pales before she appears to flinch at my tone. I don't blame her, but at the same time, I *wholly* blame her. She broke me when I was already in the process of breaking. How dare she act like she didn't! She has to know why I'm here. You can't just do that kind of damage to a person and expect to walk away without answering a few questions.

"Well. First off, you never asked me to wait. You just said we needed to talk. Historically the most awful words in the human language." Delilah clears her throat before continuing. "I can tell that you're still upset, and I can't say I really understand. However, I want to tell you a story before I answer your question. Will you listen?"

At my nod, she continues.

"On the plane ride from Houston to LA, I was seated next to this sweet little old man. The ride was short, but he struck up a conversation. He told me I was the prettiest *seatmate* he'd had since his wife passed. He went on about all the places they would go together and how they met. I could see his love for this woman who had been such a massive part of his life that even five years after her passing, he was still madly, irrevocably in love with her. He still remembered their first date, how much her dad didn't like him, and laughed about the time he told her they couldn't get a dog, so she went out and got three ducks instead. Her only excuse when he confronted her about it? *Well, you said I couldn't have a dog! You didn't say anything about ducks!*"

When Delilah chuckles at her story, so do I. Because I can fully see her saying something similar. "Dee. That's a cute story, but I don't see where this is going…"

"I'm getting there," she says before pinning me with another glare. "After talking to that little old man, I realized that that was what I wanted. What I *want*. I want to be loved like his wife was loved. I want to be someone's entire world, and I just didn't see how anything like that was possible—" Her voice trails off, and the unspoken "with you" hangs in the air.

"Delilah Rose Callahan, how do you not know I already love you like that? Jesus, you're EVERYTHING. I've been trying hard to wait and let you graduate high school. Every dance performance, every night spent eating pizza and watching movies... I've wanted nothing more than to claim you as my own every single second of every single day for the last two years. But I couldn't do that. I had to wait. But then, when I asked you to please have faith and wait for me—" This time, I let my voice trail off.

We both know what happened after that. She left.

I expected Delilah to understand where I was coming from. To apologize. Then we could work toward a reconciliation that resulted in her finally being mine. So no one is more surprised than I am when her cheeks flush red and a deadly fire crackles in her eyes. Gone is the contrite girl who can't meet my gaze for too long. No, that Delilah isn't in the house anymore. This version I know intimately, and before she even opens her mouth, I also know this will not end well for me.

She sets her mug carefully on the table before wiping her lips and folding her napkin in half. When she looks up again, I can feel my mouth go dry. Delilah gently places her hands, palms down, on each side of the table before shoving her chair back. The resulting screech is loud in the relative quiet of the diner. All conversation immediately stops, and I can feel all eyes on us.

"All right. Let's just address a few things first. I've already apologized—" Delilah holds up a hand, effectively stopping me from interrupting her. "I'm speaking now. You're listening *now*. Like I said, I've already apologized several times for leaving the way I did. So you want to talk about my actions on the night I left? I was going to wait. I was going to give up coming here, give up doing the one thing that I've always wanted to do... for YOU. I was going to give us a chance. Then I found out you're nothing but a liar, and it's like I never even knew you at all. Grow up, Peter Pan! You need to learn Neverland doesn't exist. This is the real world, and our actions have consequences. My leaving just happens to be yours." Delilah snatches her purse from the table and storms out of the diner while I sit here, once again trying to wrap my brain around what just happened.

I stand, my legs shaky as I pull a twenty from my wallet and throw it on the table. I'm still in a daze as I stumble out of the diner.

On one hand, Delilah was glorious. The Delilah I knew never would have lit into me the way she did. She would have just decked me and moved along. That said, I can't help but feel confused as her words keep ringing in my head. They don't make sense. I didn't do anything that night but ask her to stay... to wait.

Something else must have happened, but what?

One thing is clear, though. I won't get a second chance to talk to her until she calms down. If she thinks this is over, she's the one with her head in the clouds.

That's what I tell myself and silently *promise her* as I head back to my hotel to regroup.

Chapter 25
Delilah

I wait until I'm back in the comfort of my bedroom before I lose my shit. Straight into the fluffy decorative pillows my mom always loved and *I* always thought were dumb.

Why have a pillow if you aren't allowed to sleep on it?

I scream and scream until I get woozy. Then I sit on the edge of my bed and slowly slide to the floor. I can't hold myself upright. Leaning against the frame, I sit here as the sun begins to rise. Thoughts are swirling in my head, and I can't tell where one ends and another begins. I replay the events of that night at the hospital, the texts coming through, and how it felt being in X's arms. Every moment is a kaleidoscope of feelings in my mind. Eventually, I can hear everyone move around, preparing to head over to the studio.

Mia knocks, like she does every morning. When I don't answer, she cracks the door, in case I'm dressing, and walks on in. "Babe, did you hear me knocking? You okay?" She looks me up and down before sitting beside me.

I need help getting my thoughts straight. "Yeah. I mean, no. I will be. I don't know. Is Jensen up yet?"

"Yeah, girl. Lemme grab him. He was in the kitchen." She watches me, worry etched on her face as she slowly exits the room. Jensen replaces her in minutes.

"Dee." He pulls me close. "What's going on?"

My breathing hitches, and I break down sobbing. "Alexander blames me."

That's all I can say, but Jensen already knows what I mean. He's witnessed everything from that one night to now. Not even my mom knows the whole truth of what happened. He says he asked me to wait but he didn't. What he did do is destroy my world with a text conversation. How he expected me to stay after seeing what I saw is beyond me.

Jensen pulls me closer. "If he blames you, he isn't the man I thought he was, and he doesn't deserve you. No matter what, you have me. How do you know he blames you?" Jensen leans back to try to look me in the eyes, but I do my best to avoid him while scrubbing my face clean with my shirt.

"I met him last night at this diner down on 46th. I thought it would be good to hear what he had to say, but all he kept repeating was how he didn't understand why I didn't wait, left like I did, and didn't trust him. He just kept poking and poking. I was sitting across from him, and he acted like I broke him. Like he'd done nothing wrong. It was like I was in the Twilight Zone." I let out a loud sigh. "I know I shouldn't have met him, I knew it would be hard, but I didn't think it would be this hard. He hugged me, and it was all I could do not to come unglued. I still love him. I don't want to love him, but I do." I collapse onto Jensen, and he pulls me close.

Of all the things I thought would come out of his mouth, what he says next throws me for a loop. "Do you want me to call Gio?" It's whispered into my hair, but the words hang in the air.

"*Tesorina*?"

I wince at the sound of Gio's voice before glaring at Jensen, who holds up his hands in surrender. Then I hear the front door slam.

"I didn't call him. I've been in here with you. It must have been one of the others." Jensen pushes up from the floor when my bedroom door flies open.

Giovanni enters my room like a whirlwind of expensive linen and cologne. He flicks a dismissive hand toward Jensen and then plucks me from the ground as if I weigh nothing. "*Tesorina*, you will tell me immediately what that *idiota* did to you. He'll regret his actions. Just say the word, and I'll put my men on it." Gio's tone is sincere, but the thought is so ludicrous that I can't help but laugh.

Which draws the rest of our crew into my room.

I shake my head, waving my hands in the air. "Okay, everyone. Let's just take a moment. Sorry to derail the morning. Let's postpone the meeting about the tour for an hour. Maddie, can you call Cora and see if we can move it here? Thank you."

I watch Maddie duck out of the room at my request. Grayson is quick to follow her. I file that away to think about later.

Then I turn to Gio, lay my head on his shoulder, and wrap my arms around his waist. He pulls me close, and I take comfort in the familiarity of his arms. "Gio. I'm fine. I had a moment. It's okay. You don't need to send your men anywhere. But since you're here, you could make me a coffee and stay for the tour talk. I know it's all so very *boring* to you, Mr. Toured-the-Country-Already."

He chuckles before kissing my head. "Fine, *bella*, but we will be talking later." He gives me a pointed glare from the doorway.

As soon as Gio is out of earshot, Jensen pulls me back into his arms. "Are you sure you're okay, Dee? It's okay if you're not okay. The tour can wait a moment."

"I'm fine, Jensen. Promise." I force a smile on my face and head for the kitchen.

Gio is at the sink making my coffee. You've never had coffee until you've had *his* version of coffee. He uses the same machine and beans that we do, but it tastes much better somehow. Gio slides the cup across the bar with a wink, and I pick it up without slowing down.

Walking around the counter, I see Maddie and Grayson in the breakfast nook signing furiously. I'm decent when it comes to the art of sign language, but they put me to shame. I can only catch a word or two of their conversation, but from what I can tell, they are most likely arguing. I flicker the lights to grab Grayson's attention, and he throws his hands up in frustration before walking over to me.

I sip my coffee, setting it down to sign, before he rests his head on mine. *"You okay?"*

"Yeah, I'll be fine. Stubborn as a mule." Gray's irritation is almost tangible, making me chuckle. He's always had the ladies eating out of his hands. Good for Maddie for making him work for it.

"I *resemble* that remark." I hip-check him as I walk into the living room and settle onto the plush sofa. Gio lowers himself down next to me and we sit in comfortable silence. Until we hear the front door open and the click of Cora's heels on the tile entryway.

"Well, there they are! I was on my way to the studio when I got the message that you wanted to meet here! Love it! So much more comfortable. Now, let's get down to business." Cora perches on the coffee table, her legs crossed and her tablet open on her knee.

I grab my phone for notes and get comfortable. I can tell we're going to be here for a while.

"So. We have twelve more weeks in the studio to finalize your EP. Once that's done, we can move straight to your first tour. You are slated for a hundred cities across thirty states. I know you've been chatting with Giovanni about the process, and as such, you are further ahead than most of my new recruits. This is a marathon and not a sprint. You'll have some downtime between shows, but most of your time will be spent on the bus. I hope you all get along because it will be close quarters for a while on the Records tour bus."

Gio lifts a lazy hand in the air. "They will not be using the Records bus. I've already arranged an alternative." I gasp, and he shrugs a shoulder. "It was my last bus before I upgraded. It's not as modern as I prefer, but it's better than what the label provides."

I kiss his cheek, and he smiles at me, obviously pleased. "Thank you, Gio. You know you are too good to me. I could never deserve you."

"That is where you're wrong, *cara mia*. You deserve the world. I'm lucky you let me give you a small piece of it. Besides, my bus has upgraded security, and it makes my heart happy to know that you will be safe on the road."

Cora clears her throat before she goes back to her tablet. "Okay. Well, the tour bus issue is sorted. I've emailed the suggested itineraries. We'll be hiring makeup and sound techs. We typically have a person we work with at each venue. But for some of the newer, smaller ones, we may have to hire local talent or bring someone down from a larger city."

The next three hours are spent chatting and discussing cities, venues, songs, and so on as a group. We view mock-ups of merch and costumes and discuss meet-and-greet options. We leave it to the label to narrow down our opening acts while stressing our preference for new indie bands like us. When everyone is finally done packing up, I stand and stretch, ready to return to my room.

Gio taps me on my shoulder. "Let's go get lunch. Do not think it's escaped my notice that you have yet to eat today. Throw on some shoes and let's go."

I roll my eyes but do as he says and slip on my flip-flops. Then we head down the elevator in more comfortable silence. During one of the breaks in our tour discussions, I told him what happened that night at the hospital and explained the situation with Alexander. And now things seem better between Gio and me. He called Alexander a fool and swore to be there for me no matter what. No matter when.

I chuckle a little to myself at the thought. *My dramatic Italian.*

When the elevator door opens, I'm surprised and more than a little pissed to see a familiar face standing there. "Alexander, what the hell!? What are you doing here?"

"*What am I doing here*? I'm here to try to talk to you, Dee. You blew up at me last night and left without giving me a chance to get a word in edgewise. *SO*, I thought I would come here to see if you would talk to me in person like an adult, since you've been ignoring my texts all morning." His jaw is clenched so hard I can almost hear his teeth cracking.

However, his accusations push me right over the edge. I tuck my hair back from my face before storming out of the elevator and into Alexander's personal space. "First, *you* never allowed *me* to get a word in edgewise. Second, I wasn't ignoring you. We had a critical band meeting about our upcoming tour today, and I didn't have my phone. Third, when I wasn't answering your texts, your first thought was to AMBUSH me outside my HOME? That's what goes through your head when you just HAVE to speak to me? HAVE YOU LOST YOUR MIND?"

"You. Weren't. TALKING TO ME!" Alexander roars back, and Gio shoves me behind him.

"It appears you both need to calm down. However, you do not yell at a lady. Any lady. Especially this one. If you do not find a way to calm yourself, I'll have to do it for you, and you will not like my methods. Are we clear?" Gio's tone is deceptively cool, but I can feel the vibrations from his body. He wants nothing more than to drop Alexander onto his perfectly sculpted ass. Right now, I don't think I would mind that either. I'm so done with his mantrums.

"Look. My life is here. My band is here. I'm not leaving, and you're not staying. You and Megan had big plans to be the next power couple of Havenbrook, and that life isn't for me. So go home. Get the life you want and leave me be. This is done, Alexander. Done." I wrap my hand around Gio's and pull him out the door. He tucks me closer to his side, as far from Alexander as he can place me, and we push through the glass doors into the sun before slipping inside the waiting town car.

Chapter 26
Alexander

I stand here and stare after her as she walks out the door. I can't even comprehend what just happened.

What am I doing? Another thought quickly follows that one. *Is this really it?*

I feel myself getting angry all over again. I storm outside and hail a cab to the airport. Where I purchase a ticket back to Texas and spend the rest of the time waiting on my flight, distracting myself with the inventory reports I never finished before my impromptu trip.

This went way differently from how I planned it. I briefly think about texting James, but the last thing I need is for him to figure out that what I really want to do with my life is marry his little sister. Frustrated, I close my phone and slide it back into my pocket.

When the flight lands in Texas at six that evening, I head straight to the office. I don't want to go back to my empty apartment. My anger is still coursing through me, and I grumble about Delilah to the vacant space. I can't help but replay every moment of my brief conversations with her.

She was happy to see me again when she first entered that diner. I didn't imagine that. Then something changed. I didn't imagine that smile on her face either. It was there before something stole it away.

What was it she said before she stormed out in a glorious, sexy rage?

I don't miss the irony that her reaming my ass is something that I find attractive about her. She's beautiful on a good day, but when she's angry, she is glorious.

I think back to that night in the waiting room. I asked her to trust me, to bear with me. Then things got so hectic with Dad that I never had a chance to reach out. Not that it mattered, seeing as she didn't even wait. She left the next day. Even after she said she would stay.

She did say that, didn't she?

I think back but I can't remember. However, I *do* remember that she left. I'm missing something. I have to be, but what?

Frustrated, I slam a fist down on my desk. My cell phone chimes, and I snatch it up to check the notification. It rings in my hand and I see James's name on the screen.

I click over and lean back in my chair. "Well, hello, fucker. How's whatever hellhole you're in now?"

"Listen, asshat, I don't know what you did, but you have to apologize to my sister."

I flinch. I wondered if Delilah was going to call James. I should have expected him to reach out to me by now. "I don't know what you're talking about." I try to play innocent but know that dog won't hunt.

"Look." His tone is no nonsense. "I don't know what happened between you two, and honestly I don't care. I'm not thrilled about Dee dating that Santoro guy, and I agree that he's too old for her, but he treats her right. Plus, she likes him. She's an adult and can make her own decisions."

"She's been an adult for all of thirty seconds. There's no way she can make her own decisions."

"Well. She has, and as a family, it's our job to support her. Like I said, I don't know what you did exactly, but I know you need to fix it. Now. Get over whatever bullshit you disagree with her doing."

I stare at my phone for a moment. Letting my best friend's words sink in before sighing into the receiver. "I'm not saying I agree with you, but I can see where you're coming from. You know I care for Dee." I swallow roughly before plowing on. "I only want what's best for her. And I don't think it's that Santoro guy. I'm not saying he would hurt her, but that she may end up hurt regardless." The idea of Delilah being hurt in any way or shape has me clenching my jaw.

"You know, it's funny. I always figured you and Dee would end up together. You've been in love with her for years." His casual tone catches me by surprise, and I choke on the spit in my mouth. James chuckles, and I have to catch my breath.

"I—uh—I mean..." Stumbling over my words, I try to accept the fact that my best friend knows I'm in love with his little sister, and somehow I can still see from both eyes. "Well, I thought we would be having a very different conversation right now. I honestly thought that you would be wiping the floor with my ass and threatening to end me if I didn't stay away from her when you found out..."

"Listen. I know you. I've known you all my life. Which means I also know I would be hard-pressed to find a better man to love my baby sister. That said, something's happened, and she is spitting mad at you. So what did you do?"

I go on to give him the short version, starting with the night Dad had the stroke and ending with the final confrontation at the elevator. "I honestly don't know why every time I try to get her to acknowledge what we could have, it just implodes. She called me Peter Pan."

"Peter Pan?"

"Yeah. *Peter Pan.* She said—and I quote—*Grow up, Peter Pan! You need to learn Neverland doesn't exist. This is the real world, and our actions have consequences. My leaving just happens to be yours.*"

James whistles. "Boy, you really pissed her off, huh?"

"Yes, but I still don't know what I did, and she won't tell me!" I can feel myself getting mad again, so I take several deep breaths.

"Listen, when she gets mad, she needs time to calm down. So give her time. Work on you and build the kind of life you know she deserves. The rest will come. Delilah never stays mad for long. She'll text you soon." James sounds certain. I'm not so sure.

"You didn't see her, James. I've never seen her this worked up. She kept talking about returning to my perfect life and the life I wanted. And all I *wanted* to do was shake her stubborn ass and tell her she's all I've ever wanted, but she never gave me that chance!"

"She didn't say anything else? Just that? That's all she said?"

I lean back in my chair and think, sifting through the conversations over the past forty-eight hours. I jerk upright in my chair. "Megan. She mentioned Megan."

"Why would she mention her? You only dated for what? A few weeks? Months? It was never anything serious. It wasn't like you ever chose Megan over Dee."

Groaning out loud, I bang my head on my desk.

"I'm not going to like this, am I?" James grunts into the phone.

"Probably not." I sigh. "The night my dad had his stroke, a bunch of us went to a bonfire. Megan rode along and I was chatting with her. Delilah and the group were performing. And I may—" I hesitate. "I may have reacted badly. Everyone was drinking, and I was too, and then I was trying to find Dee but couldn't. I must've been more drunk than I initially thought and sat down when Megan came up and started making out with me. Dee saw it all." My tone is resigned, and I can feel a headache brewing.

"Well. That does not bode well for you, my friend. The good news is that Dee will get over it. Eventually. You're like her second favorite person, after yours truly, so the chances are good she will text you back soon." He's being placating and sounds hopeful, but he wasn't there. He didn't see her, how she looked at me.

I lean back in my chair again and stare at the popcorn ceiling of Dad's office. It just doesn't make sense. I have to be missing something....

"Hey, man, I gotta go. Look, I'll be out of pocket for a bit, but I'll try to put in a good word for you the next time I talk to her, all right?" James says, drawing my attention back to him.

I can hear the noise of trucks in the background and some people calling out. "Hey, you're safe, right? You're not going to do anything stupid?” James is a wild card, also my best friend, and I want him to remain that way for many years to come.

“I’m being as safe as possible. But what I need is for you to remove your head from your ass regarding my sister. Or I might have to break your legs when I come home.” I can hear the steel thread underlying his teasing tone.

“I don’t want to hurt her either, James. You know that. I just don’t know what I’m up against.” I close my eyes, willing my headache to subside.

“Yeah! I’m coming! Hang on!” James yells to someone before addressing me again. “I’ll find out what I can, but like I said, Dee can never hold a grudge for long. Don’t give up. She’ll come around. Talk soon.” With that, he hangs up.

“Yeah. Dee can’t hold a grudge forever,” I whisper to my now empty office.

Boy, were we wrong...

Chapter 27
Delilah

*T*hree Years Later

We've just finished up the last venue of our Little Whiskey Girl Tour. The roadies know how to throw an after-party—that's for sure. I'm laughing, bouncing off the walls, as I stumble down the hallway toward my hotel room. When I get closer, I realize someone is sitting outside my door. I squint and take a hesitant step forward.

"Who's there?" My vision is still blurry from the stage effects and copious amounts of tequila that followed. I stumble into the wall, the high-heeled boots causing my ankles to twist and hit the floor with a resounding *oof*. The person sitting on the floor straightens to their full, *tall* height. I quickly back away from the imposing figure.

"Jesus Christ on a cracker. Dee. It's me. James. Your brother."

I gasp so hard I start to choke on my own saliva. Coughing violently, I struggle to push to my feet. James is there immediately, lifting my arms while helping me stand. I roll my eyes. Mom always swore that raising your hands above your head would help if you were choking.

Fun fact? It doesn't.

"James! Big bro! What are you doing here? I've missed you, broski!" I lean against his arm and start giggling.

James rolls his eyes and guides me down the hall back toward my room. "Where's your key, Dee?" He holds out his hand impatiently, and I pat myself down, trying to find it. However, I'm not having much luck locating that little bit of plastic keeping me from the mini bar I know is waiting.

I'm patting my chest when I feel something and grab it out triumphantly. "Ah-ha! There you are, you pesky little doohickey!"

James snatches the card from my fingers and opens the door before picking me up and carting me into the room. Dumping me onto the bed, he stands in front of me with his hands on his hips and a scowl on his face. "Delilah Rose Callahan, WHAT do you THINK you are DOING?" His tone only has me giggling more.

I attempt to school my features into a matching scowl. "James Michael Callahan, I THINK I'm PARTYING at the end of my tour!" I giggle again, falling back against the bed as I lose my balance. "Oops!" I slide sideways, but my brother catches me before I fall completely off the mattress.

Sighing, he walks away, returning a few seconds later with a glass. "Drink this. Where is Gio? Why isn't he watching you?"

I take it from him. "Oh, what is it? Vodka? Tequila? Rum? Gin? You look like a gin drinker."

"Water." James's expression is grim, and even in my drunken haze, I sense he's over and done with me and my bullshit.

I screw up my face but drink the water under my brother's watchful glare. "Gio is doing his own thing now. We decided that it was too much. What are *you* doin' here, James? I thought you were overseas somewhere?"

He sighs, rubbing his eyes before raising them heavenward. "I get a break before I go overseas, Dee. I told you this. I emailed you, saying I would meet you here before you returned to Cali."

"You did?" I try to think back, but everything's fuzzy.

James swings my feet back up and around into the bed. "Go to sleep, Dee. We'll talk in the morning."

"James?" I call out as I lie here clutching the comforter.

I can hear him sigh before he replies, "Yes, Dee?"

"The bed is spinning."

James chuckles. "No, it isn't, babe. Trust me. Go to sleep. We'll talk tomorrow." His voice is the last thing I remember before the darkness takes over.

***

The room is still dark when I jerk awake, several hours later, with the scent of coffee pulling me from my sleep. Groaning, I sit up and immediately fall off the bed before hitting the floor with a *thud*. "Ow."

"I thought that might happen. Of course, you'd wait until I was far enough away I couldn't catch you." A male voice from across the room has me scrambling back up on the bed with my back pressed to the headboard.

"What the hell! This is my room!" I start chucking pillows at the strange, blurry, male blob.

"Jesus. Not this again. Dee! It's me! James! Damn it! Stop! You make me spill this coffee, and you'll be mad!" His annoyance breaks through my panic at the same time recognition does. It is James.

"Jesus, Mary, and Joseph! What are you doing here and why does my mouth taste like ass?" My vision is clearing, and I can finally see him standing at the entrance to the suite holding a to-go tray of coffee cups and a couple of paper bags. The smell of pastry fills the air and I realize I want what is in those bags. Badly.

James sighs before walking over and setting the coffee on the desk by the window. "I knew you wouldn't remember. I'm on leave before I ship overseas. I emailed you, *remember*?"

I groan in frustration. I do remember. *Now.* "I'm so sorry. It completely slipped my mind! I was too busy finishing the tour and getting ready to head back to LA and start on the next album. I lost track of the dates."

James sits on the bed across from mine, still unmade from where he slept on it last night. He rests his elbows on his knees before cupping his hands under his chin. "I'm not going to lie to you, Dee. I'm worried. Ma is worried. A lot of people are worried about you. Over the last three years, you've been all over the tabloids, pictured with different male celebrities. Drunk and partying. You can't keep going like this, Dee, baby. Talk to me. What's going on?"

I pull a coffee from the to-go tray, take a sip, and sigh in relief. Then I sit back and cross my legs as I consider his words. James knows me well enough to not push for an answer when he can tell I don't have one. I sift through the last few years. The good, bad, and average. Lower my coffee and take a deep breath.

"I wasn't in the best place when we left to go on that first tour. It was such a change compared to everything I knew, and it was a rush. I felt like flying and never wanted to lose that feeling. I lost myself in that feeling. Being on tour is like being on a mer-ry-go-round. It's constant lights, parties, music, and fun. Then, one day, you realize it's been three years, and you're still spinning, but suddenly it's not as fun. The lights are too bright, and you want to stop. You try to stop, but you just don't know how." I sigh before leaning forward, propping my elbows on my knees. I grab one of the paper bags and pull out a sandwich with a famous and *familiar* white-and-orange logo. "OMG. You got me a Sausage Bob!" I take a big bite and hum happily.

At least there's something good about this day!

"It's a breakfast sausage on a bun. I don't know why you keep calling it that ridiculous name. Also, I know you're trying to change the subject, Dee. It won't work. Listen. I don't want you to go back to Cali yet. I'll stay here too, and we can explore the city and spend time together. We'll get through this. Deal?" He holds out his fist, and I bump it in agreement.

We take turns showering, and I pull on my favorite cutoffs and slide into my flip-flops. We head down the elevator, and I stop by the front desk to extend my reservation for another two weeks. Before heading out the sliding glass doors, I grab an extra key card for James.

Walking into the overcast day, the slap in the face I receive from the humidity reminds me why Portland makes me miss home. All that's missing are some mosquitos the size of butterflies, and it could *be* home. I see James standing beside a rented Jeep in the parking lot, talking on the phone. Between the look on his face and the wild gestures he's making, I can tell the conversation isn't going how he wants it. He curses under his breath before angrily ending the call as I approach him.

"Everything okay?"

My brother whirls around and plasters a smile on his face. "Of course, it is, baby sis! Let's get this *road* on the *show* and have some fun!" He opens the door for me.

I climb in, while rolling my eyes to the back of my skull at the lameness of his joke, before he runs around and gets behind the wheel.

Pulling out of the hotel, he tosses a guidebook into my lap. "Start picking some stuff for us to do. I know what we are doing first, so you get the next pick. Fair warning—you are going to want to buy different footwear. Can you find us a shoe store nearby?"

I haven't seen James grin like this in years, and I quickly Google the nearest shoe store. We pull in and head inside to grab a pair of hiking boots and thick socks. I thought my brother loved me; it turns out he might be trying to kill me with exercise. At least that's what I'm assuming until he pulls into the Oregon Zoo parking lot, and I know for a fact he loves me.

"The ZOO!" I'm jumping up and down while clapping my hands. This will be the best day EVER! I grab James by the hand and tug him toward the entrance. I'm already over the waiting.

I want to go see the animals! I want to go to the gift shop!

Hours later, we take a break at the polar bear exhibit. I'm leaning against the fence, as James settles in beside me. "Dee. Tell me about X." He's glancing around at the trees and various scenery instead of looking at me.

"What about him?" I swallow harshly. "He showed up in LA three years ago, completely unannounced, and was a total ass to me and even worse to Gio. I told him off, and he went back to Texas." I cringe because, while technically accurate, that rendition leaves out a LOT of details. I'm not particularly keen on telling my older brother about his best friend.

James hums and continues to stare at the sky. "Are you sure that's all that happened?"

"What are you getting at?" I'm already tired of the back and forth. If he has a question, I wish he would just ask it.

"Dee, Alexander has been hung up on you forever. I'm honestly surprised he never made a move on you before you came out here. I was away and may not have been available when you needed me. That's on me. Still, even I can see something's happened between you two since then, and I need to know if I'll be kicking my best friend's ass or not." My brother tries to appear nonchalant. His posture tells me otherwise.

"No. You're not kicking his ass. While I'm unhappy with how he acted, it is what it is." I take a deep, exasperated breath. "The night his dad had that stroke, I went to check on him and his mom. Bring them food. Alexander and I had fought recently, and I felt bad he was going through all that alone. Nobody should have to go through something like that alone."

My tone is solemn and quiet. James takes my hand and nods, so I try my best to explain.

"Well. He told me we needed to talk, to give him some time and wait. I thought it meant he wanted me, that he loved me. Then I ran into Megan, and she showed me the messages he was sending her. They were making fun of me." My voice trails off into a whisper as I add, "He told her he loved her."

"Are you sure? 'Cause all he did was complain about her. Constantly," James asks, and I'm more than a little pissed that my brother doesn't believe me.

"Really? 'Cause he was all over her that last night at the bonfire, so he must not have meant it. They were swapping so much spit I thought someone might drown." I wrinkle my nose at the memory.

James hums but doesn't say anything before turning to me. "C'mon, squirt, let's finish and go get some lunch. Then we can decide what we are going to do next."

We're walking out of the gift shop when his phone rings. Again. My hands are full of bags—*seriously, I went a little overboard.* James uses his fob to remotely open the trunk for me while he steps to the side to take the call.

I'm loading up the bags when a string of expletives cuts through the air. "You listen to me, you dick. Touch it, and you will die. Tell Beau I'm dealing with a family situation and will report when I report. Eva's still in the field, so I have nothing to do... Where am I? Let's not play games. I know you have already had Felix track my phone. So you know exactly where I am... No, I'm not telling her hi from you!"

My brother's head snaps up and looks around before he growls into the phone.

"That's my sister, asshole. You WILL watch your mouth... No, she isn't into Army men. Okay—fine." James lowers the phone and turns to me. "Dee, will you sign an autograph for Felix? He's fangirling so hard right now it is pathetic and—"

He's cut off by another voice that has him rolling his eyes.

"Felix AND Ransom, apparently. You assholes are weird—no, I will not say that. I will definitely not say that, and I will kick your ass when I see you for YOU saying it."

I'm standing here, grinning, as I listen to my brother give shit to someone who isn't me. It feels so good to not be on the receiving end of his temper for once.

"Listen. I have to go. Tell Beau I'll be in when I'm in... Okay, I'll tell her... Send it over via email." James hangs up the phone before pocketing it.

I close the hatch and walk around to my seat. I climb in and buckle my belt, then turn to face him with a grin. "Soooooooo."

"Don't start with me, brat. Just don't start. It's bad enough Ransom was hacking the security cameras to spy on me. I don't need you adding your two cents. By the way, Ransom said he found what you were looking for and he's gonna email it over. Apparently, you've been having issues and you didn't tell me?"

I just continue to grin as James starts the car and exits the parking lot. We end up at a little bistro in the middle of downtown Portland.

After the waitress takes our order, my brother aims his glare at me. "Dee. I gotta return to duty early, not today, but before the two weeks are up. Beau is being impossible. However, I will spend every second I can with you, and Beau can kiss my grits if he doesn't like it. I still don't want you heading back to LA early, though. Can you do that?" James is wearing his serious face. Nothing good ever happens when he wears that face.

Reaching across the table, I clasp his hand in mine. "That sounds perfect."

"Now. Tell me about these issues you've been having. When you asked if I had someone who could look into some stuff for you, you didn't make it sound all that serious. Ransom seemed to think it was something that needed his immediate attention."

Picking up my coffee, I proceed to tell my brother about Jensen and his grandparents and all the weird things that have been happening lately. Things we chalked up to them... but may not have been after all.

"So, you're saying that someone's been leaving weird-ass notes in Jensen's dressing rooms, and you didn't think this was something to mention to your brother?"

"Look. We thought it was his grandparents trying to get him to come back, but now we're not so sure."

"What changed?"

"Well, for one thing, the last note said they were meant to be together and *she* couldn't wait to carry his babies."

"That is deeply disturbing."

"Very. So I asked Ransom to look into it. And, according to you, it seems he's found something."

Chapter 28
Alexander

The phone ringing wakes me up. I roll over with a groan as I check the bedside clock and see that it's 3 a.m. Snatching up my phone, I answer it.

"Someone better be dead or dying," I grunt, without even checking who my mystery caller is.

"Shut up, asshole. It's me."

I sit up at the sound of my best friend's voice. I know he went to Portland to see Dee. "James? Is everything okay? Is Dee okay? What's going on?"

I can feel my heart racing. I've waited three years for Delilah to reach out or acknowledge my many reconciliation attempts. When James said she couldn't hold a grudge forever, he may have underestimated her stubbornness.

"She'll be okay. Look. I got called back in. Something's happened, and I have to go. I don't want to leave Dee here on her own. I need you in Portland. Now. Get up and get to the airport. There'll be a plane waiting for you. Ask for Ransom at the private gate. I'm swapping my room over to you—it's been paid for the next two weeks." His tone is brisk and matter-of-fact.

"James, she doesn't want me there. She's ignored every attempt I've made to talk to her for years now. She will lose her mind if she wakes up and I'm there. You can't do this to her—or me—I don't want to get my ass handed to me by your sister 'cause she's mad at both of us, but I happen to be the only one within ass-chewing range." I'm already pulling on jeans and a button-up. Then I throw a couple of days' worth of clothes into a duffle. If I need more, I'll buy some while I'm there.

"I don't have time to go into this. I have to go. I wouldn't even be doing this if I didn't need to leave. Please listen to me and listen carefully. Dee isn't in the best place. You can make it better or you can make it worse, so you need to get your head out of your ass and think about that." He doesn't say anything else before he hangs up, and I stare at my phone in shock.

Shaking my head, I finish packing and head out. I spend the whole hour-and-a-half drive replaying the conversation with James. And by the time I arrive at the airport, I'm determined that Dee will talk to me. I won't let myself be swayed on the matter—the whole world could be burning, and we would still be having this conversation.

I head to the private gate, which is more of a lounge. There are a few people dotted here and there, most drinking coffee. The front desk attendant is smiling when I approach.

Who smiles at five in the morning?

I ask for Ransom, and a man in the corner stands.

"You must be Alexander." He looks me up and down, then shakes his head. "Well, there's no accounting for taste."

"What the hell does that mean?"

"Nothing. Just think Dee could do better. Oh well, let's go. We got to get you to Portland so you can fix the shit you fucked."

Ransom grabs my duffle and walks down a hall to the side that leads to the tarmac.

I stride after him, angrier than I've been in years. "Look, I don't know who you think you are or what you think you know—"

I'm cut off sharply when the guy turns and shoves me into the wall. "I know EVERYTHING." His voice is low and radiates danger. "There is no way to keep secrets from me. I know how you've been dating Megan for the last three years. I know that you haven't told James, and you like to play off that you're waiting for Dee to forgive you. I know your father's business is doing better than ever, but you don't love it—your heart isn't in it. I'm not even sure your heart is all there for Dee. However, for whatever reason, she's picked you." He shoves off and continues to walk down the hallway.

I narrow my glare, shake the wrinkles out of my shirt, and follow behind him. "Seems you care a lot about Dee for just an acquaintance. How do you know her and why are you taking me to Portland if you think I'm so bad for her?"

"Because James is my brother, and he asked me to do it. If it were up to me, I'd be dropping you somewhere in the middle of the Pacific, and that would be that." He glances at me over his shoulder. "That said, don't forget there's nothing you do, nothing that happens around Dee that I'm unaware of. So the next time you get that tingling in the middle of your back like someone's watching, know that I am."

We step onto the tarmac, and the Texas heat has already started to bake the ground. I stare at Ransom's angry gait as I continue to follow him, ignoring the sweat that drips down my spine. "Look, you're right about some things but you're also wrong." He snorts, but I continue. "I went on a few dates with Megan *years* ago. Before Dee left, I explained that nothing would come of us, and she accepted it. We're strictly friends. That's all we've ever been."

"I know what you think you told her, but all that girl heard was *try harder*. She's poison, a cancer. She wants prestige, power, and money. Let me guess? She hasn't been messaging you as much this past year?"

He laughs at my shocked expression.

"Yeah, that girl's been trying to trap you for years, and if you'd given in to it, I'm betting dollars to donuts she would have come up pregnant. You are just too blind to see how evil she is. You said all that to her before Dee left for LA?"

The abrupt change of topic has my head spinning, but I nod.

"Yeah. Before Dee left. Why?"

Ransom hums thoughtfully. "Interesting. That's not what Megan said."

We've reached the small plane by now, and Ransom opens the door to pull down the steps. Then we board, and I find myself in the copilot's seat.

"What do you mean that isn't what Megan said?" I buckle the lap belt while Ransom starts flipping switches and toggles.

"I mean—" He shoots me a look that suggests he thinks I'm an idiot. "That girl has been telling everyone who can listen that you are essentially two steps away from marriage, and if she had her way, it would be the truth. She's been doing this for years, and you're too thick to see it, so you've been going on all these lunches with her and lending clout to her story. But that chick's resourceful. She realized something and has her sights set on someone new. You're off the hook."

I gape at him. "You're kidding me, right?" I can tell by the expression on his face that he is, in fact, not kidding. "Who has she been saying all this to?"

He raises a sardonic eyebrow at me before replying. "The better question is who HASN'T she told?"

I curse under my breath, which seems to please him for some reason.

"Now he gets it. Welcome to the present. So, whatcha gonna do about it?" The guy's tone borders on smug, but his face is completely stoic.

I think back on every interaction I've had with Dee with this new information in mind. Now I realize why she was so upset at the diner. Megan. I can feel the color draining from my face. "Jesus, no wonder she hasn't forgiven me yet." My words are little more than a strangled whisper, but in such close quarters, Ransom hears me.

"Maybe you're not a lost cause after all. Look, Megan isn't gunning for you anymore. Like I said, she has someone else in her sights. I'm telling you this because Dee knows and doesn't know what to do with the information. You need to help her."

The flight to Portland is short. Ransom tosses my bag at me as I quickly deplane.

"Look. Dee's at St. Regis, room 3246. You're right next door in 3248. Don't fuck this up!" The look he gives me makes it clear that if I do *fuck this up*, I'll be answering to him as well as James.

I head toward the terminal, and Ransom pulls up the steps and starts the engine again. He's taxied back down the runway and is gone when I enter the airport terminal.

The cab ride to the hotel is quiet, the early morning light still breaking. Portland isn't awake yet, and the nearly deserted freeway makes the trip easy. The cabby keeps up light chatter, the usual questions of what I plan to do in Portland and how long I'm here for. All questions I don't have any real answers for. Despite the forced air of the cab, I can feel my palms starting to sweat. I swipe them on my jeans as we pull up under the hotel's portico.

A few minutes later, I'm entering the lobby. I approach the front desk attendant and give her my name. She hands me the plastic hotel key, a sealed envelope, and two copper coins. I thank her and head toward the bank of elevators while turning the coins over in my hands. They have bears stamped on them but no other identifying information. I punch the button for the third floor, and when the doors close, I open the envelope.

Alex,

I've made a reservation for brunch at the hotel restaurant. I left Dee a note to be there at 9:30. Wait for her to sit down before you approach her. Talk to her, keep your cool, and LISTEN to what SHE SAYS, not what you THINK she's saying.

The coins are for a private tour of the red panda area at the Portland Zoo. Dee loves all things red panda. You'll have two hours alone with her, behind the scenes.

I've done all I can do. Don't fuck this up. If you do, I'll know.

—James

I exit the elevator and make it to my door by the time I've finished reading the letter. I stop and stare at Dee's door. I could knock, wake her up, make her listen. But that would only make things worse.

Christ, I need to get my head out of my ass.

I unlock the door to my own room and walk in, collapsing onto the bed and reaching out for the bedside lamp. When it clicks on, I notice a set of clothes hanging up by the desk and chuckle to myself. James really did think of everything.

I check the clock—7:30 a.m. I have some time before meeting Dee in the restaurant, so I click on the TV and surf through the channels before giving up and turning it off again. I'm too worked up to concentrate. I'll jump in the shower, shave, and get ready. I plan to look my best when seeing her for the first time in three years. I already know she likes how I look, and I plan to use everything I can to make her mine.

Goodbye, Mr. Nice Guy. Now I'm going to play dirty.

Chapter 29
Dee

I wake up to the sound of the shower turning on next door. James must be up and getting ready. What are we going to be doing today? He said he had a surprise for me but not what it was—which, yes, I know is how surprises work. However, James has never been able to keep a secret to save his life.

Stretching, I look at the clock and groan at the blinking numbers... 8:00 a.m. There's an envelope on the bedside table that wasn't there last night. I sit up against the headboard and open it.

Dee,

Meet in the hotel restaurant for brunch at 9:30 if you want your surprise.

—James

I'm not sure what we're doing today, but I know I'll be late if I take the time to tame the monster that is my hair, so after I shower, I throw it up into a messy bun and pick out my favorite sundress to wear. It's the perfect summer outfit, both cool and fun, while the deep navy with white daisies material hits me around the knees. I grab my room key on the way out the door.

I recheck my phone, and I see a notification from Jensen. He wants me to message him when I'm free. He has news to share. I'll text him after brunch before we go out to do whatever it is we're doing today.

The hall is quiet as I approach the elevator, which opens when I press the button. It's empty when I step inside, and there are only a handful of people scattered around when I enter the restaurant.

The hostess walks up to me with a smile. "Ah, Ms. Callahan. We were expecting you. We have your table ready. Right this way."

I follow her as we head toward the back of the dining area to a corner spot partially obscured by a half-wall and fake greenery. I smile up at her as I take my seat out of view from the rest of the patrons. Wild Child Reckless is popular enough to be a household name in most cities, which means I often get recognized in public. James must have mentioned the importance of privacy when he made the reservation.

The waitress comes up. I ask for a sweet, milky coffee as well as let her know I'll wait to order until my brother arrives. I'm about ten minutes early, by some miracle, and considering James is always überpunctual, I'm surprised he isn't down here yet. Before the girl sets off to get my coffee, she hands me another sealed envelope. My name is scrawled on the front in what I recognize to be James's handwriting. When I tear into the envelope, I find a folded piece of paper with only two words.

Trust me.

I'm just about to pick up my phone and text him when someone moves to stand in front of my table. I look up from the note and nearly drop my phone.

"Is this seat taken?" Alexander asks me.

I look anywhere but at him as my eyes flit around the room, noticing everything and nothing simultaneously. Then I pick up my phone and text James before setting it back down. I huff out a breath when it vibrates with a reply.

James: Trust Me.

I force a laugh and gesture for X to sit. "Well. If I had to guess, I'd say my brother isn't going to show up, is he?" My voice is bitter but resigned as I sip my coffee while staring at Alexander over the rim.

His hair is a bit longer, and the clothes look new and freshly pressed. He was obviously clued in to what would go down today. I'll knock the shit out of James the next time I see him.

HOW DARE HE!

I start to get ramped up in my head again when the next sentence out of X's mouth stops me in my tracks. "He called me about six hours ago, told me to get to Portland, gave me his hotel room, and instructed me to meet you for brunch. I owe you a huge apology and an explanation."

It's now that the waitress decides to walk up. Alexander and I take this chance to order our food as silence settles over the table, broken only by the sound of us drinking coffee. I keep sneaking glances at him over the rim of my cup.

Why does he have to look so good?

I tug on the hem of my sundress, wishing I'd picked anything else to wear. "So. How is your dad doing? I heard from Mom that he's basically back to his old self. She said he retired and that you're running the company now." I blush when I realize how much I've revealed.

So I asked Mom about him? Sue me.

X clears his throat before nodding. "Yes, that's correct. I've been running it for the last three years. Dad and Mom finally took a cruise out of Galveston not too long ago. Mom was thrilled. She already wants to go back out. Dad even enjoyed himself, which was the biggest shock of all." He forces a smile. "And it appears you've been doing well for yourself—selling out arenas and touring the country. I heard your label's considering an overseas tour?"

I nod my head. "Yeah, things have been good with WCR. But we told the label no to an overseas tour right now. We'll be working on our next album for another twelve weeks before we start planning a new tour. Jensen is still in town. I'm not sure where Grayson has gone off to. And last I heard, Mia was going to head back to LA. The plan was to hang out here for two weeks and have a much-needed break before we all return to work." I glance up at X quickly before focusing back on my cup of coffee. "However, that plan seems to have changed. We may all head back early now."

"Changed because I'm here and not James?" X heaves a heavy sigh when I don't look up or answer. "Like I said, I owe you an apology, Dee. I've owed you one for a lot of years."

He's cut off when the waitress returns with our plates. We spend a few moments eating in more tense silence before Alexander speaks up again.

"I am sorry, Dee. I'm sorry that I didn't listen when I saw you last. I'm sorry that I let my temper get the best of me and I didn't ask the questions I should have asked or even saw what was right in front of my face. You were hurting. You were hurting, and it was my fault, and I turned that around on you like you were the one to blame. I'll spend the rest of my life trying to make it up to you, but I need you to know, right now, at this moment, that I'm so incredibly sorry for the way things happened." His tone is sincere, and his eyes, as they meet mine, show genuine remorse.

I give him a small smile before dropping my eyes to my plate. I push the food around and shrug a shoulder. "It was a long time ago. Ancient history at this point. I appreciate the apology, but we should just forget it happened. It was childish of me to get upset anyway. I should have known better. I should have trusted you, but it was all so convincing, and at the time, I felt like I was just your best friend's baby sister. I didn't want to be seen that way by you but at the same time I didn't see how you could possibly see me as anything else. I spent years trying to get your attention and it never worked. "

Alexander's hand, warm and rough, settles over mine, pressing my fork down onto my plate before tilting my chin up so that I can meet his eyes. "Oh, it worked. I noticed you, Dee. However, I couldn't do anything about it. As for the rest, it wasn't childish of you—you couldn't know better. It's me who should have known better. You trusted me, and I betrayed that trust. I should have listened to you. I should have chased you. I never should have doubted you for even a moment. I know it won't fix everything but hopefully this will be a good start." He slides two copper coins over to me, and I pick them up before squealing with joy.

"The red panda exhibit! These are tokens so you can go behind the scenes and interact with the animals!" I turn the coins over and over in my hands. I love red pandas. I love all pandas. Of course, X would remember that. "Can we go now?"

He chuckles at my enthusiasm. "I'm ready if you are. We can stop and get snacks at the zoo's deli."

I signal the waitress to charge brunch to my room before jumping up and heading to the door. I can still hear X chuckling behind me as I rush outside. I head straight for the Jeep James rented for his stay and bounce on my toes as X pulls out the keys. I'm not silly enough to think this fixes everything but I will admit it's a damn good start.

We ride silently for blocks, with X stealing glances at me when he thinks I'm not looking. Joke's on him. I'm always looking.

I clear my throat before whispering, "I never loved him."

I don't have to elaborate on who *he* is. X knows. I see his fingers clench around the steering wheel before his shoulders relax. Then he holds out a hand to me, and I slide mine against his. He entwines his fingers between mine, and they are rough against my smoother skin. We ride like this for several more minutes before his voice breaks the silence.

"I never loved her."

I turn and look out the passenger window with a smile playing on my lips.

Chapter 30
Alexander

She doesn't love him.

I know I must have a stupid grin on my face, and I don't care. We still have so much to discuss, but it all seems inconsequential with the news I just received.

Is it me, or is the sun brighter? The sky bluer?

I pull into a parking spot and have to release her hand to kill the engine, which just won't do. I move around the front of the car to open her door and reclaim her hand. When Delilah's fingers are wrapped in mine again, I guide us toward the front of the zoo. I show the token to the lady at the ticket booth, who directs us to the red panda exhibit and lets us know that our appointment is for 1:30 p.m. so that we can assist with feeding. I can practically feel Dee vibrating with excitement. Chuckling, I lead her into the zoo, and we stop at the giant map at the entrance.

"So, while we wait for our time slot, what do you want to see first?" I already know the answer but wait for her to respond anyway.

"I want to go see the Primate Forest."

I nod and pull her toward that exhibit. Some things never really change. We stroll side by side, our hips and shoulders bumping every couple of steps.

"This is nice." Her voice is quiet, and I have to agree.

"Yeah. It is." I clear my throat. "We still have to talk about what happened. I don't want any secrets or misunderstandings between us."

"Not today," Dee insists. She has a point. I don't want to ruin today either.

I bring our clasped hands to my mouth and kiss her knuckles. "You got it, princess. Not today."

We arrive at the primate exhibit and slowly work our way around to the red pandas. We talk about the animals and all the little things that make up small talk. She tells me funny stories about being on the road, and I tell her about the craziest houses we've constructed as we wander around the zoo for several hours. Just easy company and conversation between two people whose lives have been entwined for years.

"Look, Dee—" I'm cut short as my phone starts ringing with a number I don't recognize. "Hello?"

"It's me," a familiar voice says on the other side.

"Ransom?"

"Yes, you moron, now listen. They're coming. They just entered the zoo and are spreading out to look for you."

"Who?"

"The paparazzi. Someone spotted Delilah and followed ya'll—" He's cut off as Dee's ringer blares like crazy. Stepping off the walkway, I watch as she pulls her phone out of her pocket to check it before swearing profusely under her breath.

Dee continues clicking on her screen. Then she groans and turns it so I can see what she's seeing. There are pictures of us.

Several. Sipping coffee at the restaurant, leaving the hotel, holding hands, and walking into the zoo under the headline.

New Prince for the Pop Princess!

and

Wild Child Reckless Lead Singer Off the Market?

"Oh, shit." I swallow quickly and return my attention to Ransom. "How do you know they're coming?"

He scoffs. "I hacked the zoo's servers."

At the same time, Dee starts looking around. "That's Ransom? On the phone?" She waves at the camera at my nod before returning to me. "We need to move away from open areas. The paps will eventually give up, but we have to find somewhere to go before they find us." She grabs my hand and starts to stride down the path.

"I'm guessing you've had to do this before then?"

She shrugs and continues walking. "When we first started to get popular, we had some problems. James told us he had a tech guy who could help if we needed him. At this point, I think we should change James's last name to Bond with how little he tells us. He introduced us to Ransom and his brother Felix. They know all things tech."

"Listen carefully. Take the next left, then right, then left again. That will put you by the panda exhibit. The coins give you access to a private waiting area," Ransom says, and I nod because I know he can see me. I hang up and shove the phone into my pocket. Grabbing Dee's hand, I take off at a jog.

We've just reached the first turn when I hear someone shout, "There she is!"

We both glance back to see three men with cameras around their necks. Heading straight for us.

"Shit." Dee giggles, and we take off running, dodging the other zoo-goers as we try to reach the red panda exhibit.

When we make the last turn, I see the arrow pointing toward a rocky recess. I tug Dee that way and pull her close to me so that the stony exterior keeps us out of view. We're both laughing when I notice how flushed her face is. Her eyes are sparkling and bright and there's a big grin on her lips.

She's never looked more beautiful to me.

I slide my hand up her neck and into her hair before lowering my mouth to hers. I can feel her breath catch before she gives in and opens to me. Deepening the kiss, I pull her closer. Then turn us so my large frame continues to block her from view. I glide both hands down her sides and grip her hips, sliding around to cup her ass under her sundress.

The noises Dee makes are like gasoline on a fire, and I pick her up. Before I realize what's happening, she's wrapped her legs around my waist, and my achingly hard cock is pressed against her center with only a thin strip of cotton keeping me from the promised land. I can feel a growl building in the back of my throat when the hard tips of her nipples press into my chest. I hitch her up higher, getting a better grip on her, while my fingers slide dangerously close to her center. I flex my hands against her lush thighs, and she answers with a breathy moan.

I pull back and rest my forehead against hers. We stand here for several minutes, our breaths mingling in the quiet.

The moment is broken when we hear the scuffle of feet rush past us. I reluctantly lower Dee back to the ground and pull the two tokens from my pocket, slipping them into the coin slot by the door. The light flashes green with each one, and a door automatically opens. We walk into what appears to be a kitchen with table seating and deep industrial sinks.

We are met by a zoo worker who greets us with a handshake and a pleasant smile. "Hello! Welcome to the Portland Zoo. My name is Amelia, and I'll be your guide today. You are one of our first visitors to our new pilot program. Your generous donation will help ensure this exhibit remains active, which is necessary to fund the survival plan in place for endangered species like the red panda." Amelia gestures for us to follow her farther into the exhibit.

Dee walks in front of me, hanging on Amelia's every word. I must admit that my focus is mainly on how Dee's ass looks in the flirty little dress she's wearing. Still, when I hear the guide mentioned that there are less than ten thousand red pandas left in existence, I pay more attention.

The next area is more like how I expect a zoo to look. There's hay all over the concrete pad and various ropes, ledges, and boxes for the pandas to play and rest inside. Multiple toys—*enrichment activities,* as Amelia calls them—litter the floor, and another worker walks in with a tub of apples, grapes, bananas, and blueberries.

"I thought pandas ate bamboo?" Dee peers into the bucket with fascination.

"They do!" Amelia chirps. "However, these are called enrichment treats. The pandas also eat insects, bird eggs, and small lizards. So, we'll have you two return to the area with the tables. Where we'll let our oldest breeding pair in to visit with you. Pip and Gomer have been with our zoo for eight years now. While red pandas can live to be as old as twenty-three, they start to show signs of aging at around twelve."

The other worker hands us smocks to wear over our clothes while Amelia leaves to get Pip and Gomer.

I take a moment to grab Dee's hand and give it a kiss. "You having fun, princess?"

The way her face lights up makes me feel ten feet tall. Fuck, I don't know how I'm ever going to repay James. "So. Much. FUN! This is absolutely the best thing to ever happen in my life. I can't believe this is even something that you can do!"

I swear she would vibrate straight off the chair if she were any more excited.

When Amelia walks in with the pandas in tow, I hear Dee suppress a squeal. She immediately sits up and begins grabbing some of the treats left on the table. Which has our new friends hopping down and running to her. Climbing over and around her arms and begging for bites. Her delighted laughter will forever be the best sound I've ever heard.

The zoo workers are enamored with Dee, and I can't blame them. I have been for years.

We stay way later than the intended time frame. They let her help with grooming and playing and give her a nursery tour in the back, where the babies are weighed, measured, and given any necessary injections. We are shown back to the main area, where

Pip and Gomer are joined by NiNi, Adi, and Nico running rings around the older pair.

Chuckling, I turn and watch Dee as she views the room, capturing every detail of her expression and committing it to memory. She doesn't even realize I'm watching her with the same intensity she gives the pandas. After not seeing her for three years, I want to get reacquainted with every freckle, every tilt of her lips and thought in her head. I can never go back to the way we were before.

If there was ever any doubt, there isn't now. Delilah Rose Callahan is *mine*.

Chapter 31
Dee

We're out of sight long enough to have the paps chasing some other lead. I haven't stopped smiling since X and I left and went to the food court. Now, sitting here in the afternoon sun eating overpriced hot dogs, I can't help but feel content. I try to remember the last time I was this relaxed doing everyday things, and nothing comes to mind.

"So." I clear my throat. "What are we doing after this?"

X finishes chewing his last bite before wiping his mouth. "I didn't have anything planned. We're eating a bit later than I intended, so that doesn't leave room for an early dinner. What were you thinking? Was there anything in Portland you wanted to do?"

My first instinct is to say *you*. I want to do you.

However, I manage to catch myself and shrug my shoulders instead. "There's supposed to be another get-together tonight, just the main crew. We generally drink, play, sing, and goof around to wind down after a stressful tour."

"I haven't been to a party in years. That sounds fun. Plus, I want to meet Mia and see Jensen and Grayson again officially."

I wince at the mention of Mia. To say she isn't Alexander's biggest fan would be an understatement. Hopefully, Lawrence will be around. She may be upset about the burly bodyguard, but he's good at distracting her and deescalating tense situations.

I glance at my phone. It's 4 p.m. "Well, the zoo will close soon, so we better get out of here."

I text the group to let them know that X is in town and will be joining us at the tour party. The last thing I need is for the guys to freak out and a fight to ensue.

Gathering up our trash, we head toward the entrance. The parking lot is nearly empty, which is an excellent sign, and we're both quiet as X helps me into the car before he gets in on his side. He wraps his palm around mine again for the drive back to the hotel, and I use my free hand to check the gossip rags. They've added very little since the earlier posts. Still, the feed on the photos is full of all kinds of commentary, and some are not very nice. I roll my eyes as I read a few out loud and can tell X is agitated.

"X?" I jiggle our joined hands. "You simply can't get upset by every little thing these people write. It's nothing more than a cesspool of insecurities, jealousy, and straight-out lies. We know what is true. We know what happened and who and what we are."

He grunts his agreement as we pull into the hotel's parking garage. He refuses to let go of my hand when we enter the elevator, holding it tight for the ride until we arrive on our floor. The band has taken over a little conference room about halfway down the hall. So we head that way and see that they've started without us.

Jensen, in particular, has an impressive collection of shot glasses in front of him. I slide into a chair at the round table, and everyone calls out a greeting, which I return before introducing X.

"Everyone not from Havenbrook, this is X. He's going to hang around with us for a while." I catch Mia throwing him the stink eye across the table. I raise my eyebrows at her. "So, let's all be very welcoming."

Mia wrinkles her nose and calls out for tequila. Fuck. Mia *cannot* hold her tequila.

The bartender walks over with a tray of shot glasses, and I take two.

"So, who hired the barkeep?" Jensen raises two fingers off the top of his glass before picking up two of the SIX and quickly downs them. He hisses at the burn before following it with a swig of what is probably Jack. X looks at me in shock, and I subtly shrug a shoulder. I have no idea what's going on with Jensen, but obviously something is.

"So. AleXander." I don't miss the way Mia emphasizes the X. And cringe. "How long are you here?"

X reclaims his seat after grabbing a beer and takes a long drag. "I have to head back for an important meeting with some vendors in a few weeks. However, most of my work can be done remotely, so I plan to return to Dee as soon as I can and then we can go from there." He smiles at me, and I can feel myself blushing.

"Is that so?" Mia's tone is contemplative as she takes another shot. "So." She claps her hands. "Let's play a drinking game. Let's play *Never Have I Ever*. Bartender! We need a round of Scooby Snacks, Adios Motherfuckers, and some Jameson neat!"

I groan out loud as the bartender starts to prepare Mia's very long drink order. I hate this game, and she knows it. Which is precisely why, four hours later, I'm well on my way to being completely blitzed out of my head.

"Okay, my turn!" I giggle as I try to think up a really good one. "Never have I ever stolen panties!" To my surprise, I'm the only one who doesn't take a drink. I laugh while pointing a finger around the table. "Okay, some of you owe me an explanation."

Mia snorts and takes another sip. "Not on your life. I will take that one to my grave."

I throw an eaten lime wedge at her, and we dissolve into another fit of giggles. I notice that Jensen is still silently staring at his drink, so I nudge his shoulder. "You okay?"

"Yeah. Fine." His curt response pulls me up short.

"Yeah, I totally believe that. Try again."

"Look. I'm fine. It's nothing. And even if it weren't, it would still be none of your business." Jensen slams back in his chair, stands up, and stalks off.

The table falls silent until Mia breaks it. "Never have I ever thrown a tantrum and left the room like a little bitch."

Laughter erupts around us but I push to my feet and follow him. "Jenner…"

Jensen stops and turns, rubbing his hands up and down his face. "Look. I'm sorry. I shouldn't have… but… I can't. I'm sorry I snapped at you but I'm going to go now."

I watch him walk to the elevator. Then I turn back to the table. Where it's clear the mood has been dampened. We slowly start to peel off. Lawrence is supporting Mia as she gives him hell, and X and I are leaning on each other and laughing over a story that Mia told us about the time she pranked Lawrence. His hair ended up green for a month.

X leans close as we head for my room, pressing my back against the doorjamb. "Tell me to leave." His voice is raspy as his hands slide up my hips, and he rests his head on mine. He continues his lazy exploration with a deep inhale. "Tell me to leave you alone and go to my room. Tell me you don't want this. Tell me any of that, and I will leave."

"I want this."

A shudder works through X's body at my declaration, and a growl leaves his throat. He pushes me tight against the door, slanting his mouth over mine. His tongue comes out, coaxing me to open up. "You've done it now, princess."

He takes my key card out of my hand and opens my door before picking me up and striding into the room. I wrap my arms around his neck and my legs around his waist, my mouth hungrily moving over the skin between. My sundress ends up around my waist as X slides his hands inside my panties. He dumps me onto my bed, and I bounce, my legs falling open. X stands there staring at me. His jaw clenched and his nostrils flaring. My hair disheveled and my dress pushed up. He stares for so long I start to get self-conscious and close my knees, but his hand reaching between my thighs stops me.

"No, princess, don't close your legs. Don't hide that pretty pussy from me."

My legs fall back open, and he drops to his knees, reaching to pull my panties down my thighs. His hands slide up and a high-pitched whine fills the air. I look around before I realize the sound is coming from me.

X slides a finger through my folds, and I gasp at the contact. He pulls his finger back. It shines with moisture before he licks it clean, his eyes closing in bliss. When they open again, they're blazing with need and possession.

"I'm going to eat this pretty pussy, princess, and you'll watch me. When I'm done with you, there will be no doubt about who this belongs to." He cups my pussy in a dominating grip.

My back arches off the bed as my hands scramble for his shoulders. "Please. Please. Please," I beg, almost sobbing, and I swear I'll go up in flames if he doesn't do something soon. At the first swipe of his tongue, I shatter, wailing my release as I shake under the assault of his tongue.

He chuckles darkly. "That was beautiful, princess, but we're just starting. Hold on tight."

My head is spinning, my breath stuttering in and out of my lungs as I do as he says

Chapter 32
Alexander

Dee falling apart under me may be the best thing I've experienced. Her soft cries are the sweetest song I've ever heard. However, I am far from done. By the time I finish with Delilah Rose Callahan, there will be no doubt who she belongs to. Who I belong to.

I chuckle as she collapses against the mattress. "That was beautiful, princess, but we're just starting. Hold on tight."

I tighten my grip on her ass, pulling her closer to the end of the bed before falling on her like a starving man. I'm licking, sucking, and nibbling as her wetness coats my lips. I lick my way up to her clit, flicking it hard and fast with the tip of my tongue. Dee is a sight to behold as she writhes and moans on the bed, her hands grasping at my head, shoulder, the comforter, whatever she can reach.

Growling, I double my efforts and own her pussy, trying to eat it all at once so I don't miss a taste. It's not enough, though. I want more. I work my tongue into her tight channel, fighting the urge to spill into my jeans. I've never been this hard in my life, and all I want to do is shove my pants down and slide into her slick heat. My balls draw up, and I grind my cock into the mattress for some relief while Dee screams my name, rocking her hips against my tongue and prolonging her orgasm, while I drink every bit of the cream.

She's panting, sobbing when I slide up her body and remove her little sundress. Wrapping my mouth around a nipple, I flick it with my tongue as I pinch the other. Dee squeals, and I grin around her breast. I roll over until I rest between her luscious thighs, my cock pressed snuggly against her pulsing center. I rest my hands on each side of her head and wait until she opens her eyes and focuses on me.

Smirking, I kiss her nose, lips, and cheeks. Before I lean down next to her ear and whisper. "I'm going to fuck this pussy now, Delilah. Is there anything I need to know?"

She shakes her head.

"I'm going to fuck it bare, and you're going to be a good girl and take it all, right?"

At her nod, I push to my feet and shuck my clothes before crawling back onto the bed, shifting her closer to the center. Where I spread her legs, making room for myself, until her pussy nestles wet and needy against my cock. I start with shallow thrusts that do nothing but tease us both in the best way. Dee moans and I can feel the flood of wetness coating us.

Pulling her legs up around my hips, I notch at her entrance and slide slowly into her, my eyes rolling back into my head at her slick heat. She's so tight. As her walls flutter around my shaft, I clench my jaw and count back from ten, refusing to come this quickly. I bite down on her shoulder with a growl, relishing her deep moans as she arches her back. She writhes under me, seeking friction. I tease her, licking a line up the side of her neck before nipping at her ear.

"Now it's time for you to sing for me, princess." My voice is rough as I pull back out and slam home.

Every unsettled piece of my soul clicks into place. I'll never be able to deny this woman anything. She's *it*, and she doesn't even realize it as she bucks against me.

Thrusting faster, I change my angle, our hips clashing in a punishing rhythm while beads of sweat slide down my chest. Dee writhes and gasps, her hands tangled in the sheets. I can feel her pleasure building, and I want to howl. I want the world to hear that I'm the one to bring this woman pleasure.

When her orgasm hits, it's a tight strangulation of muscles coursing through her in waves. She cries out hoarsely, and I slide my hands down her legs to her ass, gripping it tightly.

"I'm not done with you yet, princess." I swing her into my arms, wrapping her legs around my waist and moving to the windows overlooking Portland.

I reluctantly slide out of her heat and let her feet touch the ground before turning her to face the skyline. I bend her at the waist and thrust back into her. At her whimpering moan, I bite her shoulder, moving harder and faster. Watching the pleasure cross her face through the reflection in the glass may be as close to heaven as I'll ever get.

Even now, with her twitching around my cock, all I can think about is how perfect she is. Red hair cascades down her arched spine as she leans back and meets me thrust for thrust, sweaty palm prints on the window with the Portland skyline lit up, framing her in their glow.

"Please."

The word trembles between us, and I lean forward, pressing her firmly against the glass, my hips never slowing in their relentless pace. "Please, what, princess? What do you need? Tell me," I demand, my voice rough and guttural. Sliding my hands between her body and the window, I pinch her nipple, rolling it with my thumb and forefinger. The gasp and moan that follow have me grinning devilishly. My smile widens when I meet her eyes in our reflection. "Fall, princess. Fall apart for me. I'll catch you."

Watching her eyes close and her head tilt back, I can feel her pussy convulsing, trying to draw me as deep into her channel as it can, and I can't hold back any longer. Thrusting forward, I hold still as my release follows hers. Our harsh breaths break the silence as I slide out of her. And instantly miss the connection.

I tilt her jaw and cradle her face as we gaze at each other, neither of us speaking. I swing her into my arms and return her to the bed, *and* the rumpled sheets, before sliding in beside her. Her breath is warm against my neck as we lie here, our hearts pounding. I relish the quiet of this moment where words are not needed. Where she's mine, and I'm hers.

And for once, things make sense.

We must drift off to sleep like this, because Dee wakes me up as the sun breaks the horizon by slinging her leg over me and settling into my lap. She rides me slowly. Lazily. The outline of her perfect body silhouetted by the rising sun is a sight I will never tire of seeing. Her long, tangled, red hair like a flame in the gloom.

I slide my hands up the soft skin of her legs to grip her hips, and we continue moving together like we were born for this moment. Leaning forward, I take a nipple in my mouth, pulling her down to me. I take over, pounding into her with a hard and fast tempo, one hand fisting her curls, keeping her close. Her hands glide up my chest to my shoulders, using the leverage to meet my thrusts with a force of her own, fucking me just as much as I'm fucking her. Our breaths are harsh in the quiet; the slap of our bodies is the only noise. I can feel myself getting close.

"Dee." Her eyes meet mine, and I almost lose control. "Princess, you've got to come for me."

She nods while holding my gaze.

"Dee. Come. Now," The command cracks through the air, causing Dee to fall apart around me. I delight in my ability to make her do it as I follow her, my release coating her walls and causing my back to arch.

Delilah collapses onto my chest, her fingers drifting back and forth across my arm. I settle her closer, running my hand over her spine in tandem with her movements.

We lie like this for hours or minutes. Time is moving differently with this amazing woman in my arms. It's entirely too fast and, at the same time, remarkably glacial. I smile into the darkness as her breathing evens out. Then I pull the sheet up over us.

"I love you." My voice is a whisper as I fall comfortably asleep.

Chapter 33
Delilah

I wake up, head pounding, body deliciously sore, and more than a little confused as to where I am. Stretching, I roll over and am greeted by a very naked, very sexy Alexander in my bed. I take a moment to appreciate the expanse of bronzed skin glowing in the morning light. In all the times I dreamed about him, I never had any idea how much better real life could be. I roll back over with a grin and grab my phone to check the time, pausing when I see all the notifications on my screen.

"What the...?" I whisper before my heart drops into my stomach at the headlines.

Hometown Home-wrecker! Princess of Pops Steals Family Man!

Pop Princess Poaches Family Man!

I just want my fiancé back! Exclusive interview inside!

I glance at the man sleeping beside me and quickly click the first link. By the second, I'm sick to my stomach. And by the third, I'm ready to smother him with hotel pillows—room charges be damned.

I can't stay here. I have to go. I shoot off a quick text, and when the reply comes, I slip out of bed and throw my hair up and clothes on from last night. I have to be careful. The paps will be every-where, and I may be unable to control my actions if I see them.

Grabbing my room key, I try to walk as quietly as possible before knocking on a door that gives way.

"It's open." The room is dark, the curtains pulled to block out the morning sun, and it reeks of booze and sweat.

I stride over to the window and throw open the blackout curtains. "Jesus, Mary, and Joseph, it stinks in here, Jensen! What the hell?"

I stare at the empty bottles, the fast food wrappers, and the clothes all over the room. The sheets are half on the bed, and the pillows are missing. Jensen is in the corner, guitar on his lap and a half-empty bottle of Jack on the table in front of him. I don't recognize the song he's playing, which means it's new.

"Jensen. Have you seen the news?" I sit on the coffee table and steal his bottle of Jack, taking a healthy swig.

"No." Jensen never stops strumming, and I eye him, noting the more than 5 o'clock shadow on his face and the stained shirt on his chest.

"He's engaged. He came here, slept with me, and he's get-ting married. The slag rags are crucifying me. There's article after article about how Megan is the wronged woman. She's pregnant with his child, and I stole him! *Stole him.* Like he's a purse from Macy's." I throw my hands in the air, Jack sloshing in the bottle. "After everything he said to me, all the... all the..." I can't finish the sentence without tearing up, so I take another gulp of liquor instead.

Jensen swipes the bottle back from me. "Yeah. Well. That's about par for the course. I always thought he was as useless as tits on a boar."

I roll my eyes, aware of how his view of Alexander has changed since we were teens. I throw an empty cup at him before stealing the bottle back. "You're grumpier than usual. Who peed in your Cheerios?"

"It's nothing."

I snort. "Oh, it's something all right. You forget I know you better than anyone, and even I know this is a different level of pissy for you. You weren't even this pissy when I stole your truck and got it stuck in the Myers' pasture."

Jensen glares at me. "That tow cost me three-hundred bucks, Delilah."

"Oh, *Delilah*. We are in a pissy mood," I try to tease, but it comes out snarky. Sighing, I take another drag on the bottle before Jensen swipes it back. "What are you playing, anyway?"

Jensen shrugs his shoulders. "Nothing. Something. I don't know."

"Start over. From the top. Do you have words?"

Jensen nods and begins to sing.

"When she gets married,

She wants it perfect.

Her daddy gives her away,

Somewhere in the country,

Magnolias in May,

Not too many people.

It's not about the money.

Ohhhhhhh!

She's making her plans now.

Yeahhhh!

I can see it all right now.

I'll wear a black suit

And a bowtie.

I'll never be by her side.

I'll take a shot of Jack,

While hiding in the back.

So I won't make a scene.

So nobody sees.

Yeah, she's gonna get married.

But she won't marry me.

Whoa-oh-ohhhhhh.!

She's got the perfect dress now.

She'll welcome the guests now.

I could find her, tell her now.

I won't mess it up, won't fess up.

So I'll wish her the best.

I can see it all right now.

I'll wear a black suit

And a bowtie.

I'll never be by her side.

I'll take a shot of Jack.

While hiding in the back.

So I won't make a scene.

So nobody sees.

Yeah, she's gonna get married.

But she won't marry me."

"Jensen." My voice breaks. "You know I love you, right?"

He chokes out a chuckle. "Of course you do. I'm the best thing that's ever happened to you, and we both know it."

"Yes, yes, I know. You're the only man in my life who has always been there for me, ya know?" I blow out a breath and stare at the ceiling before standing up. "I can't stay here. It smells like the summer we spent playing D&D in that weird kid's bedroom. We'll have to dodge the paps, but what do you say? Wanna go day-drinking with me?"

"I have booze here." Jensen strums another chord before reaching for his bottle of Jack.

"Yes, but we both need to forget about this day, and we can't do it here. C'mon. Please? For me?" I put on my best puppy-dog face, the one that usually got me whatever I wanted growing up. It's no different now.

Jensen curses before setting his guitar aside. "Fine, but you're buying." He stands and moves to grab his leather jacket, but I jerk it back from him.

"Hell no. You're showering first. You smell like corn chips, booze, and regret."

He glares at me but stomps into the bathroom. I grin when I hear the water start. I text our driver to be ready.

Half an hour later, we sneak out of the back of the hotel. I can hear the cameras clicking and the paparazzi yelling our names, but we don't stop.

"Teardrop Lounge! Step on it!" I cry, ducking below window level.

The car squeals and takes off from the curb, and I laugh as the crowd scrambles out of the way. Jensen is cursing next to me and trying to get situated on the seat.

We pull up to the lounge and grab a stool at the bar. They've just opened, so it's the employees and us. I raise the menu to my face and take a look at their specialty drinks. The bartender tosses a couple of coasters in front of us.

"I'll take a cheese charcuterie board and an…" I squint at the menu. "…Unfinished Business, please. He'll have a Jack and Coke, easy on the Coke." I gesture to Jensen. "Thank you." While the bartender moves away to put in our order, I turn to Jensen. "So. Spill. What's going on?"

"I'm not drunk enough for this, Dee. What about you? What's going on with you?"

I grimace before blowing out a breath. The bartender, whose name tag reads Tom, takes that moment to arrive with our drinks, and I down half in one swig. "Like I said, Alexander happened. He came to town, talked the right talk, said all the right words, and I fell into bed with him like an idiot. Worse than that, I believed him. I believed every honey word that came from that perfectly sculpted mouth."

"That son of a bitch. I'm going to hang him by his balls." Jensen slams down his drink and goes to stand.

I grab his arm and try to hold him down on the bar stool. "Jensen. No. He isn't worth it. Stay here with me. I need you here. With me. Okay?"

When he finally nods and settles, I gesture for another round. We're three drinks in and picking at a decimated cheese board when I try to ease it out of him again.

"So. You sure you don't want to talk about what's happening? That's a great song you wrote, but it seems kinda..." At his glare, I hesitate but finish. "...sad."

"Yes, I'm sure I don't want to talk about it."

My phone chimes, and I check the notification. "Damn it. The paps caught wind of where we're at. We gotta move." I settle the tab, and we rush back out to the car. "Bar of the Gods!" I cry, enjoying the game of dodging the cameras.

"Where on earth did you find these bars?"

"They were in the *Guide to Portland*. I remembered from when we arrived. I had them on a list of places I wanted to see when I had time. We have time! Now step on it!"

We hit three more bars before we end up at the Pink Rabbit. The bartender is a chick with pink hair and legs for days.

"You really are my best friend, Jensen. What did I ever do to deserve you? You've always been there for me. Why can't men be like you? I don't want to die alone." The room is spinning slightly, so I lean against his shoulder.

"Marry me."

I straighten so fast I almost fall off the stool. "Do what? Jensen. Are you nuts?"

"No. It's perfect." At my scoff, he shushes me. "Think about it. We don't want to be alone. We both love people we know it'll never work out with. If we get married, then we don't have to deal with all the bullshit. We can just be us and music forever."

I think I'm more drunk than I realize because it sounds like a good plan. I tell Jensen as much, and he pulls out his phone and starts typing. "What are you doing?"

"I'm making the announcement."

"What announcement?"

"Our engagement."

Chapter 34
Alexander

"You're what?" If I thought I was livid before, it has nothing on how I feel right now. Walking into the sixth bar of the day and seeing my woman leaning all over her best friend while he announces their engagement.

Over his dead body!

"Whoa." The female bartender gives me a once-over. "How tall do you have to be to ride that ride?"

I shudder when she licks her lips. Dee's head whips around to look at the woman before tipping back to down the last of her drink. "Go ahead. Apparently, not only is he a lousy lay, but he's a cheating bastard as well."

I grit my teeth and pray for patience. Delilah, on a good day, is a lot to handle, but a drunk and pissed-off Delilah? Well, I would rather wrestle alligators blindfolded.

Unfortunately, I don't have a choice, and I'll have to get creative if I want her to listen to me and not that drivel Megan spread all over the internet. I chewed her ass when I woke up and found myself in bed alone and then saw the notifications lighting up my phone. Combined with this latest BS Ransom sent me about what the woman's been doing behind the scenes to not only me but Delilah and Jensen, she should be packing to leave town at this very moment. If she isn't, well, she will be soon. She has hurt the people in my life far too much, and I refuse to let it happen again.

"Lil Bit, I need you to come with me." I approach her slowly, making sure to maintain eye contact.

"Nope." She pops the P. "I'm getting married. Jensen and I are getting married, and there's nothing you can do about it." Her petulant tone makes me want to turn her over my knee to redden her ass *and* kiss her at the same time.

"Oh, that's where you're wrong, princess. If you're marrying anyone, it's me."

"You're already engaged. I can be engaged too. You can't stop me. Can I get another drink?" Delilah turns toward the bartender, and while her back is to me, I stride up behind her and grab her waist. "Alexander, what the hell?"

She pivots to lay into me and I use the momentum to throw her over my shoulder before striding out the door to the car I have waiting.

"Let me go!" Delilah is kicking and thumping her fists on my back. Her heart-shaped ass is at eye level, so I do what any man would do in the same position. I smack it.

"Dee, calm down before I drop you. We are going back to the hotel. We are having a conversation, and you will listen to me for once in your life!" Opening the car door, I deposit her on the seat. She glares at me from inside but makes no move to exit the car.

The ride back to the hotel room is silent. However, the second the hotel room door closes, all hell breaks loose.

"You sorry son of a bitch."

I duck when the vase of flowers on the table in the room smashes against the wall next to my head. "Delilah, listen. Please."

She laughs before turning to look for something else to throw. When she reaches for the Bible, I tut her, and she sets it down.

I stalk toward her until she's backed against the wall. "Megan. Lied." I lean forward, my body pressed flush against hers.

"You. Lied," she hisses, and if looks could kill, well, my ass would be ash.

"No."

Delilah tries to shove at my chest again, and when I don't move, she hooks my knee and puts me on my ass before trying to bear down on me with her weight. "Remind me to thank James for that one later."

How ever much she may want to hold me in place, I still outweigh her by a solid hundred and fifty pounds. Rolling us over, I pin her to the floor, wedging my body between her legs. Her pupils dilate, and I smirk.

Now that I have her settled, I try to get to her again. "Megan. Lied."

She sucks in a quiet breath, and I press on.

"There should already be a retraction being printed. I clarified that if she didn't leave town, things would become very uncomfortable for her. She has also been the one feeding information to Jensen's grandparents and causing issues with the tours. It's all in the report Ransom put together. You told me yourself *they only print lies.*"

When Dee opens her mouth to interrupt me, I roll my hips, causing her eyes to roll back in her head.

"You would have known this already if you weren't running across the width and breadth of Portland, drinking all their booze and attempting to get engaged to someone else. Like I said, if you're going to marry anyone, it will be me." I punctuate the last three words with hard thrusts against her core.

Her breathy moans are music to my ears, and it takes every bit of my willpower to stay focused on the task that is sadly *not* fucking her sweet pussy into next week.

"No, I'm not." Her defiant tone makes my cock harder, and I have to grin.

"Say that shit again, princess, and I'll spank your ass. You are mine. You will be getting married to me and no one else. I'm yours and no one else's. I know that you're still upset with me. I know you will not be able to forgive me for everything immediately, and you know what? That is my cross to bear. It's up to me to prove to you, every single day for the rest of our lives, that you can trust me with your heart again."

"X..." The way she whispers my name tells me everything I need to know, and I crash my lips onto hers, devouring her. Demanding entry.

As soon as she parts her lips for me, I spear a hand through her hair, positioning her head right where I want it. Sliding my other hand down her side, I hitch her legs up to my waist and rock in tandem with her moans.

Fuck, she's hot, and I can't picture waking up without her in my life. When I realized she was gone this morning, I almost lost my mind with worry.

Delilah whines at my inattention, and I double my efforts and am rewarded with another rush of wetness. Slipping a hand between us, I capture a nipple between my thumb and forefinger, tugging roughly while grinding my cock against her clit through our clothes. I press my face into her neck, breathing in the scent of magnolias and something that is uniquely Delilah. It's heat and sex and all that's good in my world, and I never want to be without this scent for the rest of my days.

Suddenly frustrated with all the layers of clothes between us, I shove her shirt up and over her head, and she flings it across the room. I work my way down the front of her body, placing love bites along her soft stomach. Tracing lazy circles around her belly button with my tongue before biting sharply. Her gasps and moans are driving me crazy. My name on her lips in that tone may be my new favorite soundbite. Popping the front clasp of her bra, I palm her supple tits, pushing them together so that I can lick and suck on her deliciously pink nipples.

"X, please. Please." She helps me remove her shorts, offering herself up to me, and it's a gift I accept willingly. The shorts go the same way as her shirt, and I sit back on my knees, staring at the bounty that is the woman before me. She's exquisite, my girl, and I almost lost her.

Cum is leaking into my pants. I'm so desperate to be inside her. I quickly pull my clothes off, tossing them aside with little regard to where they land. Delilah is a twisting, moaning mess.

"I'm going to fuck you now. Hold on tight." Hiking her legs up over my hips, I slam into her, and her nails dig into my back, clawing at me as she pants for more.

My hips snap forward, and my balls slap against her skin in a rapid staccato as I bottom out while bumping against her cervix. Delilah whimpers and moans, pleading with me for more, and I'm happy to oblige. I'm pounding into her heat again and again, growling and snarling my satisfaction against the sweat-soaked skin of her throat. Delilah takes it, takes all that I give, and gives it right back to me with the undulation of her hips, her breathy cries and the way she claws at the carpet, her eyes unseeing.

"Mine." My voice is rough sandpaper. "You are mine. You have always been mine. Do you hear me, princess? You. Are. Mine. Need someone to settle you down? Call me. Sick? I'll take care of you. Sad? I'll hold you tight. Horny? Come ride this cock." I fuck her hard and deep and feel her muscles start to tremble before her pussy locks down tight around my cock.

"X!" Her cries are music to my ears even as her nails shred my back, and the combination of pain and pleasure causes me to come immediately, stealing my ability to think.

I slam into her one last time as cum shoots from my cock. So forcefully that it causes my muscles to cramp while the excess drips between us. My heart is pounding and the only thing I can hear is the blood rushing in my ears. We collapse limply onto the floor, and I roll, pulling her into my side. And I know, without a shadow of a doubt, there will never be another woman for me. If Delilah walked out of my life tomorrow, I would never love anyone else.

We lie in the silence for what seems like hours before Delilah stirs. "If you think that was a proposal, Alexander Brian Stephenson, you are mistaken."

I start to chuckle before breaking out into full-blown laughter. There she is. There's my girl. I position her onto her back and kiss her deeply. I can feel an answering smile on her lips. "Don't worry, princess. When I propose, you'll know it. I love you, Delilah Rose Callahan." Propped above her, I stare down into her green eyes shining with love and find the peace I've been searching for my whole life.

"I love you, X. Always have, always will." She cards her fingers through my hair, bringing my lips down to meet hers in a kiss that quickly becomes heated.

Rolling us over until she's straddling my hips, her hands on my chest for balance, I give her a cocky grin. "Prove it."

Chapter 35
Delilah

I'm rushing around backstage. Looking for the lead singer of The Velvet Waistcoat. I rolled my eyes when the label said the band would open for us for the last half of the tour. I wanted to grab the nearest trash can and lose my lunch.

"Have you seen Dravyn?" I stop Maddie as she rushes past me.

She shakes her head and keeps going. I catch a glimpse of tears and don't have time to check if she's okay. We're due on stage in three hours and still have prechecks to go through. I make a mental note to check in with her later. She's a sweet girl, efficient, intelligent, driven, a little naïve, and she has a crush on Grayson. I've caught her staring when she thinks no one is looking. However, Grayson is firmly in his hoe phase, taking delight in the scores of groupies who follow rock stars around. They would make a cute couple if the situation were different, but it's not, and I don't want to see her heartbroken.

Grayson is taking our upcoming break from touring hard and is looking to do guest spots with other bands. It hurts. I won't lie, and it's caused several arguments within our dynamic, but I will never hold one of my friends back from something they want to do. He will always have a spot with us. He's family.

"Jensen! Have you seen Dravyn?"

My bandmate looks up from his guitar when I call his name but shakes his head. I still need to find out what happened after our "engagement" hit the paper. I know it wasn't good. It was the next day before I could extract myself from X long enough to get with my publicist to have a correction printed. However, by then, the slag rags had run wild with the story. It took weeks to get everything set straight and publish the retractions.

I storm off while muttering to myself. When I find this guy, I'm going to kick him right in his *waistcoat.* I pull my cell phone out of my back pocket and fire off a text to X. He hasn't answered me all morning. It's almost as annoying as not being able to find Dravyn.

I take a moment and lean against the stage with a sigh. The past six months have been... magical. X has been with us on tour, flying home occasionally to check in with the family business. Since most of what he does is remote, we plan on splitting our time between LA and Texas when the tour is over. While I've loved being on the road, I want to focus on making my music. I've lost that fire, the joy I used to have writing songs. Things are stale, and taking a break might be the best course for all of us.

Maddie rushes up to me, clipboard in hand. "Dee, we need you in hair and makeup, and the wardrobe is running late. Something about a zipper breaking and a tech not passing a background check?"

"Since when do we run background checks on the wardrobe techs?"

Maddie scratches her neck. "Since Law started working for Mia. I don't have all the details, but I do know that he runs a security company, is a friend of her family, and is here helping her with something."

I don't know much about Mia's new bodyguard either, and the few times I have seen them interacting, things have seemed tense. I also know Mia has been having problems and that Lawrence was here to deal with them. I just didn't realize things were as serious as having to do background checks for *everyone.*

Sighing in frustration, I turn back to Maddie. "Okay, I'm heading to my dressing room now. If you see Dravyn, tell him to find me. I want the pleasure of kicking his ass myself. Also, if you hear from X, tell him if he doesn't text me back, he can suck his own dick tonight." I pivot on my heel and stride into my dressing room to start the dog and pony show that is hair and makeup.

I am just zipping up my last boot when there's a knock on the door. "Come in!"

Maddie enters with her usual air of efficiency. "We are T-minus twenty to the opening act. We need to get you wired up."

"I never did see Dravyn. Did you tell him to come see me?" I check my cellphone for the millionth time. "X still hasn't texted me back either. When I get my hands on that man, he will regret the day he was born."

Maddie clears her throat with a strangled cough, and I glance up at her.

"Oh, don't look at me like that. You know what I mean."

Shaking her head, she follows me out of the dressing room as I make my way over to tech to get wired up.

"Maddie, are you sure you're okay with being in LA full time? I know you joined us to get experience and travel, and I would hate to lose you. You're the best PA, but I don't want you to give up your dream because you're afraid you'll be out of work."

She wraps her arms around her middle before smiling at me. "No, I'm sure it'll be fine. Who knows what the future holds, right? Things can change at the drop of a hat. I do know that I love working with Wild Child Reckless, and these past few years have been the best of my life."

I pull her into a hug before the tech guys start clipping me in. I'm standing in the wings when I hear the emcee announce the opening act, and my jaw hits the floor.

"Ladies and gentlemen, please welcome Alexander Reckless to the stage!"

The applause is scattered and muted, but tears fill my eyes when I watch X walk up to the mic. "Good evening, Memphis. My name is Alexander. You've probably seen me in the papers lately, but there's more to the story than what you've read. See, I have known Delilah Callahan almost all my life, and her brother is my best friend." He then turns, looks at me, and holds out his hand.

When I meet him on stage and take it, the crowd goes wild.

"Delilah Rose Callahan is the best person I've ever met, my reason for getting up in the morning, and the thankful prayer on my lips at night. We've had some rough times, but I've had some of the best times of my life with you by my side too. So, Dee, my darling. This one is for you."

X drops my hand, pulls up his guitar, and begins to sing.

"Your eyes aren't blue; they're green.

You aren't the woman of my dreams.

Loving you isn't quite what I had planned.

Five foot three, you're not tall.

You're not the one I pictured at all,

In the teenage fantasies of my mind.

So you took me by complete surprise

When I lost my heart to your green eyes.

Yeah,

You're not at all what I was looking for.

You're more.

It wasn't love at first sight.

I'll admit I had to look twice

To see the woman I was born to love.

Your laughter calms my soul.

I don't think that I can ever let go.

When it comes to your love, I can't get enough.

So you took me by complete surprise

When I lost my heart to your green eyes.

Yeah,

You're not at all what I was looking for.

You're more.

More than I could hope for.

More than I could ever deserve.

I couldn't ask for more than a love like ours.

So you took me by complete surprise

When I lost my heart to your green eyes.

Yeah,

You're not at all what I was looking for.

You're more."

When the final note echoes, X drops to his knee, and I sob and laugh when he pulls out a ring. My mom's ring. The one my dad bought her before he left for basic. Seeing this ring in his hand now is more than I can take, and I fall to my knees in front of him in a mess of tears.

"Delilah Rose Callahan, I love you. I love you more than I thought I would ever love anyone. Would you do me the honor of becoming my wife?"

The crowd goes wild again. This time chanting, "Yes. Yes. Yes. Yes. Yes."

My throat is so constricted that all I can do is cry and nod. X picks me up and swings me around in a circle to the crowd's cheers. Then he takes my lips in a demanding kiss that quickly turns heated. When he finally sits me back down on the stage, he kisses my forehead.

"I love you, princess."

"I love you too, but I have a show to do." My tone is teasing as I glance back out at the packed stadium that seems to be hanging on our every move.

X grins back at me. "I'm joining you for this set. Then we're going home, where I can show you how much I love you." His voice is pitched just for me, and the heat in his tone makes me pant.

Clearing my throat, I grab my guitar off the stand and turn to the crowd, who cheers louder. "All right, ladies, calm down. I saw him first. Now. Where were we?"

The End

Epilogue
Chapter One

Six Months Later

The scorching Texas sun shines bright in the summer sky, and the wind blows a rogue dandelion into puffs. I find myself in my old bedroom, as Mia puts the finishing touches on my makeup. It's our wedding day, and though it feels like it's been a million years in the making, I'm more than ready to see X waiting for me at the end of the aisle. Just then, my mom walks in, and her eyes start to tear up at the sight of me sitting at the vanity.

"Oh, honey…" Her voice wavers. "If only your daddy could see you now. He always knew you'd grow up but dreaded the day he would give you away."

I glance back at the picture of my dad on the wall. My mom is not wrong. He would have given X fifteen different kinds of hell for daring to steal his baby girl. At the same time, I know he would have been proud of who I've become and what we're doing with our lives.

I push to my feet and step into Mom's embrace, and we both take a moment. A knock breaks us apart as James slips through the door.

"Hey, sis, you ready?" He smiles at us both before someone bumps into him, and he stumbles into the doorjamb. "Damn it, Ransom! I told you to sit down with the other guests!"

"I'm not just a guest! I'm Dee's favorite guest. Here to offer my services as a getaway driver." Ransom bends at the waist before taking my hand and kissing it. "I live to serve, madam. Your wish is my command," he says, and I can't help but laugh.

Ransom is devilishly handsome, with bright-blonde hair and sea-green eyes that are even more deadly when you realize there are two sets of them. I pity the woman who falls for either of the Jasper boys. Identical twins shouldn't be allowed to be this good looking.

"For the last time, I'm not running away. I love Alexander. He is my forever."

Ransom grins at me before kissing my cheek and tucking a curl behind my ear. "I know, sweetheart. I just have to make sure you know that there is nothing I wouldn't do for you if you needed it."

I smile as I return the peck. "I know, and I appreciate it more than you know. I appreciate everything that all of you have done for me. Especially bringing James home safe and sound."

Ransom leaves the room with a wink, only to be replaced by Maddie. We officially ended our last tour three months ago. You wouldn't know it by looking at Maddie. She looks more and more exhausted as the days go by.

"Dee, the guests are ready when you are."

"Thanks, Maddie. Are you okay, babe?"

Her strained smile doesn't convince me, despite her assurances that *she's fine* and *just ready to go home and see her family.*

Mom embraces me one last time before positioning herself at the end of the aisle. James holds out an arm, and I link mine through it. "You ready, brat?"

"More than ready."

"Then let's go get your happily ever after."

Alexander

The music starts, and I adjust my tie. If you'd asked me last year if I saw this in my future, I would have called you crazy. But now, it's the only future I can see. And it's all because of her—Delilah. She was made for me, and I was made for her. We've been through so much together, but we're still here and always will be.

The music swells as our guests rise from their seats, and then she appears at the end of the aisle, on James's arm. I have to suck in a quick breath as I watch her. Ivory lace caresses her body in a tight sheath, and magnolia blossoms hold back her riot of curls. I hear the photographer clicking away but can't take my eyes off the angel walking toward me. I've been waiting for this day forever, and now that it's finally here, I want to pinch myself. I don't know what I did to deserve her, but I do know I'll spend the rest of my life proving to her that her trust in me is worth it.

James steps back as Delilah reaches the end of the aisle, and I greet her with a kiss on the hand. "I thought you'd never get here."

"Well, to be fair, I got here as soon as possible." Delilah glances back at Ransom, who is jingling his keys in her direction, and I roll my eyes. "Still harping on that, is he?"

Delilah chuckles, and I can't help but join in. "Oh, absolutely. I can't wait for the day he meets the love of his life. I hope she gives him all kinds of trouble," Dee whispers, mischief glimmering in her eyes, and I can't resist kissing her.

The pastor clears his throat. "That comes later, young man."

The audience shares a laugh as the pastor proceeds to open his book and begin the ceremony that will unite us forever.

The wedding reception follows with a flurry of activities, including cake-cutting, speeches, and dancing, which is my favorite part. Holding Delilah close as we sway on the floor settles a piece of me I never knew existed.

"Dee?" My breath ruffles her hair.

"Hmmm?" I can tell she's tired by the way she snuggles against my chest.

"Do you think we can sneak out now?"

She lifts her head and looks at me. "You ready to go?" she asks, and the desire I see in her eyes is almost my undoing.

"I'm ready to have my wife to myself."

She smiles at me. "Then let's get out of here, husband." Dee practically purrs before I grab her hand and pull her after me as we dash around the house to the waiting truck.

Delilah

We arrive at the rental property after a three-hour drive. As soon as I walk in, I'm captivated by the beauty of the house Alexander rented for us. I set my bag down and walk over to the large windows, which showcase the picturesque view that makes Garner State Park one of the best scenic adventures in Texas.

Opening the kitchen's sliding glass door, I walk out onto the balcony and inhale the crisp, clean air. Summer may be in full swing. But right now, at this moment, I can hear the distant promise of fall as a whisper in the wind.

X saunters up behind me and slides his hands along my waist. "Well, wife, what do you think?"

Turning to face him, I close my arms around his neck. "I think it's perfect. I may never want to go home after this."

His chuckle makes me smile as his lips brush mine. "I think several people would not be okay with us running off and disappearing."

"They'd get over it." I shrug before turning back around to admire the river's lazy path through the countryside.

Warm lips brush my shoulder as X's teeth nip my skin. I roll my head to the side with a moan while granting him better access. His breath is hot, raising goose bumps along the surface. I pivot to wrap my arms around his neck again, and X swings me up into his hold and stalks back into the house. We reach the kitchen, but our hands and lips quickly become distracted. He swipes out an arm to clear the counter and places me on the chilled stone.

"I completely forgot to have my dessert." X's grin is positively lethal, and I can feel my thighs growing slick with need.

As he reaches for the dress's side panel, the sound of the zipper breaks the silence, barely audible over our heavy breathing. Then he slides his lips over mine again, his tongue teasing until I open for him. He peels the material from my body, his breath catching at the sight of the white silk basque.

He groans when he gets to the silk thong and garter set. "Oh, you naughty girl. Hiding this from me all day? Things would have gone very differently if I'd known you were wearing this." He catches the thong with his teeth and slowly slides it down my legs before slipping his tongue between my slick folds.

I wrap my hands into his hair, my back arching as he buries his face between my thighs, his tongue darting and thrusting inside me over and over.

He pulls away to pin me with a smirk. "I need you to come for me, princess."

I call out his name when he attacks my clit with the flat of his tongue. Batting and teasing it, making my whole body tremble. I scream as my back bows off the counter, and waves of pleasure rack my body.

Alexander doesn't let up. He licks and sucks and teases and pushes me higher and higher until I think I might pass out. As the orgasm rushes through my body, my thighs grip his head, holding him closer. When the tremors start to die down, my legs fall open, and I can see him grinning up at me with my release coating his face.

"That's what I'm talking about, babe. Best dessert on the planet." He reaches down and pats my pussy.

"Did you just pet my pussy like it did a good job?" I laugh incredulously.

"I sure did." The mischievous grin he shoots me has an answering smile gracing my own lips.

"Well, you know what they say…" I keep my tone light and teasing.

"What do they say, princess?"

"Turnabout is fair play." I slide off the counter and drop onto my knees in front of him, and I can hear his breath hitch as I slide down the zipper of his suit pants. Wrapping a hand around his erection, I stroke him slowly, watching him from under my lashes. He throws his head back and moans, unable to stop himself as I swirl my tongue around his tip.

Alexander

The sight of Delilah in front of me will never get old. She's sporting a disheveled post-orgasmic glow, which makes her a vision. When she swirls her tongue around the head of my cock, I nearly lose the ability to stand. I can feel my breath quickening as she takes me in her mouth and strokes. I grab her hair loosely in one hand and slowly plunge in and out of her while grazing the back of her throat.

I look into her eyes, full of love, as my cock thrusts in and out. I remove myself from her perfect mouth. Gazing at her tenderly, I caress her face. "Go to the bedroom. I want you on all fours on the edge of the bed so I can admire you, wife."

I smack her on the butt as she rushes off to get into position, and I can't help but smile. For all her spit and fire, my girl loves it when I take charge in the bedroom. I find myself intoxicated by the trust she places in me every time she submits.

I walk into the room behind her, admiring the view of her pale skin, offset by the country night that's fallen outside the windows. Climbing up behind her, I run both of my hands over the curve of her ass cheeks and down her thighs, testing her readiness for me with one hand as the other slides up her spine and into the curls.

Grabbing a fistful, I tug her head back, arch her neck, and kiss the sensitive spot at the curve of her shoulder before I plunge into her wet heat in one smooth stroke.

God, yes.

I grip her hip harder as I thrust forward, dragging the head of my cock over that one spot that I know drives her crazy. The sounds falling from her lips make me smile all over again. I adjust my angle slightly, and her wails increase in pitch.

I lean into her, thrusting harder. "That's right, princess. I want you to scream for me."

"Oh, God," she whimpers, and I have to chuckle.

"No, God can't help you now. You're mine, Delilah Rose Callahan-Stephenson. Now be a good girl and come for me."

My hand on her hip tugs Delilah back against me even as my thrusts shove her forward on the bed. I can feel her starting to ripple around me, so I pull her up on her knees, her back to my chest, and spread her legs wider as I pound into her harder. This way, her ear is right by my mouth, and I proceed to whisper all the dirty things I want to do to her over the next two weeks. When she cries out more, begging me, I slide my hand down her stomach and circle her clit, moving in time with my thrusts.

"Be a good girl and come for me like this. I need to feel you tighten around my cock as I fill you. C'mon, princess, let me feel this pussy coming around my cock." I can sense her pleasure increasing. "Yes, princess, that's right. Give me another one."

I snap my hips harder, fucking her through her climax and into another one. I capture her lips with mine as my own orgasm tears through me. I fall forward, turning so that Delilah lands on top of me. I pull her close, whispering over and over again how much I love her.

I've waited for this moment all my life, and now that it's here, I can only hold the woman I love tighter in my arms.

Delilah

The sun shining through the skylight wakes me up, and I stretch. My muscles are sore and protesting, but I smile when I remember why. I finally force myself upright and realize I'm in bed alone. And I definitely do not like it. I'm reaching for my phone when the bedroom door opens, and X walks in. Hair ruffled, sleep pants riding low on his hips, and two cups of coffee in his hands.

"Oh, yes, please." I make grabby motions for a cup, and he chuckles as he passes me one and kisses my forehead.

"Good Morning, princess. How'd you sleep?"

I smile around the rim of my cup. "I think we both know the answer to that question."

"Just asking. I want to ensure I care for my woman in all facets of her life."

I pick up a pillow, throw it in X's direction, and… miss. I watch as it topples to the floor instead.

"You still can't hit the broad side of a barn."

"Shut up. What are we going to do today?" I take another sip of coffee when my phone rings. I swipe it off the bedside table and show X the screen. "Who do we know in New York?"

"No one. Put it on speaker."

I click the green answer button, and an automated voice comes over the line. "This is a collect call from Jensen Parker at the Manhattan Detention Center. Do you accept the charges?"

My eyes fly up to meet Alexander's as he grabs the suitcases still piled up by the door and pulls out clothes for both of us.

"Yes, I accept the charges."

From the Author

Thank you for reading This is Growing Up. I hope you love Delilah and Alexander as much as I do. This book started as a dare from Author Morgan Elliott and went from there. I always loved reading, and now I have a separate love of writing. I hope you stick around and join me in getting to know Jensen a bit better in This is Meant to Be, the next book in the Wild Child Reckless Book series. I am always looking to connect! You can find me in the following places.

SmutTok Made Me Do It Facebook Group

Juliet McKinleys Book Nook

Sign Up for my newsletter here so that you never miss a beat, giveaway or sneak peek-

Newsletter   julietmckinley.myflodesk.com

TikTok   @JulieyMcKinleyAuthor

Instagram   @JulietMckinleyAuthor

Facebook   Juliet McKinley